Lis... ...nore inte... ...way.

"I'm at ... why I'm telling you all th... Sorry."

"Comes with the job description: pour drinks, nod head, and listen." Tonica's voice was calm, soothing; the kind you'd unload your troubles to.

"Joe and I worked too long and too hard for the deal to fall through. I have to figure out where Joe is, get the papers, and get them filed on time."

Ginny knew a cue when she heard it. "Maybe I can help?"

The look she got from Tonica would have amused Ginny if she weren't so focused on selling herself to the client.

"My name's Ginny Mallard. Mallard Professional Concierge Services." Her card was ready and in the guy's hand before he knew what hit him. He looked down, an automatic instinct, and read the text out loud.

"We Do What You Can't." He flipped it over, looking for something more, but there was just a phone number and website: mallard.net

"We handle tasks that our clients don't have the time—or skills—to handle. Appointments, errands, research . . . both professional and personal. I'm fully bonded and insured. If you—"

"Oh. Yes." There was a gleam in his eye that might have been relief, and his hand swirled the remaining Scotch in his glass, making the ice cubes clink against each other. "God, that would be perfect. What're your rates?"

Ginny had not expected it to be that easy. Probably a little too late, warning alarms went off. . . .

COLLARED

L. A. KORNETSKY

G

GALLERY BOOKS

New York   London   Toronto   Sydney   New Delhi

Gallery Books
A Division of Simon & Schuster, Inc.
1230 Avenue of the Americas
New York, NY 10020

First Gallery Books trade paperback edition November 2012

GALLERY BOOKS and colophon are registered trademarks of Simon & Schuster, Inc.

For information about special discounts for bulk purchases, please contact Simon & Schuster Special Sales at 1-866-506-1949 or business@simonandschuster.com.

The Simon & Schuster Speakers Bureau can bring authors to your live event. For more information or to book an event contact the Simon & Schuster Speakers Bureau at 1-866-248-3049 or visit our website at www.simonspeakers.com.

Designed by Renata Di Biase

Manufactured in the United States of America

10   9   8   7   6   5   4   3   2   1

Library of Congress Cataloging-in-Publication Data

Kornetsky, L. A.
  Collared : a gin & tonic mystery / L. A. Kornetsky.—1st Gallery Books trade paperback ed.
     p. cm.
   1. Personal concierges—Fiction. 2. Bartenders—Fiction. 3. Missing persons—Fiction. 4. Cats—Fiction. 5. Dogs—Fiction. 6. Seattle (Wash.)—Fiction. I. Title. II. Title: Gin & tonic mystery.
PS3557.I4545C65   2012
813'.54—dc22

                                                                                              2012015021

ISBN 978-1-4516-7164-3
ISBN 978-1-4516-7166-7 (ebook)

For my Twinling and her DH,
their Diva and Snark,
for taking a weary traveler in,
and giving her a warm place to rest

Acknowledgments

All due thanks to Barbara Caridad Ferrer, Aynjel Kaye, Janna Silverstein, Kat Richardson, and Jacqueline Pruner, who gave me their Seattle, and let me in turn give it to Ginny and Teddy. Any missteps, mistakes, or misrepresentations are the work of the author, not her advisers.

COLLARED

The cat contemplated the distance, readied her muscles, and leapt. Her paws landed within an inch of her intent, and her hindquarters tucked in nicely. Cats did not preen over basics like that, but there might have been an extra curl to her whiskers as she continued along the rooftop.

Cats also did not admit to boredom, but there might have been a bit of it, padding along with her. Hopefully, the day would provide something worth venturing outside for. And if not, she would stop by the busy place, where there would be food she didn't have to catch, and a human or two worth marking.

There were four buildings on this block, then she would have to go down to street level and cross to the next block to reach her destination. But when she came to the edge of the final roof, she instead sat down and watched the street, her tail curled comfortably around her, only the tip twitching.

There. The cat's ears pricked forward as two figures came around the corner. One human, female; the other a square-chested dog with skin that seemed a size too large for its body, its head about knee-high to the human. They were clearly out for a walk, but neither seemed particularly anxious to get where they were going. The woman was walking slowly, as though she were deep in thought,

1

and the dog, rather than sniffing at the ground, kept lifting its head to peer down the street and up at the sky.

The cat made a coughing noise, and the dog's head swiveled that way. On seeing the cat, the dog's tail, short, skinny, and curled up over its rump, wagged once. Then, as though revitalized, it picked up the pace, waking its owner from her trance, and setting forward to their destination with renewed vigor.

Satisfied, the cat groomed her whiskers once, and then leapt gracefully onto the metal fire escape and made her way down to the street level. Things were looking up.

1

S eth!"

"What?" A man's voice yelled back, clearly irritated.

Teddy, used to the older man's moods, ignored the tone. "What's on the menu tonight?"

He waited. There was a muttering and a clanging noise from the little kitchen behind the bar, as Seth decided if he would answer or not.

"Meatless chili. And pork sliders." There was a pause. "And a salad." Seth pronounced *salad* like it might bite him.

"Thanks," Teddy yelled back, then turned around and erased the previous day's menu—chicken club, chicken soup, and the ever-present green salad—and wrote in the new offerings. People didn't come here for food, as a rule, and the kitchen was about the size of a shoebox, but the boss wanted food available beyond the usual chips and nuts. Food meant people stayed longer. People staying longer meant they spent more money on booze.

It wasn't as though people didn't have their choice of where to drink. There were three bars just in this portion of downtown Ballard, within shouting distance of each other. Nickel, on the other side of the avenue, was where recent college grads went to relive their escapades with cheap beer and drink specials on Thursday nights. If you were looking for a higher-end experience, you could walk down the street and around the corner to the Fish and pay twice as much for your drinks and small plates.

And then there was Mary's.

Teddy put the blackboard back in place, and turned to contemplate his domain. With its bare wood decor and booze-and-snacks menu, Mary's was where you could let your hair down a little and walk home afterward, where strangers were noticed but not bothered, and the regulars looked after each other. That was exactly the way he liked it.

Mary's was also, for a popular bar, surprisingly quiet. Except for the weekends, and Tuesday, which was trivia night and got a little hectic, you could always hear yourself think, and conversations could be held without having to yell. Teddy liked it that way, too.

Unlike other places he'd worked, Mary's had no jukebox, no band tucked into a corner as "value added." There was a little stereo behind the bar that only played jazz— pleasant background noise if you were sitting at the bar, while if you took one of the booths or tables, you didn't hear it at all. Acoustic tiles and careful placement of half walls splitting the bar into two distinct areas, one for mingling and one for serious drinking, helped keep the conversations from overrunning each other. Mary's was where you met up with buddies to catch up, or stopped by to unwind after a long day; rowdies went elsewhere.

On this particular Thursday afternoon, it was in the pause between the comfortable silence of the early drinkers and the full push of an evening crowd. Other than Seth in the back, there were only half a dozen people scattered through the space: three at a table together, starting the weekend early; two more sitting alone at the bar; and the sixth being Teddy.

Teddy was using the quiet to prep for the later rush to come, taking clean glasses out of the compact commercial dishwasher below the counter and inspecting them for spots before placing them on the rack, his easy movements suggesting that he had experience, and all the time in the world to do this one thing exactly right.

Being a bartender was occasionally chaotic, but there were moments of quiet calm, too. He had learned to appreciate both.

One of the figures seated at the bar, a man, finished his drink and slid it a few inches across the polished granite bar top. "Another?"

Teddy checked the glass first, and then looked up at the customer's face. He hesitated, and then smiled. "Vodka tonic, lime, right?"

The customer smiled back, pleased to be remembered. "Right."

Teddy took the glass and dumped it into the bin below

the counter, then pulled down a fresh glass and mixed the vodka tonic quickly, with economical motions, ending with a wedge of lime slipped onto the rim and a cocktail napkin placed under the glass. The man slipped a bill back in return and waved off his change, moving back down the bar to a seat that had a better view of the room. He looked at the door, then shook his head and took a sip of his drink.

A woman's voice, pitched low for only the bartender to hear, said, "You shorted his drink."

That was a damning thing to say, usually a prelude to getting punched in the face—or at least refused further service—by the aforementioned bartender.

Teddy merely sighed, refusing to take offense. "I did not."

The woman leaned on her elbows on the bar top and insisted. "You did so."

He took the towel off his shoulder and gave the gleaming counter a swipe, refusing to answer her. There was a trick to baiting; you had to let them hook themselves, for the best result. He knew that.

She waited, her drink at her right elbow, her hazel-green eyes daring him to deny what she had seen. Her hands rested on the bar, nails unpainted and trimmed short, fingers slender, a single silver ring on the left pinky. Competent hands, comfortably at rest. She'd wait all night if need be; he knew that from experience.

"The guy's meeting someone," he said, finally. She took the point in that round; he couldn't let the accusation stand, not when he had stone-cold logic in his defense. "The last thing he really wants is to be shitfaced when she gets here, and that was his third drink already."

The woman's gaze flicked down to the display of her cell phone, carefully placed out of reach of her drink, and he could almost see her doing the math, little gray cells whirring. "Three before six? How long has he been here?"

Teddy was tempted to make her work for the information, but the need to defend his honor took precedence. "He came in a little before you did."

"Oh." She had only been there for about half an hour. "Yeah, he's drinking too fast." She frowned, and then her gaze sharpened on him. "Tonica, I was watching and he didn't do more than give you his order. And he doesn't look like the sharing type. How did you know he's meeting someone?"

Teddy shook his head in mock sorrow, feeling better now that she was still so clearly puzzled. That gave him the points back. Not that he kept score, or anything. "Virginia Mallard, you should know better than to doubt me, after all this time."

He wasn't joking: they'd taken each others' measure often enough. Ginny was one of Mary's regulars, stopping by for a drink two or three times a week, and she hadn't missed a Tuesday Trivia in nearly a year. Her team and his were tied for second place, overall. He and Mallard, they weren't friends, although they knew each other well enough. She was taller than he liked, blonder than he liked, and definitely pushier than he liked. In fact, there wasn't much about Ginny Mallard that he did like.

No, he admitted ruefully, that wasn't entirely true. Ignoring the fact that she was easy on the eyes, with hazel eyes that held a snap, and a figure that had just enough curve to catch the eye, Mallard was smart and she was occasionally funny, and she could kick back a martini with the style and sass of a 1940s movie moll, all things he appreciated in a woman. He might even—to himself, never her—say he enjoyed having her around to talk to.

She was also a horrible, irritating know-it-all, and there was only room for one know-it-all in Mary's during his shift: him.

Those capable hands now tapped on the bar impatiently. "No, seriously. How did you know?"

"Seriously?" Teddy took the challenge. "Fine. He's never been in here before, he's too close-shaved for after five on a Thursday night, and he keeps looking at the door like he's expecting someone, but not looking at his watch or phone, the way you do when a friend's running late."

Standard bartender skills: reading the clientele. Ginny made a face, but accepted his assessment. "Still. You shorted his drink."

He had. The guy was drinking too fast, on nerves; that was never a good combination. "Don't start, Mallard."

Before she could reply, there was a loud thud from above them, near the ceiling, and then the rattle of glassware, as though something had just landed on one of the shelves of liquor behind him. Teddy didn't bother to turn around.

"Mistress Penny, you'd best not have knocked anything over."

Ginny shook her head, and looked down at the cell phone again, this time obviously checking to see if a text or phone call had come in. She was waiting for someone, too. "If she hasn't by now, she never will. Little cat feet."

"Yeah well, all it takes is one misstep and the boss will kick us both out," he said. There was a meow, barely loud enough to be heard, and he sighed, but backed up a step, until he was closer to the back counter than the front bar, and a pair of paws appeared on his left shoulder, followed by the rest of a small gray tabby-striped cat as she took his invitation, moving from cabinet to human perch.

"You are so totally whipped," Ginny said, grinning at the pair of them.

"Yeah, yeah. Good evening, sweetness." The latter part was directed to the cat, who did not meow again in return, but rested a proprietary paw on top of his head, her claws gently pricking his scalp through his close-cut hair.

Mistress Penny-Drops had arrived about a year earlier, wandering in during a particularly bad rainstorm, drenched to the bone and meowing her unhappiness to everyone in the bar. Teddy had been on duty that night, and she had allowed him the honor of wrapping her in a bar towel and feeding her some of the left-over turkey from his club sandwich.

Within a week she had earned her reputation as a decent mouser, and within a month had laid total claim to the bar as her domain, and Teddy Tonica specifically as "her" human. Anyone else could try to coax her with treats, but most of the time she ignored them.

He had no idea where she went when she wasn't at the bar, but she seemed content with the status quo. So long as nobody complained, she stayed.

Ginny tapped the display of her phone, then pushed it away and looked up at them, scowling. Both cat and bartender looked back at her with calm eyes, one set green, the other brown. "I still don't understand why she's allowed in and Georgie isn't."

Teddy reached his right hand up so the cat could sniff at him. "Because your dog slobbers."

Ginny drew back her shoulders and raised her pointed chin, preparing for battle—their usual mode of conversation. "She does not."

He scratched behind Penny's ear, listening to her purr, trying not to flinch when she dug her claws in more securely. Her claws were small, but sharp. "Yeah, okay. She doesn't drool. Accept that life is unfair and Patrick hates dogs. You want a refill?"

His apparent peace offering threw her off stride, and she tilted her head, studying him from under a stray curl, clearly trying to decide if it was a trick, or if he really just wasn't in the mood to spat.

Actually, Teddy was always in the mood to argue, especially if it was something that didn't actually matter, but he didn't have the heart for this particular fight. If it were up to him, dogs would be fine. He'd looked it up: Washington State law allowed places to make their own rules. But he didn't own Mary's—Patrick did, even if the old man never was around much.

And truthfully, he felt bad for the dogs—not just Georgie—stuck outside, although he supposed it was better than being stuck in the apartment while their owners were here. And Georgie, at least, seemed to enjoy the attention she got from people who walked by. Never mind that she was the ugliest excuse for a pooch he'd ever seen, with peach-fuzz fur, skin hanging in loose folds on her body, and oversized ears that flopped over one eye—other people seemed to think she was adorable.

It was funny: for all his people-reading skills, four months ago, he never would've pegged Ginny Mallard for a pet owner. A workaholic, she came in here regularly to unwind, bust a few egos taking other teams down in trivia, and kick back just enough martinis to get herself politely lit. Usually, it took two, then she switched to ginger ale with a twist of lime for the rest of the evening. Friendly enough, but not buddy-buddy.

And then she got Georgie, and suddenly she went from being Mallard to Mallard-who-had-a-dog, and didn't come around as often as she used to: two nights a week, max. Not that he missed her particular company, he was just . . . he noticed when his regulars changed their habits, was all.

"You want a refill or not, woman? I've got other customers to serve, while you contemplate your calorie sheet."

She glanced again at the phone next to her, and her face showed the slightest hint of both annoyance and worry.

Whatever phone call or text hadn't come, Teddy didn't ask and she didn't volunteer. A lot of people came to Mary's to unload to the bartender. Ginny wasn't one of them.

That was another thing he didn't dislike about her.

"Time to start the serious drinking," she said finally. "The usual, please. And no cat hairs in it, this time."

Lifting Penny off his shoulder and placing her down on the floor, he turned to make the drink, giving Ginny a very clear, cold shoulder for the slur on his bartending abilities.

The cat, indignant at being put down before she was ready, let out an annoyed *mrrrowp,* and disappeared again.

It was petty, but Ginny felt herself smile, despite her previously snappish mood. Getting a rise out of Tonica could always make her mood better. There hadn't ever been any hairs, cat or otherwise, in her drinks, and as cats went, Miss Penny wasn't bad. It wasn't her fault Georgie wasn't allowed into the bar.

In fact, the first time she'd taken Georgie for a walk down past the bar, Miss Penny had sauntered out just as the shar-pei had paused to do her business. The puppy had fallen in love with the little cat in that instant and, weirdly enough, it seemed to be reciprocated. Now, every time Ginny came down to Mary's, if the weather wasn't too cold, she brought Georgie, so the four-legs could have a klatch of their own. That was probably where the cat had disappeared to, in fact—Ginny looked out the front window, craning her neck a little, and confirmed that dog and cat were now sitting nose-to-nose, for all the world like a pair of gossiping grannies.

Even if there had been cat hairs in her drink, anyone or anything her dog loved . . .

Ginny knew that she was a total sucker for the goofy, loving, half-grown dog she'd adopted on a whim. She wasn't an animal person . . . but Georgie wasn't "just" an animal. She was *Georgie.* Wrinkled and loving, with a few issues about "stay" but none at all about "come."

BG—before Georgie—to everyone she met, she'd been Ginny. Just Ginny, or maybe Ms. Mallard. Now she was Ginny-who-owned-Georgie. She wasn't quite sure how that worked, but now when people saw her in the neighborhood—even people she'd have sworn she didn't know—they asked about the dog before anything else. And she knew every dog in the neighborhood, and most of their owners, if not by their name, then by their pets' names.

It was weird how much she liked that, the sense of belonging she hadn't known she didn't have, before.

The martini appeared in front of her, as well as a small dish of Mary's special hickory-and-honey roasted peanuts that were usually two dollars a bowl. He wasn't really pissed, then. With Tonica it was sometimes hard to tell.

She looked up and studied her occasional sparring partner. He was hard to figure out, period. Truth was, Tonica looked as though he would be more comfortable working the door at a nightclub than mixing drinks at an upscale neighborhood bar. Of average height, his shoulders and chest broad and obviously muscled even under his plain green sweater, the white towel slung over one shoulder contrasting with the darkness of his hair, cut in a neat flat-top that emphasized the square lines of his face, and the sharp shape of his nose. It wasn't a handsome face, but it drew attention and, oddly, an immediate sense of familiarity, like you'd known him years ago, and forgotten until now.

Not her type, but she liked him. No, it was better to say that she *respected* him. He didn't deal in bullshit. Most of her working hours, all she got handed was bullshit.

The next time someone swore to her that they'd *sent* the papers, or they were certain they *had* given her all the names to be invited, she was going to . . .

She was going to smile, and assure them that she would handle it, no matter what. Because that was what they paid her to do.

Ginny swiveled her stool until she was facing away from the bar, and let her gaze rest on the room as Mary's started to fill up with the evening crowd, as though by not looking at her phone, it would ring.

She knew most of the people who were here, tonight. Because the bar was on a side street off the main drag, most people just wandered on by. You had to know about Mary's to walk all the way down to the end of the street, to the building that still looked like a storefront, with large glass windowpanes and a double-paned door under an arched front. It had been a dry goods store, once upon a time, back before Seattle came and swallowed up the town in its ever-expanding girth. Thankfully, the owner had been more interested in making Mary's more a nice, peaceful place for locals than a hotspot—except on trivia night, when you got folk coming in from the city proper, to try their luck. Berto, Mary's self-proclaimed trivia master and emcee, was *that* good.

Ginny tried not to miss trivia night—she freely admitted that she was a tad competitive—but the rest of the time she came here to relax after a day of plunking away at her computer. Although she was here less often, now that she had Georgie to keep her company at home.

Tonight, though, even surrounded by familiar faces, she was too distracted to relax, hyperaware of every movement in the bar, of Miss Penny brushing against her legs as the cat wended her way back across the floor, of the small sounds that filled Mary's, the clink of glassware and the waterfall sound of conversations that tonight were too loud, too intrusive, rather than becoming the usual white noise that helped her relax.

Her thoughts wouldn't settle, that was the problem. Usually she was all about focus, but she'd been waiting for two days for that would-be client to call back and confirm the contract, and there'd only been silence.

Two days was a long time in her business. It meant they had reconsidered, no longer needed her.

Ginny took another sip of her drink and scanned the room again, her gaze resting on Tonica while he chatted with a pair of brunettes down at the other end of the bar, measuring them each a glass of white wine.

Heck with that, she decided firmly. If the client wasn't

interested, then she wasn't going to play the lovesick teenager and mope around the phone. That wasn't why she'd founded her own company, to wait for things to happen.

So. She'd take the rest of the night off, stop worrying, and start fresh in the morning. Maybe she'd call Mac, see if her former co-worker could escape long enough to get together over the weekend. That would be fun. It had been a busy couple of months, between adding a dog's schedule to her own, and trying to deal with her parents, and . . .

No. Not thinking about her parents. Breathe in, breathe out. Let the bad thoughts flow away. Her parents would make her crazy if she let them, but only if she let them. Breathe in, breathe out. Think of Georgie asking to play fetch, or bringing her the leash to go for a walk, of the slippery-smooth feel of her tawny fur, and the heavy way she leaned against you when she was feeling content. Good thoughts. Unstressed thoughts.

It almost worked, when the sound of someone slamming his drink down on the counter next to her shattered her newfound calm, making her turn abruptly.

"Hey, calm down, guy," Teddy was saying, having abandoned the brunettes at the first sign of trouble, wiping up the spill without taking his eyes off the customer. "Calm down."

"I am calm. Damn it."

"Your calm just spilled half of your drink," Teddy pointed out.

The guy looked down at his hand, as though only now noticing that the back of his hand was covered in Scotch. "Oh. Yeah. Sorry. I just . . . it's been a particularly crappy day." He shook his head, wiping his hand off with his napkin. "Half my staff's out, and we just had a crisis hit that I don't have time to handle. Christ, does it always have to come in bundles?"

"Let me refill your drink," was all Tonica said, lifting the glass out of the guy's hand so easily he didn't even seem to notice it was gone.

Normally, the rule in Mary's was that a bartender confession is the same as a priest's—you leave them alone and you don't interrupt. But Ginny thought that she knew this guy—he was on one of the trivia teams. Sports specialist, with a real head for numbers and logic problems. Not her type—late fifties, probably, and too lean—but handsome if you liked the sharp-faced ones. She couldn't remember his name, but they'd traded salutes across the bar a time or three, and in Mary's, that was the same as a formal introduction. So it wasn't really eavesdropping, was it?

Listening to someone else's problems was always more interesting that being morose about your own, anyway.

He was leaning across the bar now, spilling his guts to Tonica, just like everyone else who came in here—except her. "Mind you, I run a tight ship. That's the only way to survive in real estate, these days. It's just that I don't know what to do. I mean, Joe's an adult, he's not senile, hell, he founded the company, so who am I to say he can't take a few days off? His health hasn't been good, I'd be just as happy if he did slow down a bit, let us pick up the slack."

Teddy made some kind of encouraging, comforting noise.

"But this? He's been gone for two days, says he's taking some time off and then disappears without an itinerary or a phone number where we can reach him—and without handing over the papers he had been working on. We need to file them on Monday, or this deal goes south like it was the last flight to San Diego!"

The guy took another sip of his new Scotch, and exhaled. "Hell, maybe it is early-onset senility. And of course, all this happens when we've got other things on the table I have to keep an eye on. I swear—I'm too busy to deal with this right now."

Ginny's ears pricked up at that. Her company specialized in doing things for people too busy to do for themselves. Distraction and a night off be damned, this guy was a potential customer on the hoof. But it would be tacky to just jump in . . .

On the other hand, waiting around for a client to call hadn't done her much good, either, had it? Ginny chewed on her lower lip, debating with herself.

"I'm at my wit's end," the guy said. "Which I guess is why I'm telling you all this. Sorry."

"Comes with the job description: pour drinks, nod head, and listen. You don't have copies of the papers?" Tonica's voice was calm, soothing—exactly the kind of voice you'd unload your troubles to. Ginny squelched the unkind—and familiar—thought that he'd spent hours practicing that voice to eke out better tips, and kept eavesdropping.

"Oh, yeah, but they're copies, you know? Not original signatures. And yeah, I could use them to stall . . . but the moment anything even smells of trouble, the other folk could use that as an excuse to back out." He took another long drink from his glass and put it down, this time with a deliberately careful *thunk*. "Joe and I worked too long and too hard for the deal to fall through. I have to figure out where Joe is, get the papers, and get them filed on time."

Ginny had never been in the drama club, but she knew an entrance cue when she heard it. With a mental apology to her mother for the breach of manners she was about to commit, she slid off her stool, and leaned into their space. "Maybe I can help?"

The look she got from Tonica, his eyebrows rising up into his hairline, was nothing short of "woman, what?" disbelief. It would have amused Ginny if she weren't so focused on selling herself to the potential client.

"You?" He *was* the guy from trivia night, but it was clear from his expression that she hadn't pinged any recognition lights in his memory. She'd be insulted if she wasn't already in saleswoman mode.

"My name's Ginny. Ginny Mallard. I'm sorry, I heard you talking, and"—her card was ready and in his hand before he knew what hit him. He looked down, an automatic instinct, and read the text out loud.

"Mallard Professional Concierge Services. We Do What

You Can't." He flipped it over, looking for something more, but there was just a phone number and website: mallardPCS.net.

"Services?" His tone was almost but not quite insulting, implying that she might be offering something illicit. Ginny bit back her annoyance, brought up her best smile, and explained.

"We're a concierge service. Like a hotel offers, you know: making reservations and smoothing away problems, that sort of thing, but for individual clients."

Usually she compared herself to a professional butler-slash-personal assistant, but that didn't seem appropriate, here.

"We handle tasks that our clients don't have the time—or manpower—to handle." *We,* in this case, meant Ginny. "Both professional and personal. Research as well. I'm fully bonded and insured. If you—"

"Oh. Yes." There was a gleam in his eye that might have been relief, and his hand swirled the remaining Scotch in his glass, making the ice cubes clink against each other. "God, that would be perfect. What're your rates?"

Ginny had not expected it to be that easy. Probably a little too late, warning alarms went off, and she automatically doubled her hourly rate.

"Two fifty per hour. And I can't say how long it will take." Never with a first-time client, anyway. "If you can get me the copies of the papers to be filed, I can—"

"I can handle the office side of things," he said, cutting

her off firmly. "No, I need you to find my uncle. Find him, without a fuss, and get him back here before Monday."

Ginny's alarms upped their urgency and she could feel her brain backpedaling in panic. What had she just agreed to do? "Oh. Oh, but when I said services, I . . . we're a concierge service, not a detective agency."

"You do research for people, right? I'm not asking you to go interrogate anyone, just . . . track him down." Her would-be client, having grabbed on to her like a lifeline, wasn't going to take no for an answer.

Reluctantly, she nodded. Mallard Professional Services did a fair amount of that: genealogical research, real-estate searches, chasing down random bits of information, although most of her jobs involved running errands and organizing trips for people who didn't have executive secretaries or administrative assistants to do for them.

"Just research. Backtrack his receipts or something, see where he was, find out where he's gone, and tell him to get his ass back here." He laughed then, a deep, practiced chuckle that seemed at odds with his earlier agitation. "I'm not asking you to clunk him over the head and drag him back, just find him, and remind him he's got obligations, that he needs to come back to work—or at least hand over the damn papers—so we can sort this all out. That's all."

Ginny's panic settled a little. If she looked at it that way, he was right, it was all within range of her usual jobs. Certainly no harder than scheduling three teenagers' summer trips across Europe, which she had done for a client last year. But she must have looked hesitant, still. He licked his lips, and nodded, as though finalizing a discussion with himself.

"I'll tell you what, manage this by Monday, before the close of business, and I'll pay time and a half."

Ginny almost stopped breathing. One and a half times . . . or twice what her normal rate was. Not that any of her clients were poor, but . . .

He held out his hand. "Do we have a deal?"

Ginny considered that hand for a second. If there hadn't been witnesses, she might have wiggled out somehow, money or no money. He'd agreed to almost 3k a day way too easily. When people were willing to lay down big money, in her experience, that meant there was a problem she hadn't been told about, that would bite her, eventually.

But real estate, even now, was a high-stakes game, right? With all the Microsoft money around town, God knows how many millions he might have riding on this deal. So maybe it was worth it to him, to throw money at the problem and get this done quickly.

She reminded herself of the non-calling client, and the frustration that had been building in her all week, and swallowed down the unease. It was a new challenge, that was all. A different kind of research. A lot of money.

And Tonica was standing there, elbow propped on the bar, that "whatcha gonna do now, woman?" look on his face, the same expression he wore when he was convinced her team wouldn't be able to come up with the right answer on trivia night. That look just pushed her off the cliff.

She took her new client's hand, giving it a shake she hoped conveyed confidence and competence. "A day's retainer now, clear, to get me started." Eight hours at time and a half . . . yes, that was almost three thousand dollars. That would pay for the rest of Georgie's vet bills and training, and next month's mortgage payment, too. "If the check bounces . . ." she started to say, giving herself an out.

"It won't." There was a level of confidence—no, arrogance—in his voice that shut down any objections she might have made, plus the pen her new client pulled out to write the check looked like it was solid silver, with a ruby chip set in the handle. If the check bounced, she thought, she could demand the pen, instead.

"Jacobs Realty," she read off the check. "And you're Jacobs?" That name didn't sound familiar, at all.

"Walter Jacobs." He suddenly seemed to realize that they'd gone about this ass-backward, because his laugh this time held a tinge of embarrassment. "DubJay, people call me."

That name rang a bell. Clearly, he had no memory of her at all, despite going head-to-head some trivia nights. Another time, that might have annoyed her. Right now, still in saleswoman mode, she merely held the check in her hand, and smiled.

"We run—my uncle Joe and I—we run a corporate realty firm," he continued. "Finding and leasing offices for smaller companies, that sort of thing."

Ginny worked out of her apartment, but she nodded like she walked in every morning to a rental office with a receptionist and free coffee. Always make the client believe you're totally on-key with them; that was the first rule.

He had let go of her hand, but kept looking her directly in the eyes—so directly that she started to feel uneasy all over again. "Walking in here, all I wanted to do was get a drink and bitch a little to Tony, here. Your offer . . . this was just incredible," he said. "I really had no idea how I was going to handle everything and not lose my mind."

"That's our specialty, keeping your sanity intact." She smiled brightly, her natural confidence winning through the doubts, even as she folded the check and put it in her jacket pocket.

Off to the side and nearly forgotten, Tonica rolled his eyes, just enough for Ginny to see. Her smile didn't falter, but she could feel something twitch in her cheek. He did that just to drive her insane, she knew it.

She wondered if he'd even noticed that the guy had gotten his name wrong. Probably.

"Here"—and DubJay, oblivious to the drama being enacted around them, pulled his cell phone out and started typing. "I'm sending you his digital card: all his particulars are on it, that should be enough to start, right? Anything else you need, just call me, and I'll get it for you."

A tinny little *ding* from the bar behind her indicated the card had arrived.

"Yeah, um, okay." Ginny knew that she should have offered to give him client references, done her whole spiel, but there was already a check in her hands and a deadline, and she was feeling a little like she'd just been hit by a truck.

"I'll need his Social Security number, his credit cards, his address, that sort of thing." Hopefully he wouldn't put up a fuss: she'd had too many clients who'd expected her to work wonders without any personal information at all.

"I'll have his secretary be in touch."

As easy as that. DubJay tossed back the last of his Scotch, picked up his overcoat where it had been folded across the barstool, and walked out like he had someone waiting for him by the curb.

"You look like someone just slapped you with a fish."

For once, Tonica's voice was more sympathetic than mocking, but Ginny didn't trust it. "That's pretty much how I feel. Like I just had a run-in with a very large, very confident fish that left me with a large check in my pocket."

"DubJay's like that."

"Fishy?" She turned back to her seat, and took another sip of her drink. Her hand shook a little with the weight of the glass.

"Overpowering." Tonica waited until she let go of the glass, then took it away and mixed her a new one, without asking.

"He brought a woman in here once," he went on, casually. "Pretty, younger than him by maybe a decade. Might've been a date, although he's married. Might just have been a closing a deal. He ordered her drinks for her."

"Oh, nice." Her voice dripped with the fact that she thought that was anything but nice.

"Yeah, she didn't seem real thrilled with it, either. When

25

she changed his order to something else, he laughed, but . . . well, he didn't bring her here again, far as I know. Sure not on my shift."

Ginny knew guys like that; control freaks, especially around women. Not surprising if the guy was a salesman, and owned—okay, co-owned—his own company. "So if I don't bring the guy home by Monday?"

Tonica didn't even have to think about it. "He'll probably sue you to get the first payment back for failure to put out, I mean, perform."

"Nice," she said again.

"Yeah. I don't think he'd bad-mouth you, after the fact, but . . ." He rotated his hand back and forth to indicate that he couldn't be certain.

"Shit. Four days." The unease came back, with a wallop. Now it wasn't just a matter of getting the job done, but protecting her own company, too. Mallard Services had built up a decent reputation over the past two years, but all it took was one person with a grudge—and access to online review sites—to take it down.

She turned a speculative glance on him, and *hrmmm*ed thoughtfully out loud. "You're a smart boy, and you know more about DubJay than I do. How'd you like to help a girl out?"

He held up both hands in front of him in denial. "Hell no. You got yourself into this, Ms. Mallard. You get to handle it yourself."

She watched his face, sorting and discarding ways to talk him into joining her in the insanity. Money? No. Appeal to his better nature? Definitely not. Sweet-talking? She wouldn't know where to begin.

She smiled then, and it wasn't a sweet smile. "What's the matter, Tonica? Afraid this sort of work's too much for you? Maybe you can't handle it? Think I'll show you up, or something?"

He swore under his breath, slapping the cloth down on the counter and making a few of the new patrons—those not used to their sparring—look up in confusion. Ginny didn't let her smile turn into a grin, as she practically watched the gears in his head grind around and around. She didn't know much about people, but she knew his number, for sure.

Finally, he gave in. "You're on."

Georgie lay on the sidewalk, and sighed. She did that regularly, not because she was depressed or sad, but because she liked the noise it made, whistling out her throat.

"You sound like an old man when you do that."

The scolding was accompanied by a gentle swat on the side of Georgie's head. The faint prick of claws might have caused another dog to shift, or growl in protest, but Georgie was getting used to it, and the folds of her skin protected her from such a glancing blow, anyway. The cat's restless kneading of her skin was oddly comforting, like the feel of a human hand petting her head, only smaller and sharper and more prone to swatting for no reason whatsoever.

But right now, all she could think about was how bored she was. Even the damp air, which usually carried a hundred and ten different smells, was boring her.

"How much longer is she going to be in there?" There was only one she, to Georgie.

"It hasn't been that long. You want to go home already?"

"No."

She did, kind of.

Penny backed away, then jumped up on the sill of the big window, and looked inside. *"They're talking,"* she reported back.

"They" meant Ginny and the man with the warm hands, called Teddy. He had come out a few times and petted her and given her water. That was all it took for Georgie to decide that she liked him. She wasn't sure Ginny did, though. It was so hard to tell. Humans didn't sniff or bark or show submission, or if they did, it was in ways a dog couldn't tell.

Penny might. But she might not, and make something up if Georgie asked. Cats were like that. Penny was a good friend, but she could be mean sometimes, too.

Georgie sighed again, resting her square head on her paws. *"They'll be there foreeeeever."*

Penny swatted her again. *"Yeah, at least another half an hour. Calm down, you drama hound. She always has you home in time for supper. And what, you'd rather be home on your cushion, with nothing to look at except the same old, same old?"*

"Yes." Georgie reconsidered. *"Oh all right, no. It's nice to have the change, and to get the chance to talk to you. But I miss her."*

"Dogs. Sheesh."

Georgie raised her head at that, just enough to look Penny in the eye. *"Oh yeah, cause you weren't worried when he was home sick those days and you didn't know where he lived to check on him."*

"Humans are humans. I don't need any of them. Do I look like

28

the collared type?" Penny flicked her long tail back and forth, and looked insulted.

Georgie snorted, a heavier, less elegant sound than her sigh. "You just keep telling yourself that, Mistress Penny-Drops."

Cats might be smarter, but there were some things even dogs knew.

2

Five days a week, Ginny's alarm was set to go off at 6:00 a.m. At 5:58 Friday morning, a low whine reached her brain, and she threw an arm out, as though to slap the clock. Instead, she reached a flat, warm shape, shoved up next to her bed. A flat, warm, slightly fuzzy shape that came with a long, wet tongue.

"Right." It took her brain a moment to process the information. "I'm up, Georgie, I'm up."

They both knew that was a lie. But when the alarm did go off, two minutes later, Ginny rolled out of bed with a groan, shutting the *beep-beep-beep* noise off with one hand while she pushed sweat-dampened strands of hair off her neck with the other. She needed a haircut; her curls got out of control if she let them grow too long.

"I suppose you want to be walked," she said to her companion.

Georgie's pig-curl of a tail was too short to thump but her butt wiggled, and her wrinkled face scrunched up more in anticipation. Shar-peis weren't the prettiest dogs in the world, God knew, but Georgie's expressive brown eyes always made Ginny feel better, somehow. Like the Grinch, when his heart grew.

Not that Ginny thought of herself as particularly Grinch-like, but she admitted to being a bit . . . reserved. Certainly, acquiring a half-grown dog had not been on her to-do list when she had wandered into downtown Ballard that fateful day last summer. All she'd wanted to do was pick up some coffee, and maybe look at a new pair of shoes.

The local shelter had set their cages up along the sidewalk in front of the storefronts, parading the larger dogs, encouraging people to come in and pet the smaller ones, and Ginny had come to a full stop at the first sight of that ridiculous body, the skin folded over neatly as though waiting for the dog inside to grow into it. And then Georgie had looked up at her, massive brown eyes and one ear that didn't flop right, and Ginny was lost.

She reached out now and scrubbed those ears with her hand, making Georgie's eyes squint shut in delight, and her backside waggled harder, making it a full-body squirm.

Breathe, she reminded herself. Breathe, and let the bad things go.

The past few years had been such a stress-fest, between the company she worked for being bought out, and everyone being canned that same week, and a relationship she'd thought was long term turning out to be not so much. And then her parents trying to get her to do something "more practical" instead of pouring everything she had into starting this new business? Yeah. Bad stress, the kind martinis and massages and gym workouts didn't touch.

And then, Georgie.

Ginny had not been expecting that having someone look at you with such expectant adoration would be a feel-better tonic better than anything late-night TV or magazines could hawk, and with a hell of a lot fewer calories than a hot-fudge sundae. But it was, it absolutely was.

But there were obligations, too.

"Right. Go get your leash. Leash, Georgie."

The dog dashed off, nails clicking on the hardwood floor of the condo. Ginny got out of bed and shucked off her pajama bottoms—white cotton with bright yellow ducks, a present from her friend Max—dropped them on the bed to deal with later, and pulled on a pair of gray sweatpants. For a quick pee-walk, she didn't need underwear or a bra—her yellow tank top and a hoodie was decent enough for 6:00-a.m. standards, so long as she didn't try to jog.

She was pulling on her Keds when Georgie came back, the tattered pink leash in her mouth.

"Good girl. Let's go."

She hadn't thought to look out the window before they left the apartment, and water was coming down almost hard enough to actually qualify as rain. Ginny looked up at the sky from the front steps of her building, and sighed. "Really? In September?"

She thought the cloud cover lightened a little bit as they stepped outside, but it could have been her imagination. Georgie looked annoyed at getting wet, but her need to go outweighed her dislike of the weather, and they proceeded down the block, looking for exactly the right place.

Their neighborhood—only a few blocks away from the downtown area proper—was moderately upscale, but with the feel of a place that had gentrified slowly, rather than having developers come in and force-feed the change. Old warehouses still lined the bay, and the little breakfast place that had been there since the 1920s was still in business, but there was a fancy bike shop on the corner, and a bunch of high-end restaurants and boutiques that had come in over the past ten years, despite the crap economy. Even the old buildings like hers had been renovated to compete with the newer condos uphill, although she didn't have the water view they did.

"You couldn't afford it if you did," she muttered. She'd looked at one of those condos, when she first moved here. Fancy kitchens, and with great views, but she loved her old building, with its occasionally cranky personality and pre-war curves, more.

And, as a bonus, the city had left all the old trees lining the streets down here intact during the gentrification, so in the spring there was green, and in the autumn, for a very brief time, there was a splash of red, and Georgie had a wealth of topics to sniff around during her walks.

"Georgie, leave it," she said, looking down in time to see the shar-pei sniffing at a cigarette butt. "Smoking's bad for you."

It wasn't a particularly exciting neighborhood—her friends who lived in trendier hotspots or more luxurious suburbs had laughed when she moved here—but it had a distinct, slightly quirky personality, and Ginny liked the feel of it. Plus, her mother and stepfather were happily settled in their little suburban split-level just on the other side of Seattle proper, which meant that they were close enough to visit regularly, but not so close that she was expected to see them every week.

That was another headache lurking that even Georgie's puppy-love couldn't defeat. Her parents, who still didn't understand why she'd want to work for herself, rather than get another "stable" job, who wanted to know when she was going to start dating again, who never actually came out and asked if she was unhappy but acted like they knew she was . . .

She wasn't unhappy. She wasn't particularly happy, either—no, that wasn't true. She just defined happiness differently than her parents did. And she loved her work.

Georgie finally moved to the curb and did her thing. Ginny waited, then pulled a biodegradable baggie from her hoodie's pocket and bent down to clear it away. "You know, owning dogs was probably a lot easier before pooper-scooper laws."

Georgie looked up at her, blue-black tongue hanging out of the corner of her mouth, and then turned back to sniff at where she'd just pooped.

"Oh, ew." She tugged at the leash, and Georgie, obliging, abandoned that smell for the next one. "I bet it's good to be a dog. Smell this, smell that, mark something else, chase a stick. Nobody giving you grief about what you're going to do next."

Happiness was relative. She had friends, she dated, she

wasn't lacking for work, even if lately it wasn't exactly a mental challenge. Even the panic and glee of running a small business was starting to get stale. This new job, though—that had possibilities, she thought. It might not be particularly exciting, but it would be different. And different meant adding to your résumé, which meant the possibility of new jobs even more interesting down the line.

That was what Ginny told herself, anyway, tossing the used doggie bag into the trash. And the time limit . . . she was used to working with those, too. Concierge services didn't usually work on long-term projects. Get in, get it done, get out, move on.

"Just usually not so much money riding on a deadline."

Georgie, alerted to something in her voice, looked up inquisitively, as though to ask what was wrong.

"Nothing, baby. Just Mom talking to herself. Go on with what you were doing."

Georgie did her business a second time, sniffed backsides with the poodle who lived down the street, and let herself be brought back home and given fresh water and a chew-bone. The shar-pei settled on the kitchen floor, gnawing contentedly.

Ginny stood there and watched her for a moment, soaking in the contented doggie vibes, then shook her head. "Definitely easier to be a dog. Good girl, Georgie. Don't get into trouble while I'm gone."

Ginny hit START on the coffee machine and disappeared into the bathroom, where she threw herself under the shower, letting the hot water and promise of caffeine bring her all the way to wakefulness.

The problem with this new job, she thought as she rinsed her hair, was that she had no idea where to begin. Normally, there was an end goal: get the party arranged, find the best movers within budget, bring things in for repairs and take them back home again. Even the trickier projects had a definite goal, a series of checklists she could make and follow, to reach the final solution.

This? Not so much. Was there a checklist for tracking down an AWOL real-estate broker?

"If there is, it's on the Internet. Everything's on the Internet. But I have no idea what keywords I'd use . . . 'Where in the world is Joseph Jacobs?'"

It was silly, but talking it out served the purpose in getting her brain back on track. Every job had steps. The fact that she didn't know the exact, precise steps for this didn't mean she couldn't figure them out. Finding a missing person wasn't exactly on her list of services, no, but it was just a matter of narrowing options until you saw the obvious, right? If she could figure out the perfect vacation for someone's fiftieth wedding anniversary when the participants couldn't decide—and get a thank-you postcard from them both—then this should be a piece of cake.

"Ignoring the fact that you've never baked a successful cake in your life?"

She stared at herself in the mirror, her normally unruly curls slick against her scalp, and turned her head from side to side, to better check the lines that were starting to form around her eyes. She looked tired, she thought. Or maybe it was just the difference between being thirty-three and turning thirty-four?

"Oh yeah, because thirty-four is ancient. You don't get paid for your looks, Mallard, and that's a damn good thing. Coffee. Work. And no more talking to yourself allowed. That's what you have a dog for."

From outside the bathroom, as though she heard that, Georgie let out a low woof.

"Yeah, yeah, give me a minute, will you? Sheesh. Some dogs, so demanding . . ."

She toweled off and, wrapped in the towel, went outside, pausing long enough to give Georgie a loving head-noogie before going into her bedroom to dig out a pair of jeans that had seen better days and a silk blouse from her old office wardrobe. She'd found, early on, that she worked better if she dressed like she was dealing with people in person, rather than through the phone and computer. Sweats were for off-hours only.

Dressed, but not quite ready for the workday, Ginny headed to the kitchen, with Georgie padding along behind her. Her bare feet were silent, but the dog's claws clicked against the hardwood, a sound that had quickly become comforting rather than odd.

"You want to go to the park later today, doll? If I can get things cooking along by lunchtime, and the rain goes away, maybe we'll do that, you think?"

Georgie's butt wriggled again, hearing the word "park." Or maybe it was "lunchtime."

The kitchen was small, compared to the rest of the apartment, but it had been well designed for the basics: two steps from the fridge to the counter, and another two steps to the sink. The only problem was that it hadn't been designed with a place to put a dog's water bowl that wasn't underfoot.

Ginny looked at the puddle of water where she'd once again knocked the dish with her foot, and sighed. "Coffee."

Once the spill was cleaned up and the dish was refilled, she poured her coffee into an oversized mug and carried it with her into the office, Georgie again following behind, the same parade as every workday.

The larger of the two small bedrooms in her apartment, it was arranged for maximum efficiency, with an *L*-shaped desk in the center, a twenty-four-inch monitor taking up one side, and paperwork in varying piles on the other. She ignored the paperwork, sliding into her chair and waking up the computer, while Georgie took her position on the floor underneath the desk, her head resting on her paws.

A plan of attack was starting to form in Ginny's mind, but first things first. She clicked over to her bank, and confirmed that part of the check she had digitally deposited the evening before was already being processed.

"All right then," she said in satisfaction. "We're in business, Georgie-girl."

Not that she had actually believed the check would bounce, but everyone knew that you didn't start work without confirmation, not even when you were on a deadline. Maybe especially not then.

Despite what her mother and stepfather seemed to

think, the squalid glamour of the hand-to-mouth free-lancer had not been her plan when she went freelance three years ago. She was in this to make a living. A *good* living, thank you very much.

The personal concierge business was still new, and she had to explain it to a lot of people before they signed on, but Ginny was good at it—calm, focused, and tenacious in getting things done. She was capable of handling two or three clients at a time, but disdained multitasking, prefer-ring to deal with each project in order.

That disdain didn't mean she wouldn't use *tools* that multitasked, though. A concierge's best tool was her brain, but her second best was a fast Internet connection.

Checking her email, she found that DubJay hadn't wasted any time: there was an email from someone named Elizabeth at JacobsRealty.com with the information she'd asked for, no questions asked.

"And that, children, is how you get your identity stolen. Tsk-tsk." Still, she supposed when the Big Boss told you to send info, you sent it.

With that, and the details on the digital card that Walter Jacobs—DubJay—had sent her the night before, Ginny could start the hunt.

Opening several more browser windows, she accessed a few of the national databases she maintained accounts with, typed in Joseph Jacobs's full name, address, date of birth, and Social Security number, and hit ENTER.

"So now we find out—who are you, and what have you been up to, Mr. Jacobs?"

If he had any outstanding legal issues, public financial difficulties, or had appeared in the news—either local or national—in the past three months, her sources would tell her. Odds were, nothing would show up—or what came up would be useless in this particular search—but she didn't get her reputation by being sloppy.

Acting on impulse, she also entered the name of the company itself. Real estate, yeah, but what kind, and what kind of reputation did they have? It wasn't germane to the job, but . . . Ginny liked having information. You never knew when it might be useful.

"Which reminds me . . ." She entered their URL into the browser, brought up their website, and studied it. Smart and to the point, with very little clutter. There were drop-downs for market research, properties, and a section for clients that required a log-in. The splash page merely identified who they were—commercial real-estate brokers, working with small- to medium-sized clients in the Seattle-to-Vancouver area—and how to reach them if you were interested.

They didn't market themselves to the general public, clearly.

DubJay was listed first. Interesting, considering his uncle had founded the company. But she supposed, from what the client had said, that the older man was getting ready to retire, leaving more and more of the front-office stuff to his nephew. That would explain why he felt free to disappear, assuming that DubJay would handle any problems. It didn't explain why he forgot to leave the papers with his nephew, but she supposed things did get over-looked, or shuffled into the wrong pile. . . .

Letting the background searches run, Ginny swiveled in her chair, her bare feet resting on Georgie's warm, sleeping back, and picked up her cell phone, dialing the first credit-card company's number listed in the email.

The phone tree options were listed in a mechanical voice, and she pressed 2, then 4, and then entered in the credit-card number.

"It's nice working with a client who has their shit to-gether, Georgie," she said to the sleeping form under her desk. "All the things I need, and none of the fuss I don't. And pays without a fuss."

Assuming she accomplished the task, a small voice that sounded a lot like one particular bartender told her. By Monday.

"Shut up," she told the voice, then heard the click that told her a live person was about to join her on the phone call.

"Hi," she said, aiming for brightly cheerful but obviously worried, "I can't find my card and I want to make sure that nobody else got their hands on it. . . . Yes, the Social Secu-rity number is—" and she rattled off the number smoothly, praying that they wouldn't notice it was associated with a male name, rather than a female. She had no problem claiming to be Mrs. Client, if needed, but the fewer white lies she told, the fewer she'd have to confess later.

Not that she went to confession, but childhood training had left its mark.

As expected, the man on the other end just assumed she was Mrs. Client, and gave her the last three purchases on the card. If it was an innocent query, he was doing good customer service. If she was trying to make sure hubby wasn't buying flowers or undies for another woman—or another man, for that matter—well, he didn't want to know.

The desire for a lack of fuss made Ginny's job easier, on a regular basis.

She repeated that question three more times, for three more credit cards—two more personal cards, one corporate—only once having to fall back on her little white lie.

When she hung up the phone after the last call, Ginny looked at the notes she had compiled, and chewed on the end of her pen, thinking.

"A man goes missing, Georgie. And the last things he spends money on are a fancy dinner, a car service, dry cleaning, and his monthly parking validation downtown. Not a single suspicious thing in the lot, and nothing that indicates he's about to flit. Unless he's been doing a lot of cash-only business. . . ."

Banks were harder to get information out of than credit-card companies. Normally, Ginny approved of that.

She opened her email again, and started typing.

Dear Mr. Jacobs,

He might have said *call me DubJay,* but she was on the clock, and business communications should stay formal.

It would help my search greatly if I knew if your uncle's ATM card was used in the 36 hours before his disappearance, and how much money was withdrawn. Also, if he is using it as a debit card. I realize that you might not have access to this information but if you do, it would facilitate my search considerably, and speed up the end result. Sincerely,

She checked the email for typos, then hit SEND, just as her cell phone rang. She grabbed it up off the desk, and checked the number before answering.

"Oh God, no."

The temptation to ignore it was intense, but she knew from experience that that only made things worse.

"Hello? Oh, hi, Dad."

She leaned back and put her feet up on the desk, balancing carefully in the chair. She'd lucked out. Her mother called to fuss at her, usually with the deep sighs of, "I only want what's best for you." Her stepfather tended to call when he had something to say—usually a rant—and he was looking for an audience, not a partner. All she had to do was grunt at the right moments, and not fall asleep, and she was golden.

This time, it was about an increase in property taxes, something Ginny tended to treat like an act of God—they would come no matter what she did, and there wasn't much point griping about it. But her stepfather had never met a topic he couldn't grouse about.

Finally, he ran down enough to ask her how she was doing.

"All right. Got a new client, interesting work. No, I'm not seeing anyone. And don't tell me you weren't going to ask, because you totally were."

It didn't grit quite so much when her stepfather did it. Her mother . . . better to tell him, and let him tell her.

"All right. Yeah, I love you, too. Look, I'm in the middle of something, I gotta go. I'll talk to you later."

She hung up the phone and let out a sigh, the kind that had "parents" written all over it. She had been perfectly comfortable being an only child, growing up, but as an adult she often wished there was someone to share the weight.

"Georgie, I promise, I will never grow old and drive you crazy like that."

Her dog snored in response, fast asleep.

"Yeah. Good to be a dog." She swiveled in her chair, and checked the computer screen. Her searches were still running. "Okay, dry cleaning. If you're going away, you might pick up your suits, yeah. And go out to dinner. But it doesn't tell me where he might have gone. Seriously, guy, would it have been so difficult for you to have—I don't know—booked a plane ticket, or a hotel room? Ordered a pizza?"

Underneath her feet, Georgie moaned in her sleep, and let out a nearly toxic fart.

"Oh God." There was only so much love could excuse,

and that wasn't it. "Thanks, puppy." Ginny opened the window behind her, noting that the rain had, in fact, ended, and used the need to let the air clear as an excuse to get another cup of coffee.

On her way back from the kitchen, refilled mug in hand, she had a thought. Sitting down again at the desk, setting the mug safely out of the spill zone, she picked up her cell phone and sent a quick text to the number she'd gotten from Tonica last night, before leaving Mary's.

Find what you can abt Joe's rep—or DubJay.

She was working the financial and legal aspects, the obvious first routes, but Tonica might have contacts in areas she couldn't touch. Not that she believed he had any illegal contacts . . . slightly off-straight maybe, but not illegal. Probably.

She wouldn't ask, that was all.

The point was, he might be able to dig up something she couldn't, something that Jacobs senior wouldn't have expected to be under scrutiny, and therefore hadn't been so careful about.

"If I could get my hands on his computer . . . okay, if Darren could get his hands on that computer." If someone had been dumping emails or trying to erase files, her on-call tech guy would know, and for the price of a decent bottle of wine, he'd find it. But the chances of DubJay letting a stranger in on a company computer on her say-so . . . ? Not going to happen. And that was assuming she could even find Darren over the weekend.

No, her best bet to dig up actual dirt was through Tonica's contacts. Although mainly, Ginny admitted to herself, she just wanted to let him know that some people were awake and working at 8:00 a.m. It was probably petty, but she just could never resist the urge to get a good verbal hook in. Not when it was Tonica, anyway.

In her defense, he not only took the hook, but tossed it back at her, each time.

"He's not bad, Tonica isn't," she said, settling back at her desk. "Tall, strong, reasonably smart, reasonably easy on the eyes, and he shakes a mean martini. I'd marry him if it didn't mean having to put up with him twenty-four/seven."

Georgie, who had woken up at some point, rolled over onto her back so that Ginny could rub her belly, the dog seemingly unimpressed by Ginny's admission.

Ginny obliged the request for a few minutes, then tucked her left foot under her, telling Georgie that the belly rub was over, and took a deep sip of her coffee. "Think about the checklist. Credit cards, done. Bank info, pending Jacobs. Legal write-up, pending reports. Personal gossip, pending Tonica. Is there anything you can think of right now that would be useful, not just spinning your wheels?"

There wasn't.

"I swear, at least half this job's always waiting." Still, it wasn't as though she didn't have anything else to do. There were reports to generate on another job, and invoices to file, and—being an office of one still seemed to generate enough paper to drown five people, and much of it was of the time-sensitive financial sort.

"Eeny, meeny, miny, mo. Which of these piles do I most want to go?"

Her finger settled on the one closest to her, and she placed her palm down on the top and pulled it to her. "Oh, goodie, financial filing. My favorite."

She'd gotten through about half of the pile, muttering dire things about state bureaucracy, when a beep from the computer behind her indicated the first of her searches had returned results.

"That was fast." She frowned, tapping the screen to bring up the results. "Too fast."

Too fast meant either there wasn't anything to find, or there was so much junk floating around, it would require hours of wading through to find anything useful. Neither was good.

The too-loud beep of his phone had woken Teddy out of a pleasant, dreamless sleep, and he was particularly annoyed about it.

"I should not have given that woman my number."

It had seemed a reasonable request when she made it, but he had thought she might call him, maybe. At a reasonable hour. Not blip an incomprehensible message into his ears at oh-my-God-early.

Teddy stared up at the ceiling of his bedroom, one hand behind his head, the other resting across his stomach, clutching his cell phone. The digital clock by the side of his bed told him that it was 8:09 in the morning. Mary's closed at 2:00, but he had been there until 3:00 a.m., had made it to bed just before 4:00 a.m., and normally would still be asleep until the alarm got him up at noon.

Noon was a reasonable hour to wake up, when you kept bartender hours. Especially after working a double shift. Did the woman have no clue? No couth? No kindness?

He lifted the phone again, and squinted at the message, which this time was reformed into legible words. "'Find out something about Joe.' Right. Who the hell is Joe?"

He let the hand holding the phone drop back to his side, and rubbed his eyes with his other hand, as though that would make the missing Joe show up.

"Oh, right. DubJay's uncle." They'd never mentioned a name, not that he remembered, but clearly she'd gotten more information, and forgotten that he didn't have it.

Forgotten, or just not thought to tell him. Or was she trying to screw with him, seeing how fast he was on the uptake? No, this wasn't trivia night, they weren't competing, they were working together. Which meant sharing all their information. Right?

"Right," he said out loud. "I hope to hell she remembers that."

He also hoped she was going to cut him in for some of what DubJay was paying her. Although she was a good tipper, he'd give her that. Not stingy the way so many regulars got, like the fact that they were there all the time meant they didn't have to play fair.

Not that he was working for her. He was helping her out. Did helping out include payment? He really should have clarified that before he agreed.

Teddy uncurled his fingers, letting the phone drop to the mattress, and closed his eyes, trying to go back to sleep. Too early to be awake. Too early to be poking into someone else's problems.

Unfortunately, lying there, he became aware of every single noise, from the sound of the mattress creaking slightly underneath him to the occasional rumble of traffic outside his window. There were blackout shades and curtains drawn; these muffled the light and most of the noise, but nothing was perfect. And the moment he became aware of how aware he was, the noise slipped in further, making itself at home, until his ears, his skin, felt oversensitized.

He pulled the pillow out from under his head and put it over his face. It was no use. The damned woman had woken him and he was up now. Too many years of training: even now he couldn't even bring himself to hit the mental snooze button, even though he had every right to be sleeping.

"Damn it. All right. Fine. You win." If she ever asked, he'd swear he didn't pick up the message until he woke up at noon.

Swinging his feet off the mattress, Teddy pulled on the pair of jeans he'd dropped on the floor the night before, then padded across the apartment to the kitchenette, pausing to look out the window. Cloudy, with a chance of gray.

He pressed the START button on the coffeemaker, overriding the timer, and opened the fridge, pulling out eggs and a loaf of whole wheat bread. It was earlier than he usually ate, but be damned if he was going to work on an empty stomach.

A quick fried egg and toast later, Teddy pushed his plate aside, finished the coffee that had gone cool in his mug, and stared across the apartment. Weak sunlight was starting to filter in through the windows at the far end of his studio, dappling the bare floor. He really should buy a rug, or something. Eventually.

He'd lived in this apartment for two years. He was never going to buy a rug for the floor. Teddy was well aware of that fact. But he still thought about the fact that he should, eventually.

He'd been raised to live better than this. The fact that he'd chosen to walk away from that life . . . "There's a difference between living a simple life and punishing yourself with cold feet," he said, not for the first time.

"'Find out what you can about Joe's rep,' she says. His reputation? How does she expect me to do that, start looking up his old college buddies? Start asking the bank teller? Or, I know, invite all his country-club buddies in for a drink, and get them to spill their guts. I'm sure I have a tux in my closet somewhere. . . ."

What he should do was go for a run. Or hit the gym. He was pushing thirty-four, and the body wasn't as easy to maintain as it used to be. Or he could try to go back to sleep: Friday nights were hell, and coming in exhausted tonight was not the way to start a weekend. But the look in DubJay's eyes when he gave Ginny that deadline kept him in his chair. He would refuse to pay her, if she didn't come through, no matter how hard she tried. And Teddy was pretty sure that yes, Walter Jacobs *would* bad-mouth Mallard Services if he didn't get what he wanted.

"His reputation, huh?" Maybe she was thinking of a counterstrike, in case he . . . no, that wasn't Mallard's style. She was a straight shooter.

Things had gotten hectic last night, as usual at the start of the weekend, and they hadn't talked much once he'd agreed to help her. Despite the text message this morning, he wasn't sure what she wanted from him, or how much time it was going to take. Well, he knew how much time, because there was a deadline.

Teddy got up and poured himself another cup of coffee, more for something to do than because he really wanted it. This wasn't going to end well. He knew it, even if Ginny was too damn stubborn to admit anything could possibly be wrong. The entire thing was wiffy, like fish that hadn't quite gone off—yet. If it was just a matter of finding the guy, someone like Walter Jacobs could hire a PI without blinking. Hell, he probably had 'em on retainer, or something. But DubJay didn't do that, didn't want to do that. Which meant he had a reason to go outside his usual circle, which meant . . .

Teddy's thought process failed him there. All it probably meant was that DubJay didn't want a paper trail, didn't want anyone to know his uncle had gone walkabout. Lots of reasons for that, even in a privately held company. If you traded on your reputation . . .

Yeah. Going outside your usual circles made sense, then, if you wanted to keep gossip to a minimum. Had the two men been arguing? Was there something amiss in the company itself? Maybe they had disagreed about this deal Dub-Jay was so anxious to close, and walking off was the elder Jacobs's way of throwing a snit. Bad form in business, but well within limits in a family scuffle.

Some tension, which he hadn't even realized was there, eased. The job still stank like wiffy fish, but that didn't mean anything was actually wrong. Sometimes a fish was just a fish, a perfectly edible fish. DubJay might be trying to spare his uncle any embarrassment, or maybe didn't want to have to explain why he sicced a PI on the older man, so instead he was sending a good-looking woman after him.

"Yeah. That's more DubJay's style."

The question of why they'd been hired put on the back burner, Teddy focused on the task she'd set him. "All right. Fine. Uncle Joe. Joseph Jacobs? Let's assume so, since it's Jacobs Realty, right? What dirt have you gotten on you, and who would know about it, Uncle Joe?"

He felt a weird surge of energy, an excitement in his gut, and mentally handed another point over to Mallard. Ginny had been right: he couldn't resist a challenge any more than she could. He enjoyed bartending, liked managing the weekend staff, but the truth was, after three years working at Mary's, rearranging the way the bar worked to his own satisfaction, the job had become routine. It wasn't enough to keep his brain occupied.

He was bored.

"Dirt. Business. Ah. And I know exactly where to start digging." He got up and dropped the dishes in the sink, and then retrieved the cell phone from his bed. It was still too early to call most of his contacts—they were night owls, the same as him—but there was one person who would be awake now. And she might even take his call.

Elizabeth wasn't on his speed dial, but he didn't have to look the number up. Ten digits, and the sound of a phone ringing. He scraped at a bit of wax on the table, and resisted the urge to pace.

"Hello?" A woman's voice—yep, awake even at this hour—carefully modulated and controlled.

"It's Teddy. I need you to do me a favor."

A long silence, then a sigh.

"Please."

She was probably calculating what sort of favor it was going to be. Not an illegal one—she knew him better than that. Not a massively expensive one—he would have called someone else if it had been about money. She narrowed it down in her brain, finally deciding—almost palpably, over the phone—that whatever it was, she could wing it. "Hit me."

"Walter Jacobs. Runs a real-estate company out here, corporate space. Partnered with his uncle."

"And?"

"I'm curious, is all. Mainly about the uncle, but anything you can get."

He could tell that wasn't flying, but waited, and finally got another, heavier sigh in response. That one, though, was just for show.

"All right. I'll see what I can scare up. I can reach you at this number?"

"Yeah. And . . . we're on the clock."

"Jesus. Okay, how fast? Hours, days?"

"Anything you can find out in the next twenty-four?"

"Theo, if you weren't my favorite cousin . . ."

That surprised a laugh out of him. "You mean, the only one who doesn't give you shit for your choice of careers."

"That, too. All right, another call's coming in. I'll get back to you."

And the line at the other end went dead.

"Typical." Elizabeth was your textbook Type A over-achiever, even for his family, and she didn't have much use for social niceties. That was part of what made her such a good pathologist—and crap at family reunions.

Not that he was much good with those, either.

Teddy looked at the time display on his phone, and weighed his options. The desire for a run was considerably more appealing than making phone calls. Especially to the sort of people he'd have to talk to, if he wanted any real dirt.

"You promised. Why did you promise? Oh, that's right: because you're an idiot. An idiot who can't back down from a challenge. How many times has that gotten you into trouble?"

There were three things Teddy Tonica hated: broken

promises, people who broke promises, and the feeling he got when he let people down, no matter the cause. He'd managed to avoid responsibility for almost five years now, to avoid making promises he might have to break.

This was all Ginny Mallard's fault. She had talked him into agreeing to help, gotten him to promise, and now was pushing him into talking to people who took questions seriously.

And would expect something in return.

He drummed his fingers on the table. "Oh, the hell with it." The people he needed to talk to, unlike Elizabeth, wouldn't be awake now, anyway, and this sort of thing you didn't leave a message for—that gave them too much time to think about what they wanted in return. And if he was lucky, either Lizbet or Ginny would discover something, and he wouldn't have to call them after all.

The idea pleased him. "Right, there ya go, a perfect reason to procrastinate. Run first. Think. Then call, if you have to."

He wouldn't break his promise. He'd just . . . wait a while.

3

The one unexpected thing that had changed in Ginny's life since acquiring a dog was that she now had to be aware of her food at all times.

"No, Georgie."

The dog lowered her head back to her paws, sighing mournfully at her owner's unkindness. Ginny picked up the dropped scrap of chicken, and put it on the side of her plate, then took another bite of her sandwich, frowning at the notes she'd taken. The reports had, as she'd half feared, been mostly useless. In the past three months, Joseph Jacobs, age sixty-four, had stayed well within his credit limit—which was almost twice what she'd made in the past year—and stayed off the radar, except for a speeding ticket, and being named Small Businessman of the Year by not one, but two groups in the local area, mainly because of his contributions to a local community center. She'd done a quick check on the center, and it looked like a decent place for local kids, nothing even slightly shady or questionable about it. His donation, all nicely legal and documented, hadn't been large enough to raise any alarms—he'd just been the one to put them over the top, funding-wise.

If she'd been the subject's mother, she would have been beaming with pride. But in terms of finding a loose thread to pull at, some reason he might have disappeared, her morning's work was an utter disappointment. She couldn't remember the last time she'd seen anything this tidy, not even her own records.

"I don't think the man's so much as missed a credit-card payment his entire life," she told Georgie. Not that she would know if he had—that much detail was off-limits to her. But you didn't get that kind of a credit rating without a clear conscience. Nor was there a lien or judgment against him, pending or dismissed. No divorces, no children, legal or otherwise, of record. He owned his condo with a $300,000 mortgage on a thirty-year term that he'd refinanced in the past year, through the same general-services law firm he'd apparently been using since he started Jacobs Realty back in the early 1980s.

"Hrm. He started the company. His nephew came in after graduation, in"—and Ginny checked her notes to be sure she was right—"1991. All that time, does Uncle Joe still hold the reins? Or not?"

From the way DubJay had been talking, Uncle Joe wasn't the main mover—that's why she'd assumed he was close to retirement—but apparently he could still gum things up by disappearing.

"You know, Georgie, if I had to work with that guy every day, I might go AWOL, too," she said, remembering the way she'd felt worked over from just that brief encounter with DubJay. Of course, Nephew might be exactly like Uncle, in which case she saved her sympathy for the people who had to work with them both.

"Either way, doesn't matter and I don't care. I don't have to like him. I just have to find him." She pursed her lips and exhaled, letting all her frustration flow out in a long breath of air. "Managing paperwork, I can do. Threading government bureaucracies, I can do. Finding people . . ."

She looked at her tablet again, trying to see something in the notes and digital Post-its that would suddenly crystallize into a clue, a lead, a chorus of angels singing hosannas.

The tablet lay on her desk, giving her only what she had put in. Nothing useful.

"I hope to heck that you're having more luck than I am, Tonica. All right, get back to work, me. Just—"

Her phone chimed, indicating an incoming text message. Normally she would ignore it during work hours—her clients didn't text her, and her friends knew better—but with luck it was Tonica coming back with something. So she scooped the phone up off the table, touching the screen to bring the message up, expecting to see Teddy's response.

Dont play pi

Her brain refused to parse it for a second, reading it through a second time, and then a third before it resolved into a legible sentence: *Don't play PI*.

She blinked, and her heart beat a little faster, even as she was tapping the screen to check the number the text had come from.

"Blocked? What do you mean, blocked?" That offended her, on so many levels. Why would you contact someone if you didn't want them to know who sent the message? What was the point of that? She stared at the display for a while, annoyed, when it suddenly hit her: she had just been told to give up a job. By an anonymous caller. Texter. Whatever.

"Oh no you did *not*," she said with feeling, her eyes widening in indignation. "You did not just do that, Mr. Whoever You Are."

Her jaw set in a mulish fashion her parents would have recognized, Ginny deleted the text message, and then ran a save on her notes, transferring a copy of the file to her laptop, for safety's sake. And then, for the hell of it, she sent a copy to herself via email, hanging it in the cloud. Nobody ran her off a job. Especially not a job paying time and a half.

Then she stopped, common sense trumping anger and stubbornness for a moment. Who would tell her to back off? "Hell, who even knew that you took this job?" She flicked them off on her fingers. "DubJay. Tonica, natch. And that's it." She couldn't see either one of them texting her that kind of a warning. It just didn't make sense.

"There could have been someone listening in at the bar, I guess. Why any of them might care . . . DubJay wasn't the most polite guy around, maybe someone wanted him to run into problems? Or maybe they wanted me to be thrown off guard, to give up?" Ginny didn't think she had any enemies, at least not the way the cops meant it when they asked in crime dramas, but she knew she'd pissed people off over the years. She was too blunt in her opinions not to have pissed people off.

"Maybe. Someone yanking my chain. Doesn't matter. I took the job, and anyone who thinks they can push me around or scare me, with an anonymous text from a blocked number?" Well, they hadn't met Virginia Louise Mallard, then.

She looked at the clock on the monitor, and decided on her next course of action. "Georgie?"

The dog raised her head inquiringly.

"Leash, Georgie."

It was early for their afternoon walk, but the shar-pei did not hesitate, rising to her feet and trotting off to get her leash.

The walk down to Mary's was longer than their usual "doggie business" walks, but Georgie knew where they were going, and despite the odd hour seemed pleased by the thought, her entire body radiating anticipation as she trotted along at a faster-than-usual pace.

The bar wasn't open when they arrived, which surprised Ginny; somehow she had the sense of Mary's opening on the dot of twelve. But here it was, almost 1:00 p.m., and they were clearly not ready for business, the heavy curtains still drawn across the front windows, and the red-painted door held open not by the usual cast-iron doorstop, but by a wooden barstool. She studied it for a minute, realizing that the barstool kept the door open enough for air and light to come in, but not so much that strangers might come up and think they were open already.

There were noises coming from within, though: the sound of the radio playing louder than normal, and someone, a man's low voice, singing along.

Normally, she'd have Georgie wait outside, but since they weren't open yet . . . Feeling oddly daring, Ginny tugged at the leash when the shar-pei would have taken her usual spot by the bicycle rack, and ushered them both inside.

The lights were higher than normal—Ginny hadn't even known the overhead fixtures could illuminate that well. She was reassured by the fact that the place looked clean and not too shabby in full light, although the walls could have used fresh paint and the wooden floor was decidedly scuffed.

Seth, who usually worked the small kitchen at the back, helping to serve the limited menu and cleaning up afterward, was sweeping the floor. He had to be in his sixties, balding and wrinkled, but still had the upper-body strength of the minor prizefighter he'd been, back in his twenties. The story went that he'd been on his way to making a semi-decent living as a boxer when he saw one too many knockouts, and the aftermath, and decided that he'd rather keep his brains intact.

"Afternoon," he said with a nod, not seeming to see anything odd in her being there, then did a double take at Georgie. "Uh . . . oh hell, the kitchen's not open and neither are we, technically." He mock-scowled at them both. "I'm not going to see this great hunk of skin any more than I do that devil's beast Tonica insists on giving run of the place. But if the beasties get into a fight . . ."

His words trailed off as Miss Penny jumped down from the bar top and strolled over to stand in front of Georgie, sniffing up into the dog's face with all the familiarity of an old friend.

"All right then," Seth finished. "Clearly not a problem. Not seeing a thing here, nope."

Ginny laughed, and dropped the leash, giving Georgie permission to fold her legs and collapse gently onto the floor. Penny gave the dog one delicate lick on the ear, and then sat on the floor next to her, as though they were about to have a comfortable conversation. Ginny could just imagine Penny asking, "Well, what took you so long to come inside, anyway?"

"Where's Tonica?" she asked Seth, only just now realizing that she had expected him to be here, without knowing what hours he was working. Mary's and Teddy Tonica just went together, in her mind. Imagining him outside, having a life . . .

"He was doing inventory in back, couple-ten minutes ago."

Apparently, he didn't. "Thanks. Georgie, stay."

Her dog twitched one ear at her, but otherwise seemed perfectly content to rest her nose on her paws and not move.

The bartender was in fact in the storeroom, but not

counting: he was perched on a crate, his legs crossed in front of him, reading a book.

"Ahem."

He jumped a little, closing the book and shoving it on the shelf behind him.

"Hey. What're you doing here? We can't serve before opening hours."

"Wow. Nice manners."

"Sorry." She noted that he looked a little flustered; Tonica was a bunch of things, but she'd never actually ever heard him be rude to anyone. Whoever his momma might be, she'd taught him manners. Especially around women. "I just wasn't expecting to see you until we opened."

"Saw the door was open, Seth told me you were back here. You got my text? I figured we could talk easier beforehand?"

She hated the way her voice ended on an up note, making what should have been a statement into a question.

Tonica nodded, running a hand over his flattop like it might have gotten mussed. "Yeah, right, smart. And makes as much sense to meet here as anywhere else."

She couldn't even imagine seeing him anywhere else. Until that moment, she'd never even imagined him as being able to exist anywhere else, as though he were only real behind the bar surrounded by bottles and glassware. Now she couldn't stop wondering.

"Do you even have an apartment?"

The look he gave her was half disbelief, half scorn. "No. I sleep under the bar. Patrick found me wrapped in swaddling in the trash out back with a note saying, 'Please raise this baby to be a bartender.'"

"All right, I'm sorry. Okay? I just . . ." She gave up trying to explain. That stupid text message must have flustered her more than she thought. Ginny wasn't going to give whoever it was the satisfaction, not even in her own head. She had gotten the job fair and square, if maybe a little sneakily. And she wasn't playing PI, anyway. Just doing research, that was all. "Did you find anything?"

"Yeah." He didn't sound happy about it, though. "You?"

She thought about the notes on her tablet, shoved into her bag with printout of the same, just in case. "Find? Yeah. Get anything out of it? Not so much."

"All right, let's take it outside. I don't like leaving Seth out front alone too long. Safe neighborhood or not, a bar's always a tempting target and he's just dumb enough to think that he can still hold off an armed punk."

He stood up, and reached forward to grab a cardboard case of something that seemed heavy. She stepped back and gestured that he should precede her out of the room.

As he did so, curiosity took hold, and she glanced over at the book he had been reading before she came in: *The Moron's Manual for Private Investigation.*

Ginny's first instinct normally would have been to crack a joke, but she found, instead, that she was oddly pleased—and touched. She doubted he'd had the book just lying around. . . .

Then again, with Tonica, who knew?

Not that they were private investigators. Or even public

ones. Concierge services, all up front and licensed. And bonded, too. She had to be, and she suspected bartenders were, too?

A sudden shout from the front of the bar distracted her from that thought. Tonica, sounding seriously annoyed. "Jesus, dog!"

"Oops." Ginny put the book back on the shelf where Tonica had stashed it, and went out to rescue poor Georgie.

"Damned mutt." Teddy suspected his grumbling was totally ruined by the fact that Georgie was currently licking the remains of a dog treat from his palm, her eyes half closed in canine contentment.

Ginny took offense, exactly the way he knew she would. "She's not a mutt. She's a shar-pei."

He wiped his hand on his jeans, and pushed the dog away gently with his knee when she leaned in as though to ask for more. "Yeah, shar-pei and a dash of Jumped the Fence." The usual stocky body, plush, fawn-colored coat, and the loose-fitting skin that he found so odd were hallmarks of the breed, offset in Georgie's case by one ear that, rather than flopping over at the tip, was oversized and erect, and a nose that was longer than breed standard. Not that he would ever admit to anyone that he'd browsed the AKC website the week he'd first encountered Georgie, so Ginny wouldn't be able to put anything over on him.

Ginny reached down and petted the dog on her backside.

"You ignore Uncle Teddy. He's just being grumpy because you startled him."

"The damn dog almost got her fool neck broken, sleeping in the middle of the floor like that. At least Penny knows how to get out of the way of a man carrying a box."

"Bitch bitch bitch." Ginny was sitting at the bar, swinging back and forth on the stool like an oversized kid. Georgie, realizing that one apology-cookie was all she was going to get, gave his hand one last swipe with her broad tongue and went to settle in at her mistress's feet. Teddy knew he should tell the dog to get out, but he figured that so long as Seth wasn't saying anything, she could stay.

Truthfully, he wasn't as comfortable as Ginny in leaving Georgie tied outside. He didn't think anyone would dash off with her—she was a solid forty pounds, by the look of her, and not likely to go willingly—but you heard stuff about puppy mills and laboratories that made a decent person twitch.

He filled one of the shallow bowls they used for nuts with water and bent down to slide it across the floor to within Georgie's reach. She raised her head enough to sniff at it, then put her head back down.

"Stay put," he told her, although Ginny had already given the command to stay. She blinked at him as though to say "well, of course," and then closed her eyes and did a solid impression of a sleeping dog.

He watched her for a minute, then shook his head and went back behind the bar, doing a quick check to make sure that the dishwasher had finished washing. It had; he turned to see if the glassware was fully stocked. It wasn't. He did quick calculations in his head; they must've had breakage during the week they hadn't accounted for.

"Where did Penny disappear to, anyway?" Ginny asked.

Teddy didn't even bother to look around. "God knows. I keep telling you people, she's not a pet, she doesn't come when called, or stay when she's bored."

"Uh-huh." Ginny didn't sound convinced, but it was the truth. The tabby was her own cat; she hung around Mary's because she chose to, and showed up when she damn well felt like it.

He took a look at the speed rail in front of him, mentally estimating what was left in each bottle, tucked into its own niche. "Seth!"

"What?" The old man was busy hauling out the contents of the case he'd brought out, putting replacement bottles behind nearly empty ones on the shelf at the other end of the bar.

"When you get a chance, bring up some more vodka."

The old man muttered something that Teddy took for agreement, and kept unloading the bottles. Teddy picked up his dishrag and started polishing the freshly washed glasses before putting them away. Their dishwasher was a powerful beast that barely left a spot, but it was a bartendery thing to do, and looked good—and it gave him time to think.

"So, what's in the files?" He could read them for himself, he supposed, but Ginny had always struck him as more the "announce" sort.

"Nothing. Of the 'I found a lot but not a damn bit of it's useful' sort."

She had given him the printouts, but brought up the digital files on her tablet-thingy rather than take them back. It was smaller than her laptop and didn't have a keyboard, but was larger than the eBook reader Teddy had gotten for Christmas last year. Teddy admitted he didn't know much about tech, or have any real use for it, but the thing was pretty.

"I went over the records for the company, and they're practically spot-polished clean," she told him. "Ditto our missing man. Assuming that his life prior to this year— education, medical history, his past girlfriends, et cetera— has no relevance, the only things I can confirm are that he founded the company; he has no outstanding loans, liens, warrants, or debts; he is DubJay's uncle; he is currently and previously single, and to all appearances straight; he is in decent medical condition for his age, and that as of ten a.m. Wednesday he seems to have disappeared."

She paused for breath.

"*Seems* to have disappeared?" Teddy finished one glass and put it on the rack, and reached for another.

"I check everything. Always assume the client's lying, right?"

"Woman, you watch too many late-night 1940s detective movies. Not everyone's a dirty lying rat."

Ginny opened her eyes very wide. "You think everyone tells you God's honest truth?"

"Actually, they usually do." He didn't think it was his

face or manner that made people so effusive or honest—it was the whole bartender mythos. Like a priest, only you could drink his communion wine and not go to hell.

"Seriously?" Ginny looked way too impressed by that. "Okay, you're definitely handling any actual questioning of people we have to do. Anyway, there's no missing persons report on Uncle Joe, but he hasn't been seen, heard from, or appeared on the financial radar since then, so for various levels of missing we can assume that yeah, he is indeed missing.

"Anyway, my background checks tell me that Uncle Joe was squeaky clean, on paper—not even an unpaid parking ticket. Far as I can tell, he lived his entire life on record— he uses his credit card to buy everything, down to a glass of wine at the bar!" She shook her head, her curls moving as though to emphasize her disbelief.

"And he hasn't used his credit cards once, since he went missing?"

"Not once. Not his ATM card, either, which would suggest that he had a ready stash of cash on hand. If so, he's either been planning this for a while, or someone else gave him cash, because his last withdrawal was on Monday, for two hundred dollars. Seattle's not exactly cheap, and he's a little too old to be staying in hostels, or hard-flooring it somewhere, so that two hundred's not going to last him long. It's sure as hell not enough to get far out of town, not unless he takes the bus, and I don't know, I just can't see this guy taking Greyhound, can you?"

She paused long enough to take a breath, and slid a printout photo across the bar. He put down the glass he was holding and pulled the photo closer.

The man looking directly into the camera lens was in his late sixties, probably, so it was a recent photo. A full head of hair gone full silver, the skin around his mouth and eyes heavily wrinkled, despite decent texture around the neck and nose—healthy but not vain, Teddy decided, studying the picture. In good shape, probably used the gym just enough to keep the excess weight off, but not really into the whole fitness thing.

He said as much to Ginny.

"Yeah. There's a gym in his building. No idea how much he uses it, but he doesn't have any health club memberships or recent spa retreats or anything like that."

Teddy didn't want to say it, but someone had to. "Have you considered the possibility that he's dead?"

Ginny, being Ginny, had already gone there. "Called the morgue. No record of him, or anyone matching his description. And you know what? They'll tell you pretty much anything, if you ask them politely."

"That's good to know. I guess. Wait, if you're tracking his credit cards . . . how deep into his records did you go? No, never mind, don't tell me. If it's not legal I don't want to know."

"It's all legal." Ginny sounded offended. "Well, it wasn't illegal. I had permission to access the information."

"Not his permission, though."

Ginny scrunched up her face like a little kid presented with broccoli. "Details. DubJay is next of kin, I assumed he also has power of attorney. Makes it all kosher. Ish."

"Right." Teddy shook his head. "Not-illegal is as good as legal, huh? Definitely too many noir detective movies. Wait, you said no *un*paid parking tickets?"

"Yeah. He got one about . . . eleven months ago. Not a parking ticket—for speeding. He has a cute little sports car, a BMW 650i coupe, registered to the company. Man, I wish my job came with those kinds of perks."

"Make yourself CEO of yourself, and see what you can get away with? The fact that he drives too fast is actually reassuring. Someone who doesn't have any marks at all on his file is probably hiding something."

"I wouldn't have thought of that," Ginny admitted, and he was a little annoyed at himself how much her being impressed mattered to him. "Is that good, or bad?"

He shrugged, unable to answer her question. "Could be either, could be neither. He might be a law-abiding citizen, or he might never have gotten caught at anything."

"Other than a speeding ticket. Which he paid."

"Right." He paused in his polishing, and looked her straight in the eye. "Mallard. Have you considered—seriously considered—the thought that he didn't go willingly?"

From the look on her face, she hadn't. Or hadn't wanted to. "DubJay would have said something if he suspected . . ."

"Yeah. Sure he would have. And maybe he doesn't want to think about it, either. All this—none of it's making sense, not what DubJay told us, not what you're finding out. If we find even the slightest hint that he was coerced or kidnapped, we're going to the cops. Right?"

"Absolutely."

But he wasn't sure she looked convinced about that—probably thinking that if she did, she wouldn't get paid. "I mean it, Ginny." Helping out was one thing, but he hadn't signed up for this—and neither had she.

"I know, I know. Jesus, what're you, my mom? Slightest hint of that kind of trouble, we call the cops. But I don't think that's what happened. It feels too . . . clean. He paid all his bills for the month, cleared his schedule for the next week, and picked up his dry cleaning the day before he went missing. That's someone about to go on vacation, not a guy expecting to be yanked off the street and dumped in an alley somewhere."

That presumed he'd expected to be yanked . . . but she had a point.

"He paid all his bills, even the ones not due yet?"

"Yeah. But he was like that; Mr. Paid in Full, On-Time Guy. If I had a credit rating like his . . ."

"You'd blow it on new tech and shoes. What about his parking tag? Does he live near the office? I can't see a guy like that taking public transit, so he must drive in—or does he get driven?"

"With that car?" Ginny gave him a scornful look, ignoring the crack about her shopping habits. "No driver. He's pretty low maintenance, actually, for someone with a few mil. Lives in town, the offices are by the waterfront, near the piers. Mostly, the car stays in his building's garage or the office garage during the week. And yeah, he re-upped the monthly parking tag."

"Huh. So where's his car?"

She stared at him. "Oh shit."

He couldn't believe it. "You didn't think to check on his car?"

"Just that it wasn't in the garage, or in his building's lot, and the cops hadn't any reports of it being found or involved in any accident. The client had that checked out before he hired me. Us. I didn't take the next step. Damn it."

As she spoke, she was tapping the screen of the tablet, muttering under her breath. He had been sort of joking about her blowing money on shoes, but not the tech: between her laptop, her phone, and this newest toy, he'd never seen her actually unplugged for very long.

Even as he thought that, she hauled out the power cord and handed it to him to plug in under the bar, on his side.

He wasn't supposed to let anyone power their tech at the bar, but it was a rule more often ignored than honored. You just couldn't run a half-decent bar in this city if you didn't have an extra power strip or two for your patrons.

"Where the hell was that code . . . look away," she advised him, and he averted his gaze, carefully studying the hanging plants on the other side of the bar. They needed watering.

"Damn it. The cameras only go back twenty-four hours. Cheap bastards, it's not like digital storage costs you anything. . . ."

He was pretty sure she wasn't supposed to have access to

those cameras, no matter who her client was. Then again, the client was in the real-estate business. Who knew what building secrets DubJay knew? "Oh man, if these guys are connected, and I mean *connected,* I am so going to regret helping you."

Ginny either hadn't heard him or was ignoring him. Probably the latter. "The car was there, and then it wasn't. I doubt it was jacked out of that parking lot—if he doesn't have LoJack I'll eat my laptop. So, odds are he's on the road. But he hasn't used his credit cards or gotten more cash, and gas is expensive as hell—like I said, two hundred dollars won't go far, especially with that gas chewer. He could have parked it somewhere . . . bus station? The train? What about the airport?"

She groaned, planting her elbows on the bar and her face in her hands. The blond curls fell around her face, hiding her from view and muffling her words. "I donwannago-huntingdownparkinglots."

"What? Oh Christ, no," Teddy agreed, once he deciphered the whimper. "That would take . . . longer than we've got. There's got to be a better way."

She raised her head up, and stared at him. "What, hire someone else to go look? Getting a cash advance from DubJay would take more time than we've got, and I'm not exactly flush here, how about you?"

"Not everything's a matter of cash, Ginny Mallard," he said, doing his best to channel his mother's voice in reproof. "Let me check in with a few people before you freak out."

He pulled out his own phone and hit 4 on the speed dial. He'd hoped not to have to call . . . but he had promised to help. "Addy. Teddy. I'm calling in that favor, *mon ami*. No, no cash involved. I need to find out if someone's left their car at one of the pay lots in town, or out at the airport."

He smirked, the look of someone who was going to enjoy giving someone else a hard time. "Oh, don't give me that. And don't tell me you don't occasionally do sweeps to make sure everything's clean. I just need to know if it's there, is all."

He held up a hand to keep Ginny from saying anything. "No, I don't . . . no. I don't care when it came in. I just want to know if it's there. Doable?"

Penny appeared out of nowhere, as she usually did, rubbed once against his hand, and then jumped off the counter—he presumed to say hello to Georgie, who had been quietly settled at Ginny's feet throughout their discussion.

"All right. That's all I ask. And yeah, yeah, slate's wiped clean." He held out a hand, and Ginny flipped through the previously untouched paper file until she came to the sheet she wanted, then slid it across the bar to him.

"BMW, dark green, plate's seven-niner-Robert-Joseph-Joseph. Yeah, a vanity plate. Okay, thanks, man." He ended the call and slipped the phone back into his jeans pocket.

"Who did you call? He can do that?" Ginny was practically vibrating with impatience and curiosity.

"He'll try. And his try's usually damn good."

"Huh." She vibrated a little more, then figured out he

wasn't going to tell her anything more, and subsided a little. "It's a pity we can't just go beat it out of people, like in the old pulps."

He eyed her cautiously. She was kidding, right? She was. Probably. He made a note to never introduce her to Adderly, and thought maybe it was time to stage an intervention, before she started believing she was a PI, and went out and bought a gun. Or a fedora. "Ginny, you can't do that. Beating people up. Hell, you can't even talk to people, technically."

"*What?*"

"No, seriously. Without a PI's license . . . you can't do anything except research, and talk to people, casual-like." The guide he'd been reading was really clear on that, although he hadn't gotten very far in the book, yet.

"That's all I am doing: research." She looked almost too innocent when she said it. Her definition of "research" was probably closer to a hacker's than a cop's. "But hey, you can talk to people. Casually. You're a bartender."

She said the word like it solved all problems, and that light in her eye was definitely trouble. He should be running like hell. Why was he not running like hell? Right. Because she had challenged him, and he had bit like a damn dumb fish. And he had promised. "Only when I'm behind the bar. I'm a bartender behind the bar, I mean."

She made a scoffing noise. "Oh, come on . . . don't be a jerk. You know what I mean. You have that bartender-vibe thing going on."

"No, seriously. People think of me as the bartender. I'm

the guy they talk to, the one who solves their problems just by listening and pouring a beer. They're not seeing me, they see"—and he made air quotes—"'The Bartender.' I'm iconic, not personal. That's how it works."

"Uh-huh. Tonica, I've seen you schmooze. You turn on the charm, and look them in the eye, and I don't know how you do it, but you convince people that you give a damn."

"I do give a damn." He scowled at her, realizing that he'd just gotten played. Again. Point to Mallard, more fool him for walking right into it. "And yeah, okay, people like to— or they're *willing to*—tell me stuff in return, if I ask. It makes them feel like they're even on the scales, or something."

"Like that Addy person."

"Adderly's different." Adderly's job was information: he assumed that if Teddy was asking, there was a reason, and not to waste time. Purely business. "But yeah. People—especially people who have bartender-worthy troubles—like to feel needed." He'd never bothered to break it down before. "And they like having me owe them favors. It makes them feel important, like they weren't just complaining into the first sympathetic ear they could find."

"And that's what we need, to get people to *want* to talk to you." She tapped the screen of her tablet thoughtfully, opening what looked like a to-do list. "But first, we need people to talk to. And better—more useful—questions to ask."

"That's your area, Mallard." He was willing to help, but this was her job, not his. He frowned at the rail, and re-arranged the order of the limes and lemons. Someone had moved them, and he didn't want to grab the wrong one, during a rush.

Movement out of the corner of his eye made him look up. "Teddy." Seth approached them diffidently, as though afraid to interrupt, but needing to say something. "It's almost time."

Teddy looked at the windup alarm clock shoved under the bar. "Yeah, thanks, I still have some things I need to get done," he said to Ginny. "You going to hang around a bit, after we open?"

"Not sure we should talk about it with other people around," she said dubiously. "But yeah. Until it gets crowded, anyway. Okay if I set up in the far corner table"—she waved at the small table for two nearest the front window—"and work there? We need to figure out what to do next."

"Yeah, that's fine."

"And hey, Blondie," Seth called over his shoulder as he headed back into the kitchen, his sass restored. "Out with the dog!"

"I told you the next time you called me that, I'd kill your credit rating," she said, not looking around or raising her voice. "All right, Georgie, you heard the not-nice man. Out we go . . ."

The dog obediently got up on her feet, and trotted toward the door, almost as though she were relieved to be going outside, where she belonged.

"I'll be right back," Ginny said over her shoulder. "Try not to trip over anything while I'm gone."

The gesture Teddy made in response would have gotten him a dirty look from his mother. Ginny just laughed, and went out the door after her dog.

"That girl gonna get you in trouble," Seth said from the kitchen's doorway. "Trouuuuuble."

"Yeah, I'm kinda getting that," Teddy said. "Ah, it's only until Monday. How much trouble can we find in three days?"

Seth didn't even bother answering that. But Mallard did. "Scared, Tonica?"

She'd come back faster than he'd expected; he looked out through the plate-glass storefront window to double-check that Georgie was well and truly tied to her usual post. She was, curled up in a comfortable-looking flop on the sidewalk next to the bike rack.

Her owner, meanwhile, was standing in the doorway, hands on her hips and a challenging look on her face.

"Hah." Be damned if he'd back down now. "You just tell me what you need me to do."

And from the kitchen they both heard a mournful male voice call out "Trouuuuuuble . . ."

When the woman went back inside, Penny jumped down from the hood of the parked car she'd been sleeping on, and picked her way across the pavement to the shar-pei. She settled herself on one side of the dog's head, then licked one paw and started to groom Georgie's fur as though she were a kitten. "She looks worried."

"She's fine." No matter what, Georgie would defend her mistress. Her ear twitched: Penny's grooming tickled.

"I'm not saying she isn't. Just that she looked worried."

"She's not worried. Everything's fine." Georgie concentrated, trying to remember if there had been anything that might be not-fine. But it was no use: everything earlier than a few days ago was a blur of memories, her littermates falling over each other in their urgency to get at the milk, alongside the first time Ginny picked her up, as though they'd both happened at the same time.

Penny paused in her grooming, and looked up at the dog with fond disdain. "Hrmmmm."

Georgie was still fussing; now that Penny had mentioned it, she couldn't not worry. "Does she really look worried? It's because of the man they spoke to yesterday, isn't it? The one who smelled like fear?"

"Maybe." And maybe not. But there was something going on, something that had both humans putting their heads together and talking in low voices. Penny hated when they did that; it made it difficult to overhear things then.

Finished with Georgie's head to her satisfaction, Penny sat back and continued twisting the claw, gently, to make sure Georgie fell in with her plan. "It's not like her to come here two days in a row. Not so early. They're talking a lot, too," Penny added.

"So?"

The cat inspected her paw, giving it a few careful grooming licks, nonchalant as an old tom. "So, whatever they're doing, I think that we should help them."

Georgie turned her square-muzzled face sideways, interrupting *the grooming session, and looked at the cat. "I know that voice. That's the voice that got me into trouble before, with the mailman."*

Penny twitched her whiskers as though considering that accusation. "I'm a cat. Trouble's what I do. But that doesn't mean I'm wrong."

Georgie sighed and lowered her head back to the pavement. She wanted to help Ginny, wanted it more than anything else in the world. But . . . "You're going to get us all in trouble. I can tell already."

Walter Jacobs leaned back in his leather-upholstered office chair, the phone—an old-fashioned landline—held in his right hand, the other twirling the silver-and-ruby-chip pen between his fingers.

"No, everything's fine," he reassured the person on the other end of the line. "You know me, I like nailing things down and then adding a layer of glue, just to be certain. The deal will close on Tuesday, just as planned."

The lawyer for the buyers spoke, a faint buzzing sound through the wires, and Jacobs nodded, even though the other man couldn't see him. "Indeed. Every transaction of this size is a headache. But I think that your clients have chosen wisely in this building, an excellent mix of location and price. Once the renovations are done, it will be the premier space in Seattle."

He laughed, an expansive chuckle that wasn't echoed in his expression.

"All right, all right, I can't help myself. Born salesman,

me, especially when I believe in the deal. Yes, all right. You too. Relax, everything's going to be fine. See you on Tuesday."

He ended the call and placed the phone back into the cradle with a delicacy of motion that seemed at odds with his surroundings, the modern lines of the desk and credenza behind him suggesting a more brutal approach.

"That may not have been the smartest promise you've ever made. What happens if we don't get Joseph back here in time? What if he talks?"

The man sitting at the other side of the desk was twice Jacobs's size, a college linebacker not only gone to seed, but also sprouted. But the suit covering his mass was expensively tailored, and the intelligence inside was vicious.

Jacobs flicked one large hand in a "don't worry" gesture. "Joe will come to his senses, eventually. Everything will be fine. I have copies of the papers, and power of attorney with regard to all company decisions. I made sure of that, after Joe's stroke two years ago."

He had especially made sure, once the single deal he had done during that time became three, and then five, and now this. There were things happening that Uncle Joe did not need to put his hand on. The old man needed less stress now, not more.

"And if there's something that seems a bit off, or unclear, well, Stephen wants this deal as badly as we do. He won't rock the boat, even if we have to fudge a few details. And his clients . . . are idiots, who can't see anything but their shiny new building."

His own legal counsel was not so easily reassured. "Your uncle took the most recent markups, as well as the original documents. If he does anything stupid—stupider, I mean—we could have a real problem. You should have had someone deal with him before this, instead of giving him more rope to hang himself with. Because that rope could hang us, too."

There was a suggestion hanging in those words, barely veiled.

Walter leaned forward, the earlier studied casualness dropped to reveal a more intense focus. "There are two things about my uncle that are carved in granite. One is that he is, as they say, an honest man. The other is that he would die rather than bring shame to the family name."

His companion did not look away, or let himself appear intimidated. "You must have been adopted, then."

Walter smiled at that, the momentary tension broken, and leaned back. "You may be right. Don't worry, Sam. Joe will be found and talked off whatever ledge he thinks he's on, we'll file the papers as scheduled on Monday, close on Tuesday, and nobody's nose will twitch even the slightest." He said it with such confidence, he almost believed it was already done.

"And then?"

"Once the paperwork is signed, it all becomes someone else's problem. All we have to do is cash the checks, and never speak of it again. And in September, Joe can take his retirement like a good old man and worry about his health, not business."

He worried about his uncle. The man had been the only father figure he'd ever known, and the stroke had scared him more than it had the older man. His retirement would be good for them all, in so many ways.

Sam remained focused on the papers, unconvinced by Walter's reassurances. "Your uncle has never pulled crap like this before, and he's no dummy. You really think this woman can find him?"

"Unless he's left the country, which I highly doubt, then yes. Virginia Mallard has a good reputation—many happy clients."

"She bills herself as a concierge." Sam might as well have been saying that she was a maid, or a store clerk. "This is a little more important than picking up dry cleaning or arranging a birthday party."

"Tsk. Your bias is showing, Samuel. Concierge services are considerably wider in scale and scope than that—and our Ms. Mallard built quite the résumé in information services before striking out on her own—with excellent references, I might add. A judge, and two rather well-placed businessmen, all singing her praises as trustworthy and discreet. I couldn't have designed someone better suited to our needs."

"Still . . ."

"Still? Not having an advanced degree—or being a woman—does not preclude competence, Sam." His tone was still mild, still collegial, but the veiled hint of Sam's words earlier was sharper here. Tread carefully, it said.

Since Jacobs—who had only gone to a two-year college

before joining the company—paid his retainer, Sam dared not respond to that except to nod agreement.

Walter waited, then, reassured that the lawyer knew his place, continued. "Ms. Mallard is a trained researcher, used to putting together bits of information to achieve the client's desire. Her only concern is getting paid, and her career depends on having satisfied clients. Believe me, I did my own research before choosing her."

He paused, and tilted his head to look at his companion, the action oddly incongruous with his expression. "Or do you think I should have hired a private investigator to track down my uncle? Someone bound by their legal obligations—someone who might, perhaps, have been a cop in an earlier career, who might ask uncomfortable questions, or be able to fill in certain blanks on their own? Do you really believe that would have been the wisest course?"

"Oh Christ, no." The other man's eyes went wide in mild horror at the thought. "But can you control her?"

"I hold the checkbook. That gives me all the power in this relationship. And even if she does scent something off in Joe's disappearance, what might she do about it? The man's an adult, no foul play has come to him, and I've asked her to do nothing even slightly off-color."

"And if you did, I don't want to know about it," Sam muttered quietly.

"I assure you, all my dealings with Ms. Mallard were entirely aboveboard. She will do her damnedest to impress me, in the hopes of gaining my future patronage and referrals. Now, what about the other projects that my beloved uncle has left us in the lurch over? The required details in the Corkin Bay property have been filed?"

"On time, and without a peep from the other parties. So far as they are concerned, everything is proceeding according to plan, and your uncle's absence from the final meeting did not cause the slightest alarm. They were perfectly happy to accept me as his proxy in this final meeting."

In that instance, at least, knowledge of the old man's impending retirement worked in their favor. And perhaps even more: if need be, they could spin this weekend as the first crack in Joe's hold on things, a softening of the wits, where he simply walked off . . .

It might cause some discomfort with other deals, things he had negotiated might have to be reworked, but they could handle damage control later. Seize the day, seize the opportunity, that was Walter's philosophy.

"Excellent," Walter said now. "That's excellent. Now, what else is still pending, that you need to tell me about?"

4

Ginny supposed that, after she talked to Tonica, she could have gone back to her apartment. She probably should have. But there was something about the clear autumn light filtering in through the windows that made her reluctant to move. Or maybe it was just the sense of being surrounded by people while she worked: she loved working at home, but there were times that she missed an office setting, hearing other people talking quietly around her.

Other people, one of whom might have been the one to send that text message to her. The thought made her look again, this time suspiciously.

No. If she started getting paranoid, the caller had won, or something like that.

Her phone chimed at her, the third of four daily alarms she had set.

"Hey, Tonica," she called out. "I'm going to take Georgie for a walk. Can you keep an eye on my stuff?"

When Mary's had opened for the day, Ginny had claimed the table by the window, where the Wi-Fi signal was strongest, and set up the tablet and her cell phone as a portable office. She'd hate to lose the spot, leaving for ten minutes.

"Yeah, I got it." He pulled out a white cloth from under the bar and draped it over the table. "There. Go."

They made a leisurely stroll around the neighborhood, and Ginny thought briefly about taking Georgie home—but the dog seemed content where she was, and truthfully, if they went all the way home, she might as well stay there, too.

Being alone with her paranoia seemed worse than sitting in a crowd.

"You okay with hanging around a while longer?" she asked. Georgie seemed more interested in sniffing the lamppost than responding to a question, but her tail quivered enough for Ginny to decide that yes, Georgie was okay with it.

When they got back, another dog—a shaggy black terrier—was also tied up outside Mary's. Georgie and the other dog exchanged formal sniffs, then settled down next to each other.

"Guess I'm not the only one who likes company sometimes. Okay, then."

Reassured, she went back inside, reclaimed her table, and went to work tracking down the whereabouts of one Joseph Jacobs. Although right then, she was less tracking and more studying.

Walter—DubJay—had come through with the bank information, including the name of the person to talk to at Joe's bank, if she needed it. Ginny considered the phone number, but decided that it wasn't needed—yet. He hadn't closed his account or taken any major withdrawals, and that was what she'd been worried about. He wasn't using his credit or debit cards, either, which meant he was either holed up somewhere for free or where he could pay by check.

"Who pays by check anymore? Who *accepts* checks anymore?" She chewed her lip a minute, then opened a new browser window and entered a series of numbers and codes.

"All right, you haven't made an outgoing call in two days—and everything's going to your voice mail. Hm."

She felt a little dirty, getting access to his phone info. But not enough not to look. Although she did make a mental note to never, ever give anyone her mobile phone account password, even if it seemed like a good idea at the time.

Around 4:30, she finally acknowledged that she was chasing her own tail, and it wasn't going to do her any more good than it did Georgie. The digital trail had shown her where Joseph Jacobs wasn't. To find out where he was, they needed to talk to actual people.

On the plus side, finding people who weren't hiding was, in theory, an easier proposition than one man who was. Ginny turned her attention to that, starting with his date book. At some point, someone put a slice of pizza on her table, and her drink—a ginger ale with a twist of lime—never seemed to get empty, but other than that, she was in her own little world, until she suddenly realized that first, it had gotten dark outside, and that second, there were people in the previously empty spaces around her.

She took out her earplugs, letting the sounds of "St. James Infirmary" spill out of the buds, and stretched her arms over her head, hearing and feeling something in her back crack. Mary's had started to hop with the usual Friday night crowd—mostly neighborhood people decompressing after a long workweek, with a few strangers who found themselves in the neighborhood and were drawn in by the welcoming façade.

Ginny kept her place at the table, out of the way of the social swirl, although people she knew would swing by and say hello, and then move on again when she indicated she wasn't in a social mood. That was one of the nice things about Mary's—people respected the urge to be *among* without being *part of*.

She could see Georgie through the front window, her golden brown pelt highlighted by the streetlamp overhead, the smaller dark shadow to her side probably the terrier. It was misting slightly, but not actively raining, and Georgie didn't seem to mind it at all.

"Native Seattle raindog," she said fondly. Her mother's old poodle had refused to go outside in the rain without a slicker wrapped around his delicate body. Georgie? Barely even noticed. She was game for anything.

Ginny's attention was brought back to the table when her tablet dinged, telling her that an email had landed. It was from one of her other clients, confirming receipt of the requested information and invoice. It was a crazy world where someone else would pay her to research sleep-away camps for their preteen, but some people had more money than time. And thank God for that, or she'd be out of a career.

No matter how tough some days were, the thought of going back to a cube farm, or whatever configuration they were shoving people into these days, did not appeal, at all. So until someone showed up naming her the heir to a million-dollar fortune . . .

She amended that to multimillion. A million didn't go far these days, not even in Seattle. So if keeping Mrs. K happy meant finding the perfect place for Little K to spend his summer, then Mallard Services would do it, and Mrs. K would come back the next time she had money to throw at a problem.

All it took to be successful was to get the job done and never let the client know what you really thought of them.

"Hey, Ginny." It was a familiar voice, coming out of the din, and Ginny reached backward to bump fists, a gesture that felt incredibly silly to her, but Mac insisted on.

Her friend looked over her shoulder. "Girl, are you working?"

"I am."

"Phagh." Mac draped himself elegantly over the chair across the table from Ginny and made a noise of expansive disgust. "Work work work."

"Not all of us pull down a paycheck for not doing anything, Mac."

"Oh, don't you start that. You know I bust my ass. I just

do it efficiently." Mac was a former co-worker who, like Ginny, had decided not to stay in the industry, and struck out on his own. Mac now owned a catering service—where "owned" meant "hired other people to do the actual work." Mac's expertise was in talking people into hiring his company rather than someone else's.

"Sorry. I promise, I'll be more fun next week." A lot more fun, if she managed to pull this job off, and collect the rest of her paycheck.

"Don't work too hard, you. Causes heart attacks, and headaches, and other fun-killing things."

"Go bother someone else, Mac."

One strong hand squeezed her shoulder, and Mac was gone. He meant well, he just . . . he was the butterfly and Ginny was the grasshopper. No, it was grasshopper and mouse. Or something like that. He flitted, and she trudged, and they still managed to be friends, so long as she resisted his insistence that she come to work for him. That would be an utter disaster.

Left alone again, Ginny tried to ignore the noise and stared at the screen, considering the data.

Who and when, where and how. She'd managed to put together an impressive dossier on Joseph Jacobs's friends, family, and everyday associates. Maybe she had too much information? Sometimes that happened. Then you had to filter it, and filter it again, until a pattern emerged, something that actually *told* you something. Like who she needed to talk to.

"Hey."

Tonica had left the bar and headed her way, under the pretext of refilling her glass. Alcohol did not mix with working, so she was drinking ginger ale with lime, but poured into a highball glass, it could pass for alcoholic, so nobody gave her shit.

"Hey," she said to him in return. Normally, that greeting would be followed by some trash-talking before or after a trivia game, or an exchange about the Seahawks or, occasionally, the Rollergirls. Or even to thank him for the pizza, which she assumed he had ordered. But her new partner in not-crime had a look on his face that usually showed up just before his team whomped hers on a high-point question. "What's up?"

Penny, who did not suffer from the same exile that poor Georgie did, took that moment to come up and rub against Ginny's ankles, a purring figure eight. She bent down to scoop the cat up, rubbing her ears idly the same way she would Georgie, and the little cat tilted her head as though to say "right there, please."

Tonica sat down opposite her, which was a definite change from his usual "float lightly" policy when he came out from behind the bar. "One of my contacts just came through. Apparently, there's a rumor floating around that Jacobs's company had irregularities in one of the buildings they'd leased."

"Which means what? I don't know crap about real estate." She frowned, annoyed. "I need to learn about real estate. It could be useful again."

"Which means there were rumors that they'd paid off

inspectors and fudged occupancy reports, among other things." He frowned at Penny, who was now happily kneading at Ginny's sleeve. "I mean, paid off more obviously than is usual or accepted."

"That's bad?" It sounded bad, but if payoffs were normal business . . .

"That's not good. Even if it's not true—and all that anyone's heard are rumors and gossip, no actual proof—it's not what you want fueling the industry gossip mills. Especially if safety issues might be involved. I'm thinking, since our Uncle Joe looks to be so squeaky clean, it's probably DubJay who's involved. Unless you think Uncle Joe might be playing a deeper game?"

Ginny removed Penny's claws from her sleeve, and considered what she'd been able to learn about Joe Jacobs.

"He's careful," she said finally. "Cautious, even. Everything's . . . neat. A person like that, I don't think they're the type to cut corners, or let anything go by they aren't personally comfortable with." She shook her head. "No. He built the company. It's his only legacy, far as I can tell—no wife, no kids, not even any pets. It's all there . . . he wouldn't do anything that might damage it."

"And DubJay?"

They were both obviously thinking the same thing: that DubJay Jacobs was the sort of person to do whatever he thought best, and worry about the rules later.

Ginny thought about her anonymous text warning again, but couldn't see why, after hiring her, DubJay would then warn her off.

"If Uncle Joe found some evidence that Junior was doing something he didn't approve of," Tonica said, his voice thoughtful, "would he choose family, or firm?"

"The papers DubJay needed to file?" Ginny could feel the puzzle under her hands, but the pieces weren't fitting together yet. "He didn't want me anywhere near them, did he? But he wants his uncle found, or why hire me?"

Tonica shook his head, not having an answer.

"Do you think Uncle Joe took the papers? But why?"

"I have no idea. So he can hide 'em? Destroy them? Figure out how to break an agreement or dump property before they get hit with hefty fines or sanctions? But whatever he's planning, I'm pretty sure that DubJay isn't happy about his uncle's flit, and if he's as savvy a businessman as you say, Joe's going to know that. Finding him isn't going to be easy. Assuming he's not packed up in the trunk of a car somewhere."

"Oh, nice." Ginny winced. She'd never met the guy, but she'd developed a sort of proprietary fondness for him over the past twenty-four hours. She didn't want to think that he was dead.

Especially since whoever killed him might not want anyone looking for the old man.

Tonica was apparently on the same page. "Gin, I don't like this. At all. Uncle Joe may be clean . . . but I'm not so sure DubJay is. I mean, even more than being slightly on the side of shady."

Penny butted at Ginny's hand, reminding her that she had paused in the petting. Automatically, Ginny resumed,

the motion helping her think, the same way petting Georgie did. "Yeah, I'm starting to get that feeling, too. But if
he'd had anything to do with his uncle's disappearance,
why hire me? I mean, I can see why he wouldn't want PIs
or cops, but why even ask me to look for him? His uncle's
a grown man and then some, not in any way disabled or
impaired, and all DubJay would have to do was assume,
publicly, that he'd gone off on a long weekend and not
done anything about it."

Tonica sucked at his lower lip, thinking. "The missing
papers?"

Ginny dismissed them with a wave of her free hand.
"Papers can be refiled, resubmitted. Happens all the time.
This must be a time issue, probably a penalty if it's delayed.
But even if we're right and Uncle Joe absconded with
something important, they're not going to be the only copies in existence, and I doubt there's anything Joe signed for
that DubJay couldn't, too. That would be seriously stupid.
And I think we can agree that DubJay, whatever his other
flaws, does not look to be stupid?"

"Yeah. It would be easier if he was, though."

Oh, that was something Ginny disagreed with, strongly.
"Nuh-uh. Smart people are, in their own way, predictable.
They'll do things in their own interest. It's the dummies
who do stuff you'd never be able to predict, because, well,
they're dumb."

That got a laugh out of Tonica. "I never thought about it
like that, but yeah . . . the wildcard of dumb. So what now?
I mean, if we're getting into hinky waters . . ."

"Nothing hinky about it. I mean, okay, yeah." She stopped petting Penny again, and the cat batted lazily at her hand in protest. "Watch it, cat. I'm not your human, to abuse like that. Look, it's not good news about the hinky stuff, no, but we're not involved in any of that. The job's just to track down his uncle and tell him to get the hell home. So I need to go talk to people, get them to tell me where he's holed up. If you want to back off, fine. But I still have a job to do."

She took a sip of her drink, then went back to petting the cat draped over her lap, waiting for his response. She needed him; she didn't want to need him—it pissed her off to admit that there were things that she couldn't do as well as anyone else—but she was also a big fan of facing facts.

Ginny knew herself: she was fantastic at getting information out of search engines and random facts, but not so much when it came to convincing people to give up secrets. Tonica, though, had those skills. It was that bartender-vibe thing again. She was going to need that. If he backed out, she was screwed.

"I know all that. And yeah, right now all we have is a maybe-shady and a might-be-dirty. It's all conjecture, and we don't have a damn thing to take to the cops, and even if we did, they wouldn't be able to do anything before the deadline." He pushed back his chair, as though suddenly aware that he'd left the bar for too long. "I know you're not going to back off. It's professional pride as well as your damned stubbornness. I get that. But . . ."

"But?"

"Let me go with you, when you talk to people. Just in case."

Even though that was exactly what she'd wanted, Ginny felt her jaw set in what her mother used to call her "unpleasantly mulish" look. "What, you think someone's going to try and, what, lean on me? Intimidate me? Say 'boo' and make me burst into tears?"

"Oh, for the love of Pete, Mallard!" That was his "you're annoying me" voice. She'd almost missed it. "Isn't that exactly why you wanted me to help out in the first place?"

As though upset by the tone of his voice, or to echo his request, Penny meowed, and reached up to butt her head against Ginny's chin.

Arguing against something because she hadn't been the one to suggest it was exactly the kind of stupid she usually hated. And yes, he was right. Letting her ego get in the way of best practices would be as stupid as . . . something stupid. She had planned to send him off to talk to people. She just hadn't realized how difficult it would be to let go of any part of the job. This would be why she worked alone, probably.

But she needed him. And he knew it, damn it. He was just standing there, looking at her with that "don't be a moron, Mallard" look he got, that he knew made her insane. And his cat kept knocking her head against her chin, and putting her paw on her arm, with just enough claw showing to make it not-cute, like some kind of silent encouragement. Or scolding.

"All right, fine. Saves me from having to reserve a Zipcar, anyway."

"Oh for . . . fine." He shook his head, and went back down the bar to relieve the other bartender, still shaking his head and muttering something under his breath.

"So he's better at talking to people. I can handle myself just fine," Ginny said to the cat, who—job done—leapt down from her lap and headed for the door, tail held erect as she wove her way through the customers' legs. "I just hate driving."

"What's going on?" Georgie lifted her head from her paws and stared at Penny as she stepped across the damp sidewalk, side-winding around a human who tried to reach down and pet her. "You said you'd go in and find out what was going on. What are they talking about? And is there any food? I've been out here for hours and I'm bored. And hungry."

"You are not bored," Penny said, settling between the dog's fore-paws, making sure that she was out of the way of clumsy human feet. Her tail curled around her hindquarters, and flicked across Georgie's nose, making the dog sneeze. "You've been getting more attention here than you would have staying at home. And probably more treats, too."

The dog looked abashed. "I'd have saved you one, but they tasted too good."

"Ugh. No, thanks. The things you eat . . ." She licked her paw, then spread her claws out and dug at the fur between.

"Pen, stop grooming and tell me what's happening! What did they talk about? I've been thinking about what you said earlier, about her being worried, and you're right; when we went for a walk

she was mumbling to herself, and she only does that when some-thing's wrong. And something happened this morning that made her angry but she didn't talk to anyone and nobody came by, so I didn't know who to growl at and if she's upset I'm supposed *to growl at whatever's upsetting her, that's my job, the trainer said so!"*

"Calm down," Penny said, ignoring the fact that Georgie prob-ably didn't even know how to growl. "You didn't tell me about anything when you got here."

Georgie dropped her head, bonking Penny on the top of her head. "I forgot."

"Well, she didn't say anything, either, not while I was listen-ing. Mostly it was about the slick-smell man. They don't think he smells right, either."

Penny had never been impressed by the slick-smell man, when he came to the place. She hadn't liked it when the slick-smell man talked to her particular humans, either, making all smooth when he was claw-and-hiss underneath, and so she made a point to learn his name. Knowing names was important.

"I knew it, I knew it." Georgie stood, dislodging Penny, who had to scramble to her feet, her tail lashing in annoyance. "I knew he smelled slick. Was he the one who upset her? I don't like him, Penny."

"Yeah, you've said that, too." Georgie said a lot, and didn't al-ways remember it later. But she was sweet, even if she was a little dim, and she listened to Penny, which was more than could be said for most dogs. Or people, for that matter.

"Oh. So what are they going to do? Are they going to chase him?"

"Not him, Georgie. The missing-man. I told you about him, remember? They're chasing him."

"He's here?" Georgie looked up and down the sidewalk as though expecting someone who smelled like the slick-smell man to appear.

Penny tried not to get exasperated. "No, not here. Georgie, come on, you're smarter than that. They're going after him. The missing-man. Out there. Georgie, sit down. You're going to make Her worry and come out here, and maybe take you home."

A shar-pei's face fell into wrinkles naturally, but Georgie managed to add a few, scrunching her eyes up with worry, even as she settled back onto the sidewalk. "Alone? She's going alone?"

"Not alone. Teddy's going with her."

"Oh." Georgie didn't seem quite satisfied by that, and Penny twitched her whiskers. "They'll be fine, Georgie. They go outside every day, and they're fine."

"But . . . you said the slick-smell man was bad. And something upset her. I don't like any of this, Penny. And I'm supposed to protect her. We need to stop them."

Penny reached up with her paw and pulled Georgie's head down so that she could groom the dog's ear, her rough tongue barely making an impression on the shar-pei's plush coat. The action, as expected, calmed the dog down. "No, we don't. Humans do what humans do. This is good, not bad. And we can help them, like you wanted. You just need to stop worrying. You can do that, right?"

Georgie considered the question seriously. "No."

Penny sighed. Dogs.

5

At exactly 10:28 on Saturday morning, Teddy sat in his car and contemplated his cell phone. It was a stupid phone—able to make calls and take grainy photos, and text, if you were able to use the cramped little keyboard, but just then it seemed like a possible savior. All he had to do was text her, tell her that he was out. He didn't even have to make an excuse, he could just say "can't do it, good luck" and he was free. Nobody would know—just him and Mallard, and she would never say anything about it.

"No, but she'd know," he muttered. "She'd just *know,* no matter what I said, and she'd never say anything but it would be in her head, all the time. That I couldn't hack it. That I'd run, and left her in the lurch. And then she'll go and deal with the job, because she's too damn stubborn to give up, and always there'd be that, that she did it and I . . ." He was psyching himself out. How had it gotten to the point that she didn't even have to *be* there, with that Look on her face, to mess with him?

"Screw it." He dropped the phone onto the seat next to him, and inserted the key in the ignition. His semi-ancient

Volvo coupe came to life, the clutch coughing a little until he eased up and maneuvered it out of his parking spot.

Even with the stress eating at him, and only a few hours of restless sleep under his ear, as his mother used to say, the simple act of driving the coupe eased his nerves. Seattle driving was nothing compared to Boston, and he was able to take all back roads from his apartment building, so by the time he pulled into his usual parking space behind Mary's, he had achieved an almost Zen sort of calm.

"Once you get in deep, all you can do is swim." Another one of his mother's sayings. She had one for every occasion, and then another for when you didn't listen to her.

He missed her, still. The rest of his family, not so much. He loved them; he was just happy to have the breadth of the continent between visits. They could yank his chain like no one . . .

Well, almost no one else.

Ginny was waiting for him, perched on the cement stairs that led into Mary's kitchen, half hidden by the Dumpsters. The lids were ajar—they'd been emptied that morning, then.

He had worked in a place in Oregon, years ago, where trash day was just as likely to bring the cops, when body parts or worse were found in some restaurant or bar's Dumpster. He didn't miss those days, at all. Mary's was nice, clean, mostly peaceful . . .

And boring. Not that he wanted to break up bar fights every night, but these days, a shouting match over who was the better quarterback was about as rough as it ever got.

And half the time, he admitted ruefully, he was one of the ones shouting.

"I didn't realize that car was yours," Ginny said, when he cut the engine and extracted himself from the seat. He checked for sarcasm or a put-down, but the expression on her face was an odd mix of appreciation and suspicion. "Could you be any more of a Seattle cliché?"

"Ow. I'll have you know I've had her since I was twenty," he said. "She was in better shape then."

The Volvo was a beauty, still, but she cost a small fortune to keep up, more every year. Eventually, he'd have to accept the fact that she was an indulgence a bartender couldn't afford. Until then, they'd take the keys out of his cold, dead hands.

"Uh-huh." Ginny seemed oblivious to how much the coupe had cost, originally, or at least wasn't wondering how a twentysomething could have afforded it back then. Which was just as well—explaining that the Volvo had been a graduation gift would be more than he wanted to explain. Now, or ever.

He changed the topic, intentionally needling her as a distraction. "So. Do we have an agenda for today, or are we going to drive randomly around town, shouting his name out of the windows?"

"Very funny. And I have a plan." She reached into the tapestry bag at her feet and pulled out her tablet, handing it to him as she pulled herself up off the stoop. While he tried to figure out how to turn it on, she grabbed the bag from the ground at her feet, and stood up. "Did you doubt me?"

"I wouldn't dare." And he wasn't kidding. Whatever other feelings she might inspire, respect for her abilities was clearly at the top. She might be a curly-topped cookie, but she was a seriously sharp, competent cookie. And she looked it, wearing a cream-colored top that clung like silk, and dark blue pants. It was a professional look without being over the top, the kind of thing a high-level office administrator or low-level executive might wear on a casual day.

It also emphasized the fact that she was all leg and curve. He might not be affected but—he figured out how to make the screen come on again, and checked the list quickly—yeah, there were a few guys on the list, and it might favorably influence them into talking.

He would never accuse Ginny of playing on her sex appeal to get answers. Not unless he wanted to get taken down a few pegs, anyway. But he was also aware of the fact that he'd deliberately chosen an outfit that played up his own "tough guy" persona, too. You used the weapons you were given, and you didn't apologize.

That was his own motto. Although he thought that his mother would have approved.

He leaned against his car and handed her back the tablet before she started to get tech-withdrawal shakes. "How do you want to handle this?"

"You take the lead."

He hadn't expected that. "Me? But . . ." He had thought he was there to drive, ask a few leading questions and listen to the answers, maybe give the impression of muscle, if needed. But she wanted him to start it all off? To make the decisions about what to ask?

She gave him that Look. "Tonica, if I have to put aside my ego here, don't you spoil things with false modesty. We've been over this. You know how to schmooze people, put them at ease. Just imagine you're behind the bar, and they're looking to get lit. I've never seen you shy away from chatting someone up for a better tip."

He'd be offended, except it was true. You worked in the service industry, you learned how to like everyone, professionally.

"It's not the same. I *listen,* as a bartender. People *want* to spill their guts to me. I have no idea how to get them started."

"Don't worry, I'll tell you what to ask them."

That sounded more like the Gin he knew. And, annoyingly, it eased his uncertainty.

"Of that, Madame, I have no doubt. And what will you be doing while I'm schmoozing?"

"Looking harmless, and listening hard." She opened the passenger-side door and frowned at the spotless interior, as though she'd been hoping to chew him out for leaving a mess. "Look, the people on that list, they're all either friends or business associates of our missing guy. And I winnowed it down to exclude people with a known, presumed friendly connection to DubJay, too. If someone has seen Joe since he disappeared, or knows where he is—they're not going to tell us. Especially not if something bad is going down, and they know or suspect he might be in trouble. So we're going to have to work with what they *don't* tell us. The non-data."

He hesitated, halfway down into his own seat, and looked across the front seat at her, where she was already drawing the seat belt across her lap and buckling it. "The what?"

"Just drive. I'll explain as we go."

Ginny stretched her legs out in front of her as much as she could, and admitted, to herself at least, that she was impressed, and possibly a little in lust. For all that the coupe was a boxy, old-fashioned thing, with barely enough room in the backseat for groceries, and it probably jolted like a tank on the road, she understood why Tonica had kept it all these years. There was a feeling of power and majesty to it that you didn't get with newer, lighter-weight cars, and the feeling that, no matter what happened, the car would respond.

And then they pulled out of the parking lot, and Ginny made a silent apology to the car for doubting its suspension.

She looked at the first name on her list, and then said, "We're going to Upper Queen Anne. Head down Fifteenth . . ."

"I know how to drive."

"All right, fine." When he got lost, without GPS, then she'd have directions ready.

Ginny rested her bag on her lap and tried to fight down

the flock of butterflies that had been roosting in her stomach all night, fluttering wildly whenever she thought—or tried to think—about what she was about to do.

Or try to do, anyway.

"I didn't see you leave last night," he said, breaking the brief silence.

"I cut out around eight. It was either that, or bring a yoga mat out for Georgie. Pavement's too hard for her to be on that long."

"Hmmm. I should talk Patrick into setting up a doggie care station out front, or in the parking lot. Make it a selling point—'a pint with your pup.'"

"Cute." She wasn't sure she'd be comfortable leaving Georgie in the parking lot, out of sight. But a pad, and maybe a water trough, would be nice, especially in the summer.

"And shade," she added. "A tarp, something to keep the sun off."

Ginny was good at making lists. That was what she had done when she went home last night: put together the list of people she thought might be useful, adding and subtracting based on nothing more than gut instinct. She'd ended up with five people, and a sense of satisfaction in a job well done.

And then, at three in the morning, with Georgie snoring at the end of the bed, it had hit her, waking her up with one of those unsettling stomach-turning epiphanies. She had been treating it like just another job—meet the client's needs, rearrange the world so that they are not inconvenienced or delayed. Only this wasn't a party, or a vacation, or even ferrying people to and from the hospital, which she'd done once for an elderly woman facing surgery. This was someone's *life* she was trying to manage. More than manage—potentially undercut. And it was the life of someone who was neither her client nor an underage dependent of her client. Someone who might have very good reasons to not want to be found.

She had managed to get back to sleep, after a mug of tea and a few cookies, but this morning, the thought haunted her, making her second-guess everything she had done, everything they were doing. The anonymous texter had been right: she shouldn't be playing PI. She had no business doing this, no skills, no sense of where the moral boundaries were in something like this.

Now, actually in Tonica's car, the two of them en route to do this thing, Ginny struck back. Whoever the text messager was, they were trying to fake her out. Mallards did not get faked out. They occasionally screwed up, but they did not get faked out. Especially not by someone too cowardly to show their name.

She breathed out through her nose, and wished that Georgie were with them. She could use a good hand-lick and puppy-snuggle, right now, and she didn't think that Tonica would be so obliging.

"That was so an image I really didn't need."

"What?"

She had almost forgotten she wasn't alone in the car. "Nothing. Just thinking out loud." She risked looking sideways at him, but his features wore the same even, almost placid expression as usual. She'd figured out the first week he'd started working at Mary's that it was a mask, but she'd never been able to get a handle on what was happening beneath it.

Hopefully, neither would anyone they talked to, today.

"So what made you decide to become a concierge, anyway?"

"I'm good at solving problems." It was the quick answer, the pat answer, but last night's uncertainty made her stop and think about it. "I'm good at making people feel that things are being handled," she added. "It lets them get on with the other stuff they need to do, and not stress. And I'm good at follow-through and details, so things don't get dropped."

"Like a personal assistant."

"Right. Except I work for myself, not someone else. And I don't have to take any job I don't want." She made a face. "Well, there've been some jobs . . ."

"Oh?"

He actually sounded interested.

"A woman's mother was going in for surgery, and the timing was awkward for her to get Mom there in time— she had some kind of high-powered job. So she hired me to arrange the transport there, and a pickup after."

"So what happened?"

"She bitched me out the entire way out and back: everything I'd done or arranged was wrong, etcetera, etcetera, why had her daughter hired such a clueless moron—you can imagine the rest. I thought I was going to get fired. I didn't know until later that Mom was so unpleasant, nobody in the family wanted to deal with her, and the client's own PA had threatened to quit, rather than deal with it."

"Ouch."

"Someone once told me that, after enough time had passed, I'd be able to laugh about the bad jobs. They either lied, or I need more time."

"But you like your job."

"Yeah. Yeah, I do. For every crazy client, there's the person whose life I make easier, smoothing a chaotic day, or solving a problem they didn't have the ability to deal with. That's a nice feeling."

"All I do is pour booze."

She laughed. "Never say only, Tonica. Never say *only*."

The car glided down the road, Tonica managing to time the lights and traffic so they maintained a steady pace; that was a trick she'd never been able to master. There was little traffic that morning—no construction for a change—and they were soon approaching their destination. Ginny could feel something inside her tensing up, in a good way, the way she felt before a trivia game started. Not the throwing-up-sick kind of tension she'd felt that morning.

"Almost there," Tonica said, echoing her thoughts. "Who are we going to see?"

Apparently, when he'd looked at her list, he hadn't actually *looked* at it. Typical. She thought about throwing that at him, then remembered that he was driving—and being stranded in Queen Anne would be a pain in the ass, since she'd have to get the bus home.

She pulled out her tablet and looked at the list again. "In no particular order, the lawyer he met with the morning before he disappeared, the cab driver who took him home the night before, the woman he had dinner with that night, and his housekeeper. She's not a live-in, but part of the staff of the condo building he lives in. She cleans his apartment every couple of days, which means she knows his habits probably better than anyone else."

"A single guy in his sixties? Yeah, probably. She hot?"

"Don't start."

His low chuckle was annoying, not because he'd made a borderline sexist comment, but because he'd managed to get her to respond to it.

"I swear, are you sure you're not twelve?"

"Most of the time, yeah. So what's the story—how're we spinning this?"

"As close to the truth as we can stay." She had asked him to take the lead in questioning, but he was deferring to her. She was starting to believe that he hadn't been playing her when he hesitated yesterday. Teddy Tonica had an ego, she knew that for a fact; now she knew that he could put it aside when needed. That was . . . useful to know. "We're looking for Joe. We know he's gone walkabout, but we need to talk to him. It's important."

"And if they assume—rightly, I might add—that we're from his nephew, and clam up?"

She'd thought about that, too. "Then we know that

they know where he is, and push a little harder. Or rather, you do. Tell them that we know it has to do with his nephew, the reason he went least-in-sight, and we want to help."

"Lie, in other words."

"Imply knowledge we don't have in its entirety yet," she corrected primly, and honors were even again.

He shook his head, his hands tapping out a rhythm on the wheel. "You really think that's going to work?"

"I'm counting on you to make it work." She looked at his profile again, and was rewarded by the faintest down-turn of his mouth and increased wrinkle lines around the one eye she could see. "Look, if you have something better, I'm all ears." She wasn't being sarcastic—not much, any-way: she really wanted a better plan. She just hadn't been able to think of one.

"No. It's a good plan. Short of going in like bad cop/bad cop, it's probably the only plan possible. So which potential mother lode of information do we start with?"

"The housekeeping staff. I figure anyone who cleans up after a guy is going to know the dirt."

"Cute." Tonica's attention was still focused on the road, but she caught the hint of a smile on his mouth, and felt smug, the way she did when her team trumped his on trivia night. Getting approval, however grudging, from someone who could beat you, had always meant more to her than admiration from people who couldn't.

"So we're heading for the apartment building?" He moved around a massive SUV that was going twenty in a forty-five zone, and slid into the right-hand lane once he was clear. "I wonder if we could get in to look at Uncle Joe's apartment itself."

The small smugness bloomed into full flower, and she reached into her bag to pull out a key card. "I requested it last night, after I got home, and DubJay had one of his people drop it off first thing this morning. Twenty-four/seven service, just like it says on their website. The apartment is, apparently, owned by the company, same as DubJay's place, so he has every right to give us access."

"Well played, Madame. Ten points to Team Wash-and-Wear."

"And don't you forget it," she said, turning the key over in her hand. Her trivia team's name was Wash-and-Wear, his was the Cold Ducks, for some reason she'd never understood. "There, up ahead."

"Huh. I'd have pegged him for more of a modern high-rise."

"He bought it years ago, when the building was converted from a school. He probably got a professional courtesy discount, or something." Ginny stared at the building, wishing not for the first time that she made more money. A lot more money.

The neighborhood was as nice as she'd always heard—it didn't shout money, but you could tell it was there. The apartment building was a square redbrick structure with huge windows that, on the far side of the building, would have amazing water views, plus a decent view of the Needle. There was a parking garage behind, for tenants, but he pulled around the corner and—impossibly—found a parking spot on a street that wasn't at a sixty-degree angle.

Ginny shook her head, half-suspecting a setup, except he hadn't known where they were going before she got in the car, and he hadn't called anyone to clear out a space. "Seriously?"

He grinned, not having to ask what she was talking about. "I have good parking karma."

"Seriously." She extracted herself from the car—it had been easier to get in than out—and reached for her bag. The car was old enough that it had to be locked manually, rather than from the key fob.

While Tonica slipped on his jacket—a sweet brown leather one she'd lusted after before—Ginny stared up at the building's silhouette. "Tonica, I know I said you should take the lead, but I think you should avoid the charm, talking to her."

"Huh?"

"Don't try to charm her. She's used to being an employee, working for wealthy guys, and with guys like that, charm means you're not taking her seriously. We want to avoid anything that might set her back up, get her annoyed."

Tonica let out a huff, starting toward the building at a fast-enough clip that she had to rush to catch up. "Or," he said, not looking at her, "she might think it's, y'know, nice to have someone be nice to her, after a long day at work, being unappreciated and invisible."

"Tonica, that is such a guy thing to think."

He stopped, and turned to her then, and for once she didn't get the sense that it was about scoring points, or proving a point. "Look, you wanted me to take the lead because I can schmooze, right? So let me damned well schmooze. Don't second-guess what works."

Apparently, she'd hit a nerve. He was right about not second-guessing. She knew he was right. But she also had the gut feeling that waltzing in and turning on the boy charm—which, based on his worn jeans and close-fitting T-shirt under that jacket, he planned to do—would be a mistake.

Faced with a dilemma, Ginny did what she always did: she leaned back, emotionally, took a deep breath, and waited for more information. In this case, actually meeting the woman in question.

The lobby was small but felt cozy, giving the impression of being both welcoming and well maintained. An expensive-looking navy blue rug was set under comfortable-looking brown leather chairs, perfect for checking your email while you waited for someone to join you.

"Nice," Tonica said, trying to be subtle about his gawking. "Next life, I'm going to try for rich instead of good-looking."

"Next life I want both," Ginny said, both of them careful to keep their voices low. The front desk was low and smooth edged—dark granite and polished wood—with an equally polished guard working behind it. Politely but firmly, he asked who they were here to see.

"We're here to talk to Elizabeth. The service said she was working here today." They had agreed it would be best to not mention anything that might specifically tie back to Joseph Jacobs, or DubJay, just in case.

That, apparently, wasn't a good enough answer, but the guard's attitude eased a little when two folded twenties moved across the polished surface. Another pair got them the unit where the cleaning service was working.

The elevator was just as smooth and well maintained as the lobby. When they got on, Ginny looked over at her companion and said, still in a soft voice, "What would you have done if he hadn't been bribable?"

"It's not a bribe. It's compensation for services rendered. And I haven't met a doorman yet who wasn't quite happy to render services."

She shot him a sly glance. "Much like bartenders."

"Those guys get paid better," he said, again not taking the bait. She usually did better, when she wanted to get his goat. "That comes out of operating expenses, right?" The door opened onto their floor before she could answer, and he gestured for her to precede him into the hallway.

"They're down here," he said, pointing to the left.

"Yeah. But Uncle Joe's apartment is down here." Ginny pointed to the right, and waited until he joined her. At 7C, she used the key card to get in, and poked her head into the hallway to make sure nobody was actually there.

"Nice," Teddy muttered, taking a look around. The condo was large and airy, with plush carpeting in a creamy white color that suggested you'd be best off removing your shoes. The furniture—a low sectional and two armchairs—was in various darker shades and looked really comfortable. Over in the far corner, there was a desk setup, a nice wooden number with a surface too clear to actually be in use.

Three of the walls in the main room showcased large photographs, two cityscapes Teddy didn't recognize, and one he did—the George Washington Bridge, at night. It gave him a pang of homesickness he hadn't been expecting. The other wall was filled with windows, the blinds tucked down at the windowsill. Expensive, probably motorized. The lighting was recessed, with a few floor lamps set in the right places to be used for reading. "Very nice," he said again.

Ginny had already disappeared. He wandered farther into the apartment, and checked out the linen closet—everything so neatly folded it had to be done by a professional—and the bathroom, where he spent a minute poking around the medicine cabinet.

"No toiletry kit." He looked around. "Either he doesn't use cologne, or he took that, too."

He backed out, closing the door the way he'd found it, and joined Ginny in the bedroom.

"This was not a man who had company often," she said when he came in. "Two pillows, both hard. And there's only one nightstand."

"So much for the swingers' weekend theory," he said. The bedroom had slightly more color, mostly dusty dark blues and browns. There was a small wooden box on the dresser; Teddy opened it. "Two pair of cuff links, a sports watch that looks like it's as old as I am, and a man's ring." He picked it up, looked at the signet. "His college ring. Clothing?"

She gestured to the closet door. "Hard to tell. A lot of nice suits, ironed shirts, including the stuff he picked up from the dry cleaner, still in plastic. If stuff's missing from there, I can't tell. The drawers look like they've been gone through, maybe a couple of things missing. The man folds his socks."

"So?" So did he. "Does he fold his underwear?"

"Yes."

"Okay, that's a little OCD."

"And the kitchen's gourmet stocked, and spotless. Not even anything in the dishwasher, much less the sink. Counters scrubbed, dish towels neatly folded."

"Basically, what we have is a guy who works hard, has nice but minimalist tastes, and walked out of here in a calm and orderly fashion, with nothing out of place."

"Or, a guy who has a cleaning staff that put everything to rights after he left," Ginny said.

"Yeah. Or that. Time to talk to the housekeeper."

They backed out of the apartment, making sure the door was securely locked, before walking back down the still-quiet hallway to 7G. That door was ajar, but Ginny knocked anyway.

"Come in!" a man's voice yelled. They looked at each other, then Teddy shrugged, and pushed the door all the way open, gesturing for her to precede him into the apartment.

As they'd discussed, Tonica took the lead, Ginny a step behind him. "Hi. I'm looking to talk to Elizabeth?"

While he waited for a response, he looked over the crew: there were three of them, and only one female, so it wasn't hard to guess who they were looking for.

"That's me," the woman said, stepping forward.

Despite his earlier comment to Ginny, Teddy had expected a fifty-something, slightly stocky, maybe overweight woman with not much to look forward to, willing to be charmed by someone paying attention to her. Instead, they got a thirtysomething with a hard edge to her face, and better abs and arms than he could lay claim to.

"You're the head of housekeeping staff here, right?"

"Yeah. The boss said you wanted to talk to me about Mr. Jacobs. You cops?" Her voice suggested that she knew damn well that they weren't, and she had better things to do than talk to them.

Teddy leaned forward, folding his arms across the kitchen counter. "We're not cops, no. If we were, one of us would have flashed a badge by now, right?"

"Uh-huh." She looked back at her companions, who were still dusting and polishing, pretending that the two strangers weren't there at all. In an apartment—even one as nice as this one—that was tough to do.

Ginny had been right: she wasn't going to take well to being charmed. Fortunately, Teddy wasn't dumb enough to rely only on his charm with women, despite what his partner might think.

He also didn't think that the folded twenties trick was

going to work here, not with her co-workers around. Which was just as well, since he had only one left, and the thought of waiting for Ginny to dig something out of the oversized bag slung over her shoulder would turn this entire thing into a farce, straight away.

"So no, not cops. Not the IRS. Not even private investigators. Just two people, looking for some information."

"Uh-huh." She matched him look for look, unconvinced.

He abandoned the professional charm, and went for peer-to-peer exasperation, channeled entirely from some cop show he'd watched, back when he had a TV. "Look, I can't force you to talk to us. I wouldn't, even if I could—I look like a big, bad dude but I'm actually a nice guy who waits for pedestrians to finish crossing the street before I hit the gas."

Most of the time, anyway.

"We're worried about Joe, that's all. We're hoping that you can give us something—some clue, some hint—why he went away without telling anyone."

Her eyes narrowed at that. "You family?"

Ouch. And there was that line they needed to walk. Ginny might not care, but he had no desire to get yanked by the cops, if she decided they'd been scamming her. A bartender had to stay clean, if he wanted to work in the nicer joints.

"Family friends." DubJay was Joe's family, and he and DubJay . . . weren't friends, actually. Not even social acquaintances. Teddy was pretty sure DubJay saw a bartender the same way he saw his mechanic—oil the machinery and doff your cap when the guy with the Beemer deigned to pay you. But they were on a first-name basis, however it happened, and that was enough to make the lie palatable.

"Huh."

That seemed to be her default noise. Teddy supposed that he shouldn't expect erudition out of someone running a cleaning crew, then reminded himself—his mother's voice taking lead—that a man who worked as a bartender shouldn't throw stones, no matter what his college degree said.

She didn't seem ready to dismiss them just yet, so he pressed on. "You were the one who handled his apartment?"

She gave a small shrug, as though to say *what the hell.* "Yeah. It's a small place, just a one-bedroom, and it's never bad, so two people can do it. I split the team up for places like that, to move through faster."

"You get paid for the work, not the time?"

"Yeah. If we're done faster, we go home sooner. But we do good work." She wasn't defensive, but her voice tensed slightly, as though waiting for him to say something. "No skimping."

"A place like this, they wouldn't keep you if you weren't good." He said it to appease her, but he meant it—one complaint from an owner in a place like this, and she'd be out on her ear. But he needed to win her trust, fast, or this wasn't going to go anywhere useful.

"Did you talk to Joe before he left? I know that your work overlapped with his when he was home." He knew no such thing, but she seemed protective of the guy, which didn't happen unless they'd actually met.

This was harder than he'd expected, picking through the possible missteps. He could feel sweat on the back of his neck, chafing his T-shirt, and hoped none of it showed. Gin was going to have to cough up more information next time, if she wanted him to be able to schmooze properly.

"Yeah. He liked us to come in while he was still here, so if there was anything particular, he could tell us."

"A tough client?" His voice was as smooth as he could manage, the same voice he used to convince a near-drunk that he didn't need another drink, truly. "Did he make a lot of demands?"

"No. In fact, kinda the opposite. He was always 'don't worry about this' and 'don't worry about that.' Sometimes he'd tell us he was going to be hosting a dinner party, and so to make sure to get the kitchen really clean. 'Can't have my guests accusing me of an unsafe kitchen,' he'd say." Her face softened when she smiled, but it only lasted a second. "He's a nice guy. You said you're looking for him? I hope everything's okay."

"No jail, no hospitals, so I'm sure he's fine," Teddy tried to coax the smile back with one of his own. No dice. He went back to what she had said, searching for a hook.

"You said he threw dinner parties. Often?"

"No. Couple-three times a year, maybe. Usually he'd

ask us special to come in the day before. Once we came in the day after, and the place was . . . not a mess, but you could tell there'd been a lot of people there. But other than that, he didn't seem to socialize much. Everything was about work. His television was dusty, but his desk? That was always in use."

She frowned. Teddy could almost feel Ginny getting ready to pounce, like Miss Penny when she saw a mouse, and sent the strongest *shut up* vibe he could, to keep her from interrupting.

Miracle of miracles, it worked: she held that pose, but didn't speak.

"You remembered something?" He leaned forward a little across the counter, just his upper body, the same way he would if he was leaning on the bar top.

"Yeah. Maybe. I don't know, it could be nothing . . ."

"Or it could be everything. What is it?"

She spoke more slowly, but with confidence. Whatever she remembered, she was certain of it. "The last time we came in, he was still there, same as always . . . but his desk was cleared."

Teddy tilted his head. That would explain what they'd seen. "You said it was always in use, though? So . . ."

"In use, yeah, but covered. It never got dusty because there were too many things on it, piles of papers and half-empty tea mugs, binders, and things like that. And this chunk of rock that he was always picking up, like a—what do they call them? A worry stone, yeah. That was always there. But the last morning, the last time I saw him, it was all gone. Not just straightened into piles, like some people do, but gone. Like he'd chucked it all, even the rock."

Chucked it, or packed it up, as if he was going somewhere. Somewhere planned.

The woman looked over his shoulder at Ginny, then back at him, and for the first time he saw some real emotion in her eyes. "You think he's in trouble."

Teddy weighed his options, considered the risks, and made a judgment call. "He might be, yeah."

She bit her lip, and then came to a decision of her own. "One of the things we do is clean out the trash cans. And everyone knows that, so the day before, they don't bother to dump their trash, most of them. Not even him. But that day, the one under his desk was empty, which was weird. Usually he eats a sandwich at his desk when he's working, and throws away the crusts, but there wasn't anything there. So that made me curious, and I checked the recycling bin, too. We don't handle that, residents do their own recycling, someone else comes and takes that away . . . but it was empty. Like he'd already gotten rid of everything. But it was a day early for them to've collected."

Her face went blank again, and Tony figured that he'd gotten everything he was going to out of her. If she'd had a few drinks in her, he could have pushed, maybe, but not here, not in her place of employment, in front of her co-workers. He hadn't gotten far enough in the Morons book to know how far he could go before it became "questioning" rather than "talking."

"Thank you. If you remember anything else . . ." Teddy hesitated: his usual MO was to write his name on a napkin, which was just kitschy enough for a giggle, but seriously would not work here, either.

"Please call us or email. You've been a great help." And Ginny was sliding a business card across the counter like she'd been part of the conversation all along, her fingers leaving the card just in front of the woman, who stared at it, then picked it up carefully, looking intently at the lettering.

"You're really not cops, or PIs?"

"Just looking for answers," Ginny said, and touched Teddy on the shoulder, telling him she thought they were done there.

For once, he agreed.

"Thank you," he said again, and threw in just a little bit of charm, to reassure himself he hadn't lost his touch. But she had already put the card in the pocket of her company-issued smock, and turned away. Clearly, they had used up too much of her working time.

"Tonica?" Ginny was already at the door.

"Yeah, yeah. I'm coming."

Neither of them spoke until they were outside of the building and back to the car. He'd parked it in the only bit of shade on the street, so the air inside wasn't too stuffy, but they both rolled down the windows, anyway.

"What do you think?"

He might not know much about detection, but he did

know people. "Sounds like he was going to take a runner."

"It sounds like he was cleaning up before he disap-peared, yeah. Someone else might have tossed those things, but not so considerately. And you don't take something like a rock, which has to be a memento, unless you're packing up yourself."

"Yeah, all that would rule out foul play, right? Not that we thought there was any foul play . . ." He paused and looked at her. "Did we?"

"No." But she didn't sound so sure, either.

He leaned his head back against the headrest and stared at the roof of the car. "Did any of this help?"

"I don't know. He was cleaning up paperwork, not leav-ing anything behind. But he didn't sound rushed—if he'd been behaving differently, she would have mentioned it. He took his car . . . somewhere. Packed up his belongings, personal stuff, threw it in his car, and then . . ."

"And then what?"

"If it were easy, anyone could do it?" Her attempt at lev-ity fell flat.

"Right. We need more information, or we're screwed. Clock's ticking, so who do we hit next? The lawyer?"

"No. I thought we'd leave him for last."

That didn't make sense to him. "He'd be the most likely to know something useful."

Ginny shook her head. "He'd also be the most likely to call our bluff and shut us down, and make sure no one else talks to us, either."

He winced: she'd once again out-thought him. "Good

point, well made." He tried to remember who else she'd mentioned. "Dinner companion, or the cabbie, then?"

"Cabbie. I called the garage last night, and his shift starts soon, so he'll either be there or showing up soon."

"Right. Where are we going?"

"The garage is down by the Pier 91. You know how to get there?"

He gave her his best "don't insult me" look, and pulled back out into traffic to the sound of her muffled giggle.

He looked over, out of the corner of his eye, and saw that she had pulled out her tablet, and a stylus, and was jotting down notes. He was curious as to what she was writing, but figured she'd tell him, eventually. Or he'd ask. Later. He wasn't going to be *that* easy.

About five minutes later she put the tablet away and looked at the dashboard, then looked around, startled. "There's no radio."

He laughed. Everyone said that, in that same tone of voice, eventually. "Nope."

"How can a car not have a radio?"

"I took it out."

"You did what?" She touched the sleek dashboard as though expecting it to suddenly reveal the familiar knobs and dials.

"I don't like distractions when I drive. Just me, and the hum of the motor, and the shaking of the chassis, that's all."

Ginny took a minute to absorb that, then leaned back into her seat and shook her head. "You're a strange man, Mr. Tonica."

"Maybe so, Ms. Mallard, but I'm the one driving this here car."

There wasn't much she could say in response to that, so she didn't.

They had timed it almost perfectly—half an hour's wait netted them their driver, returning from a fare. Unfortunately, even with prompting, the driver was less than helpful; apparently, one fare looked just like another.

"I dunno, he was a guy, older, dressed nice, a suit, I think. Never got a call there before. Good address; the dispatcher gave me that, I knew it wasn't going to be some kids thinking it's funny to prank a call, or some drunk-ass cheapskate who'd stiff me."

Teddy didn't even try charm on this guy. Mid-fifties, with the look of a guy who'd tasted ambition and spat it out. Teddy knew the type—better to be blunt and not waste his time. Go for what would matter. "Did he tip? Like a guy who knew what he was doing?"

"Yeah." The driver thought a minute, then nodded. "Yeah, exactly. No fumbling, no trying to figure out the right amount. Decent tip, too, in cash, even though he'd paid for the ride ahead of time with his credit card, like most folks do. Like I said, the guy wasn't a cheapskate."

"Was he carrying anything? Did you put anything in the trunk? A suitcase, or even a briefcase?" If Uncle Joe had packed up, where had he taken it?

The driver tapped his fingers on the roof of his car,

seemingly oblivious to the activity around him. The livery garage was remarkably clean and relatively quiet, but it still had a dozen or so cars and drivers in various stages of readiness, either going off shift or preparing to go out, plus the actual garage in the back behind them, where a car was up on struts, being worked on. Someone had a radio blaring on a rock station, but the lyrics were indecipherable. Teddy had to force himself to concentrate.

"Nope. At least, nothing I had to pop the trunk for. He might've been carrying a bag or something. Like I told you, I don't remember."

The guy couldn't remember a suitcase, but he remembered a cash tip. Humans never changed.

"So you picked him up at the apartment, and took him to the restaurant?" Ginny had her notebook out again, checking details.

"Yeah. Place called the Table, down in the Hill. One-way drop-off, no return. I guess he figured he was going to get lucky with his dinner companion." The driver started to grin, then looked at the two of them again and reconsidered. "Sorry, man. Ma'am. Wish I could help more. But that's all I got."

Back in the car, Ginny dropped her bag on the floor by her feet, pulled out her phone and checked her messages, frowning a little at what she found. Teddy was tempted to take his phone out and do the same, but the people he'd left messages for would call him directly, not text, and he had his phone set on vibrate, so he'd know if a call came in. If anyone had sent him a text—unlikely—he knew that he'd ignore it, anyway. Which was why very few people—mainly only his youngest sister—ever sent him texts. Sometimes, he thought he was the last man standing who still preferred to actually *talk* to people.

"Hey, it's almost lunchtime. You want to grab a grinder?"

She tapped a number into her phone, clearly not really listening. "What?"

"A sandwich. Lunch. You know, bread and meat and maybe some lettuce? Something to wash it down with?"

"It's not even noon. I'm not really hungry."

Apparently, Ginny Mallard, when on the job, occasionally needed a sledgehammer to get a clue. He made note of that. "I am."

"Oh." She looked up from her digital lifeline, and he noted that she looked a little embarrassed. "Yeah. I could use something to drink, I guess."

The area around the livery garage had an assortment of meh-looking diners, all of which looked like they wouldn't pass even a half-assed health inspection, and the one food truck they saw was offering Mexican, which gave Ginny heartburn, so she pointed them in the direction of the next address on her list, and the hope that they would find somewhere decent along the way. By the time Tonica had spotted one and pulled into the parking lot, Ginny had decided that maybe she was hungry, after all.

"Good," he said, when she mentioned that as they were getting out of the car, "because I bet you had, what, black coffee and a celery stick for breakfast?"

"Oh yeah, because I look like a fashion model." Ginny might wish for ten or twenty pounds to suddenly drop off her curves, but she knew what her mother and grandmother looked like, and genetics didn't lie, so a starvation diet wouldn't leave her anything other than hungry. She exercised, and ate reasonably healthily, and that was going to have to do.

"As a matter of fact," she said tartly, "I take my coffee with cream." She studied the exterior of the fast-food establishment with caution. "I don't suppose there's anything that isn't dripping with fat and mayonnaise on this menu?"

"Live dangerously," he told her, pushing the glass door open. "Admit it, your taste buds are drooling."

She gave the menu a long once-over, her nose wrinkled, and then placed her order for a burger, no fries, a side salad, and a bottle of water.

Tonica gave the clerk his order without having to think about it, and threw in a wink at the cashier, a young girl with a row of silver studs in her nostril and close-cropped black curls. She ignored him, and Ginny swallowed a grin.

"A diet soda?"

He shrugged, collecting his meal. "You save calories where you can. So, we talk to his dinner companion next?" According to his calendar, Uncle Joe had met with someone for dinner the night before he disappeared—and according to the driver, had expected her to get him home—or take him home.

"Yes. We've already talked to everyone who could be considered impartial, who would have little personal reason to clam up, or warn the next person on the list, so next up is the personal. DubJay says his uncle wasn't seeing anyone, so she's either a friend or a business connection—"

"Or a hookup."

Ginny paused, moving over to the other end of the counter to wait for her meal. "Do sixtysomethings do hookups?"

"Based on his bedroom, I'd say not. But hell, I don't know. He took care of himself, was good-looking, so why not? Maybe he always went to her place. Maybe he was a swinging bachelor."

"Okay, that's almost as bad as thinking about my folks having sex. I don't think I want to go there. But objection noted." Their meals were delivered, wrapped in paper, and, she had to admit, smelling really good.

Looking over the crowded dining area, they spotted a small empty table—right next to an overflowing table filled with energetic six-year-olds.

"Oh God, no. Please." Ginny knew she was pleading, and didn't care. "Can we just eat in the car?"

Tonica looked at her, his face smoothing into a theatrical expression of shock. "Woman. Eat these? In my car?"

"It's not a Mercedes, Tonica. Or even a . . . all right. Point taken." He kept the car spotless, and clearly had some serious pride-of-ownership issues. "But not here. I can't stand it."

One of the kids let out a particularly piercing shriek, and they both winced. "Right. Outside."

They dumped the trays and got an extra paper sack from the cashier, who looked as though she were wishing that she could leap over the counter and join them in their escape.

The area was mostly strip malls along the main road, but set back a little was a small park, barely large enough to qualify as one, and they ended up on a bench under a tree. The earlier sun had vanished, but it wasn't raining yet. For the first few minutes, the only sounds were the rustling of paper and contented chewing.

Ginny paused halfway through her burger, stared up at the branches, and came to a decision.

"The email I picked up in the car. It was from DubJay."

He didn't comment on how long it had taken her to tell him that, only asked, "Any new information, or just a cranky 'have you found him yet?'"

She worried at her lower lip. The email had bothered her, but she couldn't quite put a finger on why. "It was more of a 'keep going, but don't forget there's a deadline' kind of thing. With a tone of . . . curtness."

"He isn't willing to wait until Monday anymore?"

"He didn't say that. It felt more like, like he was checking where *we* were, the way someone keeps rechecking their cards, to make sure nothing's changed. A control-freak twitch."

"And?"

"And control freaks don't hire other people to do their stuff. Especially not other people they don't control."

"Yeah. You have a point. So maybe it's just him feeling out of control and trying to hold on, without actually interfering?"

"Maybe. Probably." That would make sense. "I'm starting to wonder if there's something he didn't . . . no, I *know* there's stuff he didn't tell me, but I'm wondering if there's something *important* he didn't tell me. Something that changes the game."

"Like what?"

"I don't know. If this were a normal job, I'd have had time to do research, learn something about the situation—I don't know a damn thing about the kind of real-estate deals they do. It's all business to business, working with other brokers, stuff like that." She wondered if there was a *Moron's Guide to Commercial Realtors* out there, too. Probably.

He finished his burger, and wiped his mouth with a napkin. "Are you getting hinky about what's going on between Uncle Joe and DubJay?"

"You aren't? You're the one who raised these questions in the first place!"

"Yeah, and you decided not to worry about it, right?" He shoved his legs out in front of him and stared at the toes of his work boots for a while, then shrugged. "You want to back out?"

She thought about the text message, and about the terse note in DubJay's message.

"I agreed to the job. The money's in my account. If I drop the job, half finished? He can ruin my reputation. My reputation *is* my business, Tonica."

"Yeah. And we're both stubborn as two bulldogs, besides. Look, DubJay's twitchy. All right. So long as he's just leaving messages, we ignore him—we're on the job. And the job is, we find Uncle Joe. We talk to him. Then we tell DubJay his uncle's been found, collect our paycheck, and let them duke it out, okay?"

Ginny scowled, not sure why having her own logic turned on her felt so wrong. "Next time I stick my nose into a bar conversation? Cut it off, okay?"

"So noted."

"That's not an agreement."

"Next time, I'll sit back and let you stick it in without interfering," he said. "If I tried to stop you, you'd chop my hand off for the effort."

Ginny had no legitimate comeback to that, and she wasn't quite sure how to—or if she should—thank him for sticking around. Stubborn as two bulldogs. That about summed it up, yeah.

Crumpling the now-empty wrappers, along with the extra napkins, into a ball, she aimed and shot the ball at the nearest trash can. It went in a nearly perfect arc, and landed squarely in the can.

"Nice shot. For a girl."

"Bet you couldn't match it."

Once again, he refused to take the bait. "You'd be right." He got up and dumped his own trash in the can and brushed off his hands. "Onward?"

Ginny looked up at the sky, the blue scattered with random clouds. An almost perfect day, and she was spending it chasing after something she wasn't sure she wanted to find anymore. Her stomach hurt, and not from the hamburger.

But it was about more than the money, and she could probably counter anything DubJay said, if he decided to go that route. She had said she could do this, and she was going to do it.

Tonica was right; they could decide what to tell DubJay after they talked to Uncle Joe.

Standing up, she turned to her partner with a determined nod. "Onward."

6

Rooftops weren't ideal when it was wet: footing was uncertain, and your fur got damp and matted. But she liked rooftops anyway. Being up high was better than being low, in her opinion. And there were fewer threats up here: the occasional other cat, or a flock of pigeons. The former she'd acknowledge and ignore, and the latter she ignored entirely.

She'd woken up uneasy, her tail twitching hard enough that it ached. The busy place was still closed, so she'd gone to Theodore's den first. He wasn't there. Penny had stared in the window, her whiskers twitching, then leapt lightly back onto the roof and headed back into town.

Georgie was asleep, sprawled in an undignified heap on the bed. Penny couldn't hear, through the windows, but she could imagine the snore rising from the shar-pei's chest, a steady low buzz.

There was no sign of the human inside, though.

Both her humans of interest were missing. Together? Penny's tail twitched again, a full-length sweep. She hated it when something happened she didn't know about and couldn't keep a paw on. How could she keep track of them if they didn't behave properly?

Her stomach rumbled, and she contemplated the sleeping dog for *a moment before turning to leave. Food first, then she'd find out what was going on.*

The address Ginny had been given for Uncle Joe's dinner companion was out in Everest, a nice but not obviously wealthy area. The houses were all on green manicured lots, not particularly large but well maintained. Unlike downtown, there weren't people walking—there weren't any sidewalks, and really nowhere to walk *to*.

They parked on the street. "I hate suburbia," Tonica said, looking around. "The back of my neck's itching. They're watching us, from behind lace curtains."

"Aren't suburbanites too busy carpooling and killing people to peep at strangers?"

"Okay, killing people? Screw this. I'm going back to the city, where it's safe."

"Big, brave, tough guy. Come on. Number seventy-three," Ginny said, pointing toward the house midway up the street. They stared at the house. It was a cottage, really, and if she thought about it, Ginny knew she could probably identify the period during which it was built and the style they followed, but she was aware that the urge to do so was nothing but avoidance.

"So what do we know?"

She tapped the tablet that had been resting on her lap, and pulled up the list. "Her name's Zara Coridan, and she's fifty-nine. Works for a small software company, name of Branchpoint, which isn't anywhere near getting bought out by anyone—worse luck for them—but she seems to be doing okay, no public debt or difficulties, steady work history. No connection to the real-estate field, far as I could tell. Reasonably active in community affairs: belongs to a couple of groups, was arrested once for protesting."

Tonica smiled. "I think I like her."

"Down, boy. No idea where or how they met, or how long they've known each other. And before you ask, he's not signed up for any online dating sites. The only reason I know who she is is that her name was in his date book."

Technically, she was pretty sure that she wasn't supposed to have access to his date book. DubJay hadn't given her the password to that, she'd just figured it out, based on Uncle Joe's other passwords. Like her parents, he had a touching faith in family names and birthdays.

Ginny used a random password generator, herself, wrote them down in opposing order with the accounts they matched, and taped the list under her bed. It seemed about as safe as any system she'd ever heard of. If someone wanted to hack you, they would, but why make it easy?

Anyway, she'd figured that his date book would give them more information, after the financial clues fizzled, and she'd been right.

"Right. So we go in and ask her what her intentions were towards Uncle Joe? That's going to be fun. Or we could quit, you know." Tonica said it as casually as though asking if she wanted another drink.

Ginny gave him her very best Look, the one that asked if

he was really that wussy. She'd worked hard at perfecting it. "You go ahead and quit, if you want to."

He met her with an open-eyed look of his own. "I was just stating an option. There have got to be better ways to spend a nice Saturday."

"Yeah, what, sleeping in?"

"Among other things, yes. Some of us have to work tonight, remember." He cut the engine and got out of the car, not letting her get a last shot in.

"I hate it when you do that," she muttered, unbuckling her seat belt and following him. But the moment was lost, anything she said now would be petty, rather than clever.

He didn't bother to lock the car—it wasn't that kind of neighborhood. She would have locked it, anyway.

"Here's hoping she's home."

"Car's here," she pointed out. There was a nice but not brand-new sedan in the driveway. An Audi, dark blue, standard plates, not vanity ones. Between the house and the car, Ginny felt a certain sympathy for this woman. Commonsensical, the pieces said. Likes nice things, but doesn't get owned by them.

"Yeah. Like she couldn't have taken a car service, or gone off with Uncle Joe, or gone for a walk, not intending to come back . . ."

He had a valid point. Instead of answering it, she marched up the walkway curving between two bits of green lawn, and up the two concrete steps to the front porch. By the time she lifted her hand to the buzzer, Tonica was standing solidly at her left shoulder, a reassuring presence.

"May I help you?"

The woman who answered the door was definitely the woman they'd come to see. Like her house and car, she was attractive but not flashy, anywhere from mid-forties to early sixties, neatly dressed in jeans and a long-sleeved lime green T-shirt, her feet bare, her hair cropped short and left natural, the black curls showing an occasional glint of silver.

"I sure hope so." Tonica took the lead again. "You're a friend of Joseph Jacobs, yes?"

The woman's cool but friendly façade shifted, so subtly that Ginny wasn't sure if she would have noticed if she hadn't been looking for exactly that sort of reaction. She was certain Tonica caught it, too, although his own demeanor—a cross between eager puppy and door-to-door salesman—didn't change.

"Yes, I know Joe. May I ask what this is about?" Her body blocked the door, so they couldn't see inside, but there was the sound of the television or a radio in the background, canned voices turned down low.

"Oh, thank God. Because we've been trying to reach him for days, and nobody has any idea where he's gone, and someone said that you'd had dinner with him and maybe you'd know?"

Ginny was taking mental notes: he'd managed to convey the idea that they were friends of the missing man, and were looking out of concern, without telling a single falsehood. That was impressive. And a little scary.

"I'm sorry, I don't know what you're talking about. I had

dinner with Joe last week, yes, but . . . what do you mean? Nobody knows where he is? But . . ."

She was lying. Ginny would have bet everything she had on it. She knew that Jacobs Senior was missing, and she knew why—and where he was. That sudden certainty was an odd feeling for Ginny, and she was normally cautious of odd things, but she trusted this, implicitly.

"Ms. Coridan, please." She moved up to stand a little ahead of Tonica, shutting him out of the conversation and making it woman to woman. "You know he's gone away. We just need to get in touch with him, that's all. Please, if you know where he is, can't you tell us?" She wasn't good at playing people, but she wasn't playing here. She did just want to talk to him. She *was* worried. She just hadn't realized how much, until that moment.

"I didn't even know he was missing, how would I know where he is? Better to talk to someone from his office. Don't they keep tabs on him?"

She was lying, still, but bitterness weighted down those words. Whatever Zara Coridan's relationship to Joe, his work was clearly a bone of contention between them.

"The office won't tell us anything useful, just that he's not in. He wasn't in on Friday, or Thursday . . . that's not like him. It's not like him to pack up his stuff and disappear, without a word to anyone." She was extrapolating, but the evidence so far painted the broad strokes of a guy who was conscientious, and a little obsessive, so it seemed a fair guess.

"Who are you two?" The woman's dark eyes narrowed, and she studied them carefully. "You're not family, he doesn't have any family other than DubJay and his spawn. And if you were friends, you'd know better than to come here and ask me anything. So what's your game?"

Ginny shook her head, trying to reach for that connection again. "We're not playing a game. We just want—"

"No." Coridan moved forward, a measured pace, and they both saw in the same instant that she was armed; she held a small pistol in her right hand. It might have been small, but Ginny didn't doubt that it could do damage. The metal gleamed blue-black in the sunlight, and the hand holding it was relaxed, but not casual.

Any sympathy Ginny had for the woman evaporated.

Beside her, she could feel Tonica tense up, alert but unmoving, and she wondered if he was as scared as she was. "Look, we—"

"I don't care how big you are, mister, or what story you're spinning." Coridan's voice had gone icy. "You want to leave now. Or I will swear to the cops that you two came here to cause trouble, tried to shove past me to rob me."

"Hey, wait a minute, I—" Tonica tried to defuse the situation, raising his hands in a "we came in peace" gesture, and she did something to the gun that made it click once, ominously.

He stopped, and Ginny almost stopped breathing.

"You want help? I'll give you some, whoever you are. Back off before you get hurt. And if you're working for that slimy dog, tell him to go to hell. I wouldn't tell him if his ass was on fire. And yours will be, too, if you don't get the hell off my porch."

She was bluffing. Ginny was almost one hundred percent certain that she was bluffing; normal people didn't shoot strangers on their front porch for asking questions, not in this neighborhood, in the twenty-first century, anyway.

Except, her lizard brain said, when they did exactly that.

Coridan raised the gun higher, the business end pointing right at Tonica's belly. "Both of you, get the hell gone."

Ginny grabbed his elbow and, without even bothering to make her farewells, jerked him back down off the porch and onto the walkway, backing up rather than risking turning her back on the crazy woman with the gun. Ginny's arm was shaking so much, it wasn't until halfway down the path, when the woman had gone back inside the house and shut the door behind her, that she realized Tonica was shaking, too.

She wasn't sure if that made her feel better or worse.

They didn't speak, getting in the car and driving away—the clutch rattling a little as Teddy misjudged it, more proof that he was not unaffected by what had happened. With a little space between her and a gun—that did make Ginny feel better, after all.

She felt her heart beating, too fast, too hard, and tried not to throw up.

"I've never seen a gun before," she admitted. "I mean, not close up."

"I have."

Of course he had.

"I've never had one pointed at me, though. And never by a woman."

That distracted her a little from the need to throw up from adrenaline overload. "It makes a difference?"

"Damn right it does. A guy, I'd know how to handle it. And if I couldn't handle it, I'd know how to take him down, probably without getting shot, and without you getting shot. A woman, I have no idea . . . I've never been threatened by a woman before."

Normally, she'd make a wise-ass comment just then, but she was too shaken to think of anything. Her only experience with violence had been the bully-girls in fifth grade, and a couple of screaming matches between the upstairs neighbors, at her first apartment after college.

"So." Ginny stared out the car's window, watching the landscape change from suburban lots back into strip malls and interchanges, leading into the city proper. "Is it time to call the cops?"

"Normally, hell yes. But what would we say—hey, we were poking around and a crazy woman showed us her handgun?"

"Yes!" She had a distinct aversion to guns, she decided.

"And then what? Either she pulls the 'I felt threatened' card, which against me would stick, in case you haven't noticed—big white male vs. older black woman? Or she flatly denies it, we look like idiots, and any chance we have of finding Joe gets chewed up by filling out paperwork and being interrogated by cops who don't give a damn anyway."

"Sounds like someone has some experience with cops." She must be feeling steadier, if she was snarking.

"Yeah. My cousin's husband is Boston PD. Nice guy. Overworked and deeply cynical. Look, if Jacobs wanted the cops involved in the first place, he'd have called them, right? Filed a missing persons report? He hasn't, has he?"

"No."

"So. We go to the cops, and they're looking at us, and your client's unhappy with us, and we still haven't gotten anywhere for our trouble. We keep having this discussion over and over—can we just accept the fact that we're not giving up, and stop wasting time poking the other person to see if they're on the same page?"

He sounded pissed off, and she couldn't blame him: he was right. But . . . "I got a text from someone yesterday," Ginny blurted. "Telling me not to play PI."

Tonica pulled out of traffic, halting the car at the curb and letting the engine die, then turned on her, one arm resting on the wheel, the other across the seatback. For a moment she saw what he meant, about him being a credible thug. "And you were going to mention this . . . when?"

"Never. I just . . . I don't like to think about unpleasant things." Her parents used to nag her about that, saying it was a mark of immaturity, but she had always figured that if she could do something about it she would, and if she couldn't do something about it, there was no point in fretting.

"And I don't like being told what to do." She pretended not to see his "no, really?" expression.

"Anyway, it was probably nothing. Maybe even Uncle Joe, telling me to back off. Like you said, what could I do, go to the cops? Believe me, it takes a hell of a lot more than a text to get the cops' attention. A friend of mine got stalked, the guy did everything but camp out in her garden, and the cops just said they couldn't actually do anything unless he made a physical threat. This? They'd treat it like a prank, tell me not to worry, or to just give up the job."

"Jesus, Mallard." But he didn't argue with her, just stared through the windshield. His jaw was so tight, there was a tic in his cheek that looked painful. "Remember when I said I didn't like the way this gig was turning? I like it even less, now."

Her stomach hurt. "You want to quit?" she asked him again. It was different now: there was an unknown factor in the game.

"Hell no, I don't want to quit." He sounded annoyed. "Someone's telling you to back off—in my world that usually means there's a damn good reason to keep going. Something someone doesn't want us to find out. If we find Uncle Joe before anyone else, at least we have a chance to figure it out, maybe even help."

"Help who? Joe's lady friend seemed to think that Dub-Jay finding his uncle would be a bad thing. What if it *is* Uncle Joe who told me to back off?"

"That's what we need to figure out—the who, and the why. But the only way to do that is to track down Joe. Yeah?"

"Yeah." She drummed her fingers against the tablet. "Tonica?"

"Yeah?"

"I think we're in way over our heads."

That made him laugh. "No shit. So what now?" He was handing control of the job back to her, his body facing forward again, ready to turn the key in the ignition and move forward, as soon as she gave the word.

"Now . . . we go talk to the lawyer. But I want to make a stop at home first."

In a sleek modern office downtown, that anonymous text was also under discussion.

"You did what?"

Mitch Goren rarely lost his temper; he had not lost it now. He was, however, deeply annoyed and more than a little incredulous.

His assistant, a young man with impeccable credentials, an impressive CV, and balls of steel wrapped in military-grade asbestos, held his ground, but his voice wobbled slightly. "I sent her a text message, warning her away. From a prepaid phone. Impossible to trace."

"You . . . from a prepaid phone. You sent Ms. Mallard a texted threat?" Each word was pronounced carefully, inflected just so, to ensure that there was no confusion, no misunderstanding, no ability to backstep later.

"Not a threat, sir." His assistant looked disturbed at the thought. "Merely a suggestion that this might not be a job she was competent for. Sir, if she is as capable as her reputation, then such . . . advice will make her dig her feet in more. She would no sooner give up than stop breathing. And once she starts digging . . . who knows what she might find? Even the slightest hint of scandal would put Jacobs Realty in a position of weakness."

"You took initiative." There was a pause, where the conversation could have turned either way, and the assistant didn't dare swallow. "Oh, Bjorn. There are days and times when that would have impressed me. This day, this time, was not one of them. If she is as smart as Walter thinks, then in sending that text, you may indeed have alerted Ms. Mallard to the fact that something more than her stated assignment is in play. And, not being a fool, she might decide, instead, to go to the police with her suspicions."

Bjorn considered that possibility, and wilted slightly.

"While I have no objection, particularly, to seeing Walter Jacobs carted off in handcuffs, his incarceration does us no good unless I am able to make use of it. And once the police are involved, any move I make would be under suspicion as well."

Having made his point, Goren relented slightly. "We will hope that your attempt worked as you hoped, and not as I fear. In the future, however, please do not attempt to think until I tell you what I want you to think."

"Sir. Yes sir."

There was a muffled tone in his assistant's response that didn't sound like either embarrassment or fear. Goren narrowed his eyes. "All right, out with it. What?"

Bjorn had been with him for years; he rarely held back what he was thinking, and Goren usually encouraged that. "You sounded like an evil overlord. Sir."

He sat back in his chair, the leather creaking underneath his weight, and stared at Bjorn, then let out a surprised laugh. "Yes, you're right, I did. And that is why you keep getting raises, rather than being kicked out the door when you are an idiot."

"Sir." There was equal parts remonstrance and pride in that single word.

Goren waved a hand in dismissal. "Oh, go take an early lunch. Don't let me see you again until I find out how much damage you may have done, with your *thinking*. And for God's sake, stop reading spy novels. They're rotting your brain."

The phone was already to his ear before the door closed behind his assistant.

"DubJay? It's Mitch. How the hell are you? Look, I'm actually home this week—no, no travel, thank God—and I want to get the boat on the water. How about you and Gretchen join me? Oh, and Joe, too, of course."

He relaxed, the worry of the previous moments fading away while he listened to the other man make excuses for his uncle. Poor DubJay, so certain that the world could be arranged to his satisfaction, no matter what. It must have been a hell of a shock when his nearly retired uncle finally showed some backbone.

And to think that he could keep it all quiet . . . that was hubris of a dangerous sort. Mitch had nothing against

DubJay, personally, but a savvy businessman kept his fingers stirring all sorts of pots just for exactly this sort of information. Outright betrayal or careless slip, it was all useful, eventually.

And now all he had to do was sit back and wait for the inevitable unraveling.

"Lovely. I'll see you both tomorrow, then!"

It might not be kosher, this game he was playing, but real estate was no place for a conscience.

7

B y the time they got back to Ginny's apartment, they'd both mostly recovered from the shock of being threatened. But Ginny was still determined to follow through on her idea to carry protection.

Tonica wasn't thrilled. "You're shitting me."

"Humor me," Ginny said, and then turned her attention back to the problem at hand. "C'mon on, baby, into the car."

Georgie looked at the space her mistress wanted her to jump through and then back at Ginny, the expression on her sweet, wrinkled face clearly asking "No, seriously? You want me to do what?"

"If that dog slobbers—or pees!—in my car, I swear, Mallard—"

"She won't. She's already done her business for the morning, and shar-peis don't drool."

"Uh-huh." He wasn't convinced. Thankfully, Ginny'd thought to toss an old towel into the bag when she went to collect Georgie, and that was now covering the space behind the passenger seats.

Looking at it from a dog's point of view, she admitted

that the old coupe had a pretty tight squeeze between the seat and door frame. But once inside, Georgie would have plenty of room—at least as much as her training cage in the apartment.

Breaking out the big guns, Ginny reached into her pocket and brought out a pup-tart. "C'mon, girl." She tossed it into the back of the Volvo, and before her arm had finished its arc, Georgie had the treat in her mouth, her bulk through the door and comfortably settled inside the car.

Tonica stared at the dog and shook his head, then ran a hand over the top of his head, as though the flattop cut might have gotten mussed. "And what do you think that lump of puppy is going to do? Lick someone to death?"

"You know Georgie," Ginny said, getting back into the car, the bag filled with water dish and toys and poo-bags at her feet.

"Yeah. And?"

"So you know she's a sweetie. But if you didn't? Look at her. She's solid muscle; her breed was originally meant to be fighting dogs."

He craned his neck around to look at the animal in his backseat, and got a blue-black tongue in the face for his effort.

"Ugh. Georgie, down!"

Georgie, having decided that the car wasn't so bad after all, remained standing, her front paws on the back of Ginny's seat.

"Georgie . . ." her mistress warned, and with a disappointed whine, Georgie settled down on the floor, her nose resting on her paws, close-curled tail twitching in anticipation of whatever was going to happen next.

"Yeah. Hell of a watchdog." But he shook his head, and started up the car.

While he drove, Ginny pulled out her cell phone and dialed a number out of her notebook.

"Hi, is this KBJ? I had an appointment with Ian for one thirty and I just wanted to make sure that he wasn't running late? Oh he is, excellent. No, no need, I'll call again if we hit any traffic. Thanks!" She clicked off, and put her phone back in her bag.

"Nice. And if they ask him about this nonexistent appointment, or check his schedule and see we're not on it?"

"Then we'll punt," she said with considerably more assurance than she actually felt.

The law offices of King, Backer and Jacks were downtown, near Elliott Bay. Tonica maneuvered through the traffic, only occasionally muttering at the other drivers. "You know, Gin, this would have been more efficient—and used a hell of a lot less gas—if we'd talked to people in order, based on location."

Ginny did not like having flaws in her organization strategy pointed out, but he was right. "Yeah, okay, I'm sorry. It seemed like a workable plan." It *had* been a workable plan. She was just used to thinking in terms of picking up a phone or entering text, not chasing people down on foot.

Figuratively. But in-person had seemed like their best bet, especially if people were hiding something, since email and phone messages gave them time to think about what they were going to say. Every movie she'd seen claimed that confronting someone without warning got you a more honest response.

Even if part of that response involved a gun. She'd forgotten that part of the movies. Ginny reached back to pet Georgie for reassurance. Dogs were the best deterrent against home invasion; so they should be good for making people think twice before attacking in person, right?

They pulled off Elliott Avenue and cruised toward their destination, staying in the slower right lane and checking street numbers.

"This is the office?" He sounded dubious.

"Not everyone gets steel skyscrapers," Ginny said, looking at the five-story stone-faced building. It looked respectable; even the stone carvings on the corners and sills were subdued.

"I'm not even going to try for a parking spot here, not today." They were too close to the Pike Place Market, and the tourists were out in full force on a Saturday. He spotted a parking garage halfway down the block, and swung the car into the entrance ramp, grabbed a ticket, and went all the way up to the top of the garage to find the least occupied parking area.

Ginny, having already encountered Tonica's particular care of the car, didn't say anything. "Come on, Georgie. Time for a walk."

Getting out of the car was, apparently, no problem for Georgie, who wiggled past the seat and shook herself out, then proceeded to investigate the edge of the cement half-wall, sniffing for an appropriate place for her to do her business.

"She's not a certified companion animal; they may not let her in," he warned, watching Ginny bend over to snap the leash to Georgie's collar. "They don't have to."

"They will."

The front lobby had three names listed over it, each with a different typeface. KBJ was in the middle, the font simple and clean. Ginny thought that might be a good sign.

"We're here to see Ian Broderick."

"Right." They had been prepared to spin an elaborate story, or simply lie and say they had an appointment, but the guard didn't seem to give a damn. "You just need to sign in here, and—oh, that's a handsome dog, but I'm afraid he can't come in."

Tonica might have been looking smug, but Ginny didn't even check. "Oh, but Georgie has to. It's part of why we're meeting with Ian." She wasn't as good at not-lying as her companion, but the receptionist made his own assumptions, and pushed the sign-in book across the counter for them to add their names. "And I'll need to see some ID, please."

Ginny handed over her license, and then waited while Tonica did the same, and they were each issued a sticky-backed strip of paper with their name, the word *visitor,* and the name of the law firm printed on it. Ginny noted to herself, in passing, that they'd be silly-easy to forge on any home computer. The idea of office security, obviously, wasn't high on the building management's mind.

"Third floor, check in with the front desk there."

Georgie looked a little uncertain at the idea of getting into the elevator, but another treat convinced her.

The woman sitting behind the desk in the very expensive-looking lobby on the third floor didn't even blink at Georgie, but took down their names and typed something on a keyboard. She looked at the screen, waiting, then frowned.

"You're the folks who called? I thought you had an appointment?"

"No." There was no point in claiming otherwise: they were already here. The lawyer would either speak to them or not. Ginny was counting on human curiosity, and the desire to not turn away potential clients, to get them through. "We knew he was working today, and hoped he'd find time to fit us in. It's about Jacobs Realty." Ginny put on her best "confident" look, and hoped Tonica was doing the same. "It's rather urgent."

"Please, take a seat."

There was a choice between modern-looking chairs in chrome and red leather or a low-slung sofa of the same material. They both opted for the chairs, while Georgie obediently curled up beside Ginny's feet, ignoring all the doubtless fascinating smells in favor of staying close to her human.

"Who intentionally buys furniture like this?" Ginny asked in a low voice, looking around.

"Companies with a very expensive designer and image consultant," he said. "It's not supposed to be comfortable, it's supposed to say, 'We're more important than you, be glad we let you in.'"

"It's hideous."

Tonica looked around with an air that made her unsure if he was really looking or just winding her up. "I don't know, I kinda like it."

"God. All your taste is in your mouth."

"Tsk. Your middle-class roots are showing, Ms. Mallard."

"I'm okay with that," she shot back. "At least my roots are their natural color." She'd been saving that zing for the right moment.

"I went gray at twenty, got bored with it by the time I was twenty-five. And I keep my roots touched up, thank you very much."

"Miss Clairol?"

"Grecian Formula, and okay with that."

A voice interrupted whatever comeback she might have had. "Ms. Mallard? Mr. Tonica? Mr. Broderick will see you now." A woman—different from the receptionist, who seemed to have willfully forgotten their existence—was standing there, looking expectant.

The tension they'd been holding, wondering if this bluff would work, went out of them like a popped balloon, and they stood up—Georgie grumbling at being moved again—and headed for the door in the wall the woman had appeared through. She was slim and very blond, and wearing a suit Ginny quickly summed up as costing more than her entire wardrobe.

"Follow me, please."

They walked down a carpeted hallway, the doors on either side of dark wood, the ones on the left with a glass insert running along the side. There were brass nameplates next to each door on the left, and no tags on the plain doors to the right. Partners and associates, maybe. Or associates on different levels of the food chain—she thought partners, by regulation, came with corner offices?

She flicked her gaze to Tonica walking beside her, and saw him giving the space the same sort of once-over. They could compare notes later, although she didn't know what use that would be. It wasn't like Joe would be hiding here.

Although, at this point, they couldn't rule out anything, she supposed.

Their guide stopped in front of one of the offices with a nameplate. "Thank you, Louise," a voice said from inside. "You can go to lunch now—I won't be needing you for anything else today."

The woman disappeared back down the hall without a word of explanation or farewell, and the two of them stared at each other, wondering what to do.

"Come in, already. You wanted to see me, right?"

The office wasn't as lush as Ginny had been expecting: there was a large desk at the far end of the room, more a long table than a traditional piece of furniture, and a square table with three chairs, and a pitcher of water set on it. The non-windowed wall had a credenza filled with books and binders, and there were large green plants grouped at the other corner of the room from the desk.

"Come in, sit down." The man flapped his right hand at the chairs, his left still working the keyboard in front of him, his attention focused on the screen. "I'll be with you in a minute."

They seated themselves, Georgie going under the table and settling at Ginny's feet with a contented sigh, her muzzle resting on her paws. It only took another moment—the two of them trying hard not to fidget—before the lawyer sighed and pushed away from his desk.

Literally. The reason for the room's sparseness—and the three chairs at a table large enough for four—became clear as Ian Broderick rolled his chair toward them. It was a sleek, obviously expensive wheelchair, but there was no attempt to hide the braces encasing his legs.

"So. You're here about Joseph. Zara called and told me you'd probably show up."

Teddy felt his muscles tense when Broderick mentioned the woman who'd pulled a gun on them, and Ginny must have done likewise, because Georgie suddenly stood up, coming out from under the table to stand protectively at her side. He had to admit, if you didn't know better, the shar-pei looked damned unnerving, bristling like a proper watchdog.

"Good-looking bitch," Broderick said, unfazed. "You can call her off. I'm not a threat to you." He raised his hands, to show them he was unarmed. "Unless I try to run you over, you're safe."

Wiseass. Teddy liked him immediately. But he wasn't the one who gave Georgie orders.

Ginny studied the lawyer a minute, then said, "Georgie, stand down. Down."

The shar-pei looked at Broderick, almost as though trying to gauge his worthiness, then settled back down at Ginny's feet with a sigh—although she did not go back under the table. Whether because of the chair, or his smell, or something known only to dogs, Georgie wasn't entirely trusting this newcomer near her human.

Teddy could respect that kind of instinct, even when it conflicted with his own. He leaned back, consciously putting on a veneer of "tough guy," and let Ginny take the lead.

"She called you?" *She* meaning Zara, crazy gun-lady.

"After you left. Yes."

"Did she mention that she pulled a gun on us?" Teddy asked, curious.

Broderick winced. "Ouch. No. You must understand, Zara is . . . protective of Joe. And she suspected that you were working for his nephew."

There was a pause, and Teddy wondered if they were going to try and bullshit their way out of things. He would have, but this was Gin's gig; he was just along for the sweet-talking and muscle.

"Walter Jacobs hired me to discover his uncle's where-abouts," she said, and then waited for his reaction.

"You're PIs?" He sounded surprised; Teddy guessed they didn't fit the stereotype, whatever that was.

"Researchers," she said. "Not PIs, not cops, not enforcers. Just here to get information."

Broderick chewed on that for a moment. "And what will you do with that information, once you have it?"

They were sussing each other out. Teddy just hoped that Ginny's ability to read people was better than she'd shown so far, because her answer was going to determine if they got anything useful out of this guy.

"That depends on what the information tells me."

Something in his eyes sharpened. "You're not a PI—may I ask, what sort of an agreement do you have with Dub-Jay?"

"Handshake only. No NDA, no obligations."

"Huh. That was surprisingly careless of him."

They'd gone into legalese. Teddy wasn't sure if that was a good thing or not.

Now it was Broderick's turn to study Ginny carefully, then he turned that gaze on Teddy. They both sat there and waited, because there wasn't anything else they could do. Either Ian Broderick would help them or not.

"I'm not their corporate lawyer—I handle Joe's estate, his personal matters. I don't know what's going on between him and Walter, and I don't want to know what's going on with the company. Whatever it is, Joe wanted to work it out on his own, and I respected that. But Zara's worried—and I admit to some concern myself. Joe is an old friend, and a longtime client, and . . ."

He slapped the arms of his chair lightly, coming to a decision. "I don't know where he is. But if I were trying to track him down, I know where I'd look first."

Many years ago, Walter Jacobs had made a vow to himself: he would not spend Saturdays in the office. Sundays, as needed—Sunday was merely a ramp-up to Monday, after all. But Saturdays were downtime. It was for family, and relaxing, and maybe even grilling steaks in the backyard, if he ever bought a grill or had a backyard.

Two decades later, he didn't have either, but Saturdays were still spent out of the office. Unfortunately, as his responsibilities grew, that only meant that he worked from home.

Mitch's call that afternoon had been a welcome break from paperwork. Speder-Goren Management handled a number of the buildings Jacobs Realty represented, and over the years the two men had come to respect each other's business savvy and commonsense approach. The fact that Mitch had a twenty-seven-foot sailboat that Walter lusted after had never hurt the relationship, either. It would be good to see him—and the boat—tomorrow. Gretchen, as usual, would tease him mercilessly, ask him why he didn't just get a boat of his own.

"The best boat to have," he would say to her, as he always did, "is the one your best friend owns." Let Mitch deal with the repairs and maintenance: he would enjoy the actual sailing.

Gretchen was downstairs doing something in her own office: she had emailed him a question about dinner a few minutes ago, so he imagined that she was taking a break. If a good wife was a treasure, he was Midas. He had met her at a fund-raiser almost ten years ago, and convinced her to marry him within six months. She was a dynamo in her own right, her PR firm sought after not by those who wanted publicity, but those who wanted their publicity *managed*. Together, they were an impressive couple.

But any thought of play had to wait for another day: he still had loose ends to tie up.

"What do you mean, you don't know where they are?"

At home, he used his cell phone, the expensive wireless headset an annoyance that was offset by having his hands free. Swiveling in his chair, he was able to lift the small boy tugging at his leg high over his head, and make a face, causing the child to break into delighted giggles that the person on the other end of the line could not hear.

"All I asked was that you keep track of what the woman did, and where she went, and report back to me. How difficult was that?"

He put his son back in his playpen, distracting him with a toy, and paced the office. "One woman. How hard is it to keep track of one woman?"

There was a spate of words in his earpiece.

"What do you mean she got in a car? She doesn't own a car!"

That explained why she hadn't answered her phone, he supposed. He had, foolishly, thought she would do everything through records, not footwork. Footwork meant people. People were . . . more complicated. Damn it, what if they talked to that community activist woman, or . . .

He forced his hand to unclench, pushing it palm-down on his desk. It was too late to worry about that, and if the woman knew where Joe had disappeared to, so much the better. That was what he'd hired Ms. Mallard for, after all. But the addition of someone new bothered him. He had no leash on that person. "Who was driving, and why didn't you follow them?"

He listened for a few seconds, and then made a slashing gesture, as though the other person could see it and would know to stop talking. "Fine, no, fine, whatever, it's too late for your excuses now. Get your ass back here. No, wait." He stopped, his gaze resting blindly on the wall, his brain working overtime. "You can still be useful."

If Ms. Mallard was going to be out and about, he had other ways to find information.

He told the other man what he wanted, and waited for the agreement. It took a few minutes, and a renegotiation in price, but it was easily enough done.

He ended the call without a farewell, and removed the headset, placing it carefully on his desk.

"Damn it, Joe, even gone you're giving me a headache. Why couldn't you just come and talk to me when you started getting suspicious? I could have dealt with everything then and there."

★ ★ ★

Penny was worried. Not that she would admit it, of course. But she'd eaten and slept, and still Teddy wasn't where he was supposed to be, and when she had gone back to Georgie's den, she wasn't there, either, and neither was her human.

The tabby abandoned the bedroom window, and crept along to another windowsill, this one half open. She put her claws up on the screen and peered inside. It was a larger room: Georgie's bed was there, near a sofa that begged for a cat's claws to dig into it, and a little fireplace. It looked cozy, and comfortable, and empty.

Maybe they had gone out to the park. They did that sometimes, Georgie said. But Penny didn't know what park, and there were too many smells to pick out one dog on the street outside.

She could go back to the busy place and wait there. But the older man, the one who smelled like herbs and smoke, was there, and he didn't like her. And a cat with self-respect did not go where she was not wanted . . . unless she wanted to be there, that was.

She would wait. Cats could be patient, when they had to be. Penny curled up in a patch of sunlight on the fire escape outside Georgie's window, and went to sleep until the sound of someone moving around inside the apartment woke her up.

8

They left Broderick's office half an hour later with a list of places Uncle Joe might be likely to hole up in, and a sense that they were finally getting somewhere. Teddy held his silence all the way back to the parking garage before it finally escaped. "I told you we should have gone to him first."

"If we had, without Zara's apology—or at least her guilt for being a badass gun-slinging suburban vigilante wannabe—he might not have given us anything. And seeing Joe's apartment confirmed that he'd gone on his own, not been yanked off the street. Probably. It was all important."

Gin sounded pissed, and he held up his hands in semi-apology. "You're the boss."

"Hah." She wiggled her shoulders a little in mock pride. "Yeah, I am, aren't I?"

"Don't run mad with power. Especially since I still have the car keys." He reached for the keys in his pocket, and caught sight of the time. "Damn, it's getting late. Give me a second, okay?"

He pulled out his cell phone, and dialed the bar's office number. "Hey. It's Tonica."

The afternoon bartender, a new guy, sounded a little frantic. Apparently, Patrick—the owner—and Seth were having another one of their dustups

"Yeah, I know. Look, just ignore them, okay? They do it all the time. And if I run late, just cover for me, okay? I'll be there as soon as I can."

Tonica put his cell away and glared up at the sky, which looked even more like rain than before. That morning, eight hours had seemed more than enough time to give Ginny and still make it back for his shift on time. But everything seemed to take longer than expected, and ducking back for the damned dog had eaten even more time.

"Going to be cutting it close," he said to himself, trying to calculate things.

"I don't need you to take me," Ginny said. She had taken Georgie for a quick stroll down the street while he checked in at Mary's. "We can get there on our own."

"Yeah, I know. But it'll take you three times as long using mass transit, and I agreed to help you today and today's still on." It wasn't like the boss was going to fire him—he worked his ass off keeping the place in top shape, closed most nights, handled the scheduling . . . Teddy might not have the official title or paycheck, but he was de facto manager, and everyone damn well knew it. "If he's not at the first or second place, I'll dump you and run for it, I promise."

He meant it. She could hire cabs to take her around town if needed, and with Georgie with her, he wouldn't even feel guilty. Gin had been right: the dog might be a sweet doofus, but she'd proven she could act the part of a guard dog, anyway. Putting up a strong front was more than halfway to avoiding a fight, and he thought it might be closer to three-quarters of the game when you had four legs and a hard-biting jaw.

It wasn't as though Ginny couldn't take care of herself. He'd seen her arm-wrestle for a bar tab one night with her friends, and those curves weren't all soft. Ginny Mallard was hardly a frail flower, physically or mentally. So there was no reason to feel guilty. At all.

"There are seven places on this list," she said, even as she was urging Georgie back into the car. By now, the dog had figured out the car wasn't going to eat her, and hopped in without too much trouble, curling up and waiting for the humans to follow. "Five hotels, two bed-and-breakfasts. Most of them are in town, thankfully."

"So let's get going," he said. "Pick the ones that're closest to where we are, and give them a call, see if you can get a clue from the front desk if he's there or not."

She huffed a bit at that. "You really think they're going to just give out a guest's name?"

"I have learned to have the utmost respect for the incompetence of most of the service industry," he replied, most of his attention on pulling out into traffic, which had picked up considerably since they arrived. An equal number of people leaving and coming, he guessed. Tourists mostly, small families and groups of teenagers, male and female, gathering in clutches.

Ginny looked like she was going to argue the point more, then decided against it, punching in a number from the list and waiting while the call went through. "Hi. I'm calling for Joe Jacobs. Can you connect me to his room, please? Great, thanks."

She shot him a wide-eyed look, clearly amazed that it had worked.

"Hang up!" he hissed, worried that a call coming in would spook their missing man, but she waved him off, frowning to tell him to hush.

"*Ciao, è questo—questo non è Gracie? Ah, le mie scuse.* So sorry." And she hung up.

He was, reluctantly, impressed. "I didn't know you spoke another language."

"Tourist-level Italian, but hearing someone speak a different language on the phone unexpectedly typically freaks people out enough they don't wonder why, or who it might be."

"Smart."

"Well, yes." She gave him one of those looks, the one that said she thought she'd one-upped him. In this case, he gave it to her; she had.

Keeping score was more difficult when you were with someone all day, rather than just a couple of hours. He wasn't even sure who was leading on points anymore.

She pursed her lips, and then said, like a peace offering, "Talking to people is more useful than all the research I did yesterday."

It was, but he didn't think it would be politic to rub it in.

"If you hadn't done the research, we wouldn't have known what questions to ask—or what leads to not bother chasing, like a plane ticket, or stuff like that."

"Yeah. Point." She sounded happier, with that.

"It's weird, though. Do you get the feeling we've been really lucky so far, with all this?"

"No." Ginny shook her head. "I think we're dealing with a bunch of amateurs."

"Um. We're amateurs," he reminded her.

"You are. I'm a professional researcher and fact finder." Her confidence was coming back, and with it, some of that annoying arrogance.

He didn't have the energy to argue. "Okay, fine. Still. It's just been . . . too easy?"

"What were you expecting? Roadblocks at every turn? He's not some escaped convict, Tonica. Just a guy who skipped out for a few days at a bad time."

"Someone you were already warned against trying to find," he reminded her.

She made a scoffing noise. "I still think it was Joe himself. Or the girlfriend. Nothing serious."

"Nothing serious? Gin, the woman had a gun. I call that plenty serious."

"But she told Broderick, and he helped us. They're not the bad guys, just worried friends."

Teddy wasn't convinced, but if she wanted to believe the best of people, he didn't have the heart to argue. He kept quiet and focused on the traffic, thankful they weren't trying to do this during a weekday rush hour.

He just hoped to hell that she was right, and he was wrong.

The hotel was nice enough that the valet didn't ask if they were guests at the hotel, merely accepted Teddy's key and the fact that there was a dog in the car without hesitation.

"Leave the windows down," Ginny told the valet as she got out. "She won't go anywhere."

"You want I should take her for a walk?" The kid was maybe twenty, and eager to please.

"No, she's good."

"She'd better be," Teddy muttered. If there was even a hint of doggie business in his car when they got back, Ginny was paying for a full cleaning, roof to floor.

The lobby was small but it didn't feel cramped. He noticed the details—there were fresh flowers in vases along the gleaming marble walls, and a narrow, deep blue carpet led directly to the check-in counter, and then again to the elevator bank. There were people sitting in a small seating area, clearly waiting, and a handful of uniformed employees moving briskly about their business. This was no midrange chain; everything here whispered "boutique," and shouted "money."

"What now?" Teddy asked. "It's one thing to be put through on the switchboard, but they're not going to just tell us what room he's in, and I really doubt he'll invite us up if we announce ourselves at the front desk."

"Bet you he will," Ginny said, leading the way to the nearest available clerk, a middle-aged man with an expectant, professional smile.

"Hi. Could you please tell Joe Jacobs that we're here?"

"Of course. Your names, please?"

"We're from King, Backer and Jacks," she said, using the law firm's name. "He's not expecting us, but we have information that couldn't wait."

"Just a moment."

While the clerk dialed the room, Teddy jerked on Ginny's sleeve urgently, pulling her a step away.

"You lied," he hissed, low enough that the clerk couldn't hear.

"You had a better idea?"

He hadn't. And it seemed to be working, as the clerk was speaking to someone, then nodding and hanging up the phone. "Room 417. Use the left-hand elevator."

"Thank you so much," Ginny said politely, and walked away, leaving Teddy no choice but to follow her to the elevator.

"You just misrepresented yourself. Us!" This was exactly what he'd been afraid of: Mallard so focused on the goal that she did stuff like this. The book had been clear about how bad it was to misrepresent yourself. *Involving cops* bad.

"Well, Ian did send us. And we do have new information that really can't wait. So it's only technically a lie."

"It is not technically a lie. It *is* a lie!"

The elevator came, with two other people already in it,

and he had no choice but to shut up, glaring at her sideways the entire trip. She seemed oblivious.

Room 417 was actually a suite, with double doors that opened from the hallway into a large sitting room. The doors were open, and standing by the window looking out over the view, as though he'd posed for dramatic effect, was a tall, gray-haired man.

He didn't bother turning around. "I'm assuming you're here either to help me or kill me."

Ginny admitted that she was rarely caught without anything to say, but that stopped her cold.

"Drama queen, much?" she heard Tonica say, sotto voce, behind her, and had to bite the inside of her cheek to keep from replying. Now was not the time, or the place, for snark. But really, yes.

"We're not here to kill you," Tonica said, shutting the doors behind him.

"My nephew did not send you?"

Ginny blinked, but Tonica beat her to the question. "Do you have reason to believe that your nephew wants you dead?"

"At this point I'm not sure of anything, anymore."

He turned to face them then, and while Ginny saw a definite resemblance between DubJay and the older man, this was a more honed, thoughtful face. Looks, though, could be deceiving. Especially in someone who was, basically, in sales.

"Actually, Ian Broderick did send us, like we told the clerk," Tonica said. "Sort of."

"Sort of?"

"We spoke with him," Ginny said. "Also with Zara. They told us . . . where they thought you might be found."

"Everyone always hedges," the older man said, less bitter than contemplative. "Are we taught to do that, or is it an instinctive reaction?"

"I don't know, sir." The *sir* came naturally to her, although she couldn't remember ever using it before with someone not a cop.

"No. Nor do I." He came forward, looking at them carefully. "And you are?"

"Ginny Mallard. And this is Teddy Tonica."

"Any relation to the New Hampshire Tonicas?"

Next to her, Tonica made a weird jerking move, like someone had poked him in the back. "Ah. Yes sir. Distantly."

"Distantly as in 'barely related,' or distantly as in 'they're on the East Coast, and you're here'?"

"Yes sir. The latter."

Joseph—it seemed wrong, to Ginny, to refer to him as Uncle Joe, now—exhaled in what was almost a laugh, and gestured to the seating arrangement. "Come, sit down. And stop *sir*-ing me. I was an enlisted man, and I'm not old enough now to warrant that kind of respect."

It had nothing whatsoever to do with age, but neither of them argued the point, following him over to the grouping of sofas and love seats. The arrangement had them facing each other, three points across the glass coffee table.

"Interesting choice for a hideout," Tonica said, breaking the silence before it got uncomfortable.

"You think I should have been in a grungy motel, twitching aside the curtain to peer at every car that drove by?" He smiled, a little grim, a little smug. "I've watched enough cop shows to know that seedy motels will turn you over for a twenty-dollar bill, while expensive hotels guard privacy far better. They have more to lose if something unpleasant happens on their property."

The nose and eyes weren't the only resemblance between the two generations of Jacobses; the quick-thinking brains were there, too. But Jacobs Senior seemed . . . less hard, even as he was evaluating them. There was a wry humor there, and in his voice—something that was lacking in his nephew, even when he laughed.

In light of that, Ginny decided to go for broke, and hope that wasn't an unfortunate choice of words.

"Your nephew hired me—us, to find you. That was all he hired us to do: to discover where you had gone, and convince you to return."

"You're PIs?" Unlike Ian, he didn't seem surprised or disbelieving.

"I'm a researcher," she said, leaving Tonica out of it for the moment.

"And so not bound by any particular legal constraints, save those of an ordinary citizen, and not a credible witness in case of dispute. Yes. That sounds like Wally."

"Wally?" Tonica echoed in disbelief.

The nickname made Ginny want to smirk, too, but she restrained it better than Tonica.

"And Ian and Zara sent you to me?"

"After she pulled a gun on us," Ginny admitted.

"Oh. Oh, Zara . . ." He winced, much as Ian had done. "I am sorry about that. I think I frightened her when we last spoke."

"At dinner. You told her that you were going to disappear?"

"Not as such. She knew my concerns, and . . . she has never had a high opinion of Wally. She worked on a downtown improvement committee, and he had a building involved, and . . . that was how we met, actually." He smiled, some fond memory coming to the fore.

"You two were, ah . . ." She made a vague gesture in the air, trying not to be too crude, but not sure how to ask.

"No. Nothing like that. It was purely mutual interests, although I like to think that we've become friends."

"Generally, one doesn't pull a gun to defend the whereabouts of someone you don't like," Tonica said drily.

"Indeed. That's true." Joseph suddenly looked happier, as though one cloud of worry had been removed.

Ginny hated to have to push him, but sympathy didn't close the deal, and she still needed to know what they were going to tell DubJay come Monday morning.

"So you spoke with Zara and Ian, and they decided you were to be trusted, and here we are." He spread out his hands, and asked, "What now?"

That was a damned good question. Ginny had expected,

once they found him, he'd be able to answer that. Apparently not.

Breathe in, she told herself silently. Breathe out. Pretend he's your dad, handle him the same way.

"Why did you disappear?" She let her voice rise at the end, making it a question rather than an accusation—she hoped. "Your cleaning lady said you cleared off your desk, and DubJay"—she started to say *Wally,* then changed her mind—"Walter said there were papers that needed to be filed, that you hadn't handed over, so I'm assuming that's what this is all about? Paperwork?"

"Certificates." He sighed, leaning forward and resting his elbows on his knees. "Wally couldn't have told you anything, of course. He couldn't, not without breaking confidentiality agreements." He studied them again, and Ginny tried not to hold her breath or look guilty. "It doesn't matter now. The deal we've been putting together, it's not a particularly major one, but significant nonetheless. An old warehouse was going to be converted to commercial use, owned by a nonprofit that will . . ." He must have sensed that his audience was beginning to glaze over. "Well, it's all rather complicated and not germane to the point, but when I was going over the papers, I saw discrepancies in the Certificate of Occupancy. Discrepancies that, in my experience, meant that someone hadn't actually looked at the building, but just signed off on the paperwork.

"I tried calling the man whose name was on them, and was told that he'd been on medical leave for the past month. There was no way he would have signed off on those papers." Joseph's face turned stern, very much the disapproving patriarch. "Things were not done properly—and Wally had to have known. He was the one who handled this; I trained him, I know that he checks every detail. If word ever got out . . ."

"So you thought that by absconding with the paperwork, you could keep the deal from going through?" Tonica's voice was even, but Ginny thought that she could detect a faint whiff of disbelief. He knew more about these certificates than she did, she suspected.

"Delay it. At least until I decided what to do. I've been too lax with the boy lately. My health, and . . . no. No excuses. I let things slip." His face was still stern, but there was a flicker of something behind those sharp eyes that spoke of sadness and a deep regret. Ginny, knowing she should—had to—remain impartial, still wanted to comfort him.

"We don't have much family left. This—if word got out that the papers hadn't been legal, that we brokered a deal with that sort of cloud, everything we did from here on in would be suspect. It could hurt the family name. If he . . ."

"If he were suspected of fraud, your company would be ruined." Tonica was blunt, although still respectful. "Real estate is about reputation—if they don't trust the properties you bring them, you're screwed."

"It was an oversight, some failure of oversight, not a willful forgery." But the look in his eyes made Ginny think he was trying to convince himself of that, more than believing it. She tried to think about her own company being that damaged because someone she'd trusted had screwed up that badly, and couldn't imagine how angry she would be.

Angry enough to send a family member to jail? Not her parent, no. Never. She had an aunt and an uncle, and they had two sons, but she'd never been particularly close to them—they lived out in Texas, and visits were few and far between.

"You made a comment about us being here to help you or kill you," she said, remembering. "Was that for dramatic effect, or do you really think that your life is in danger?"

Joe stood up, pacing back to the window, his hands shoved into his slacks pockets. "I don't know," he said again. "I wish I could say it was drama, or some ill-advised attempt at humor, but . . . I don't know.

"When I decided to take some time off to think about it, I had my bags packed and brought them down to my car, and then had to go back upstairs because I had forgotten something. When I came back—not twenty minutes later, someone had broken into my car and stolen my things. My suitcase, my briefcase . . . but they'd left my wallet, in plain sight."

"They took the papers?"

He laughed. "No. That's what I had forgotten, what I had gone back for. But I felt . . ." He shrugged.

"Threatened," Tonica said.

"Yes. I called my local shop, arranged for them to take the car in for repairs, cancelled the original reservation I'd made, and came here, hoping they'd have a room available.

Zara brought me a change of clothes, and I've been . . . waiting, ever since then."

That explained where the car was, anyway. Ginny ticked one item off her mental list, even though it didn't matter anymore. She hated loose ends.

Tonica, meanwhile, cut to the chase. "Do you think your nephew had someone break in, to steal the papers?"

Joe looked like he'd heard a vaguely offensive joke. "Wally has the keys to my car," he said. "He wouldn't need to break in."

"Unless he wanted to scare you," Ginny said.

"Or threaten you," Tonica added. "Or sent people who like breaking into cars as a way to leave a message."

It was as though they'd hit him, the way he flinched from each suggestion, like they were cutting at him . . . No, Ginny thought suddenly, not at him, but at his certainties, the things that held him steady. She desperately wanted to talk to Tonica, to get his read on things, but there was no chance.

Then she felt his hand on her shoulder, a brief, firm grip, a faint squeeze of his fingers, as though to draw her attention to something, and she exhaled. He'd seen it, too.

"Is it possible, sir?" she asked, gently. "Not that he wanted to hurt you, but that he wanted to warn you from doing anything rash? Anything that might hurt"—she almost said *you* and then changed it to—"the company?"

Jacobs licked his lips, like they'd gone dry suddenly. "Yes. I had considered that. Sitting here has given me a lot of time to think. Wally isn't a boy anymore. He's a man. A man who has done things he knows I would not approve of. Things that would be easier to hide, with me out of the way.

"You never want to believe your own kin could . . . but then, that's where they say most threats come from, isn't it? People you know? Especially when there's money—or pride—involved."

"What are you going to do?" Ginny asked. Her entire body felt both weirdly relaxed and utterly tense, and she didn't like the feeling at all. She'd been so wrapped up in finding this man, thinking that once she did, the job would be over. She'd collect her fee and that would be that.

But her 3:00-a.m. panic attack returned, full force. This wasn't a party, or paperwork. This was someone's life. No, it was *two* someones' lives.

Even if she wasn't feeling much sympathy for "Wally" right now, though, she wasn't the one making the decision. Joe had to.

"I don't know." He must have known how that sounded, so he added, defensively, "I've been trying to figure that out for days now, going over my options, again and again. But each choice seems like a worse dead end, with no way to get out. So when you showed up, and used the law firm's name, I thought . . . well, one way or the other, time's up."

9

Teddy excused them, as politely as he could, and took Ginny by the arm, dragging her over to the far side of the suite for a "quick business conference."

"Mallard, stop, please. Think before you agree to anything. Joe is giving off all the right vibes, yeah. And he's in a crappy situation. But I know the type—he's going to look to us for the solution to his problems, so he doesn't have to make any ugly choices. I don't know about you, but that's way above my pay grade. And I don't want this on my hands—and neither do you. Trust me on that."

Her normally bright eyes were troubled, her brow furrowed, and she kept running her fingers through her curls, her dead-giveaway tell during trivia nights, when she didn't know the answer. "We can't just walk out on him."

"Yeah, we can."

"Teddy."

She so rarely used his first name, and he could hear the different strands in her voice: horror, objection, disappointment. The stab of regret that hit him was an old friend: he swallowed it, and went on. "Gin. Listen to me. We are not private investigators. We are not legal arbiters.

We sure as hell aren't family counselors. And this particular knot needs all three, not two amateurs looking to score a paycheck."

"What would you suggest, then? Just turning around and walking out of here?"

"Yes. Wasn't that always the plan? Find him, and 'hey look, the job's done'?"

He could see the thoughts going across her face: that was the thing about Ginny, she was so used to working behind a computer screen, she'd never learned to hide her thoughts. The woman shouldn't be allowed within ten feet of a poker table, ever.

"We can't just . . ."

"Yes." He nodded firmly, feeling like an utter heel. "We can."

Her eyes widened, and her jaw got a stubborn jut. "We shouldn't."

Damn the woman. No, they shouldn't. It would be like turning your back on an injured cat: it might be able take care of itself, but odds were it would just crawl off somewhere and die quietly.

"It's not like he's helpless."

"He is. He's like . . . Hamlet."

"He's not at all like Hamlet." Teddy considered the story, and the man waiting behind them. "Okay, he is like Hamlet. Nobody could help him, either, remember?" More, Teddy remembered what happened to hapless would-be heroes in Gin's beloved old noir detective movies, when they played outside their game. He wasn't going to let that happen to her. Or him, for that matter.

She tilted her head, and her eyes got a speculative cast. He had the sudden, unnerving thought that she looked a bit too much like Penny at that moment for his comfort.

"You have contacts. You could ask around, see what can be done, and nobody would connect you to Jacobs Realty, so there wouldn't be any risk."

"You have an inflated idea of who I know."

She shook her head. "No. I don't think I do. You're one of those people who's a vector—even if someone you know isn't the right person, they know someone who is. You've got that kind of personality."

"The right kind of . . . right." He knew what she meant, and she was right. He didn't know anyone firsthand, but he knew a guy who might know a guy. In this case, the second guy was a woman who worked for an organization that might be interested in knowing about things like this— interested enough to cut some immunity for the person or persons reporting said information.

Maybe.

"Even if I did . . . Joe's still got to be willing to pull the trigger. You think he's got the guts to do it?"

"I don't know." Her gaze went vague for a moment, like she wasn't looking at him any longer. "No. But what are we going to do, just leave him stewing in his own indecision?"

"For now, yeah. I've got to get to work. And it will take

a day or so to get an answer from my guy. So he's got to sit tight for a while."

Her focus sharpened again. "We only have until Monday," she reminded him.

"Thirty-six hours. Piece of cake."

"God, I hope so. All right." She turned back to the elder Jacobs, moving across the room with increasing confidence, selling whatever she was going to tell him.

"Sir, we think we know a way out of this. But it's going to take some doing. You need to sit tight for another day, all right? Don't call anyone, don't text anyone, and for God's sake, don't let anyone else in, all right?"

"I won't." Joe looked relieved, supporting Teddy's worst fears: he was hoping to lay it all on them, so he'd be blameless for whatever happened to his nephew.

Teddy wasn't sure relief was called for, not yet, but it wasn't his problem. He had one more thing to do, and then he was done, damn it. And maybe next time he'd know better and stay out of Ginny Mallard's business.

They had to wait a few minutes for the valet to retrieve Tonica's car. She could tell from the way he was shifting from one foot to another, carefully sneaking a look at his watch, that he was worried about getting to work on time. The fact that she was starting to be able to "read" him pleased her, but she also felt guilty.

"Just let me off at Mary's," she said. "Georgie and I can

walk home from there." The air felt wet and chilly, but it wasn't actually raining, yet.

"Yeah, okay, thanks. Like I said, they're not going to fire me, but Saturdays can get hectic behind the bar, and Stacy—"

"Stacy's gonna steal your job in another year or two."

"Yeah, she's got potential, but she's not there yet."

The car pulled up, and the valet handed over the keys. Georgie was sitting in the passenger's seat, her head hanging out the window, her blue-black tongue hanging out of her mouth.

"Damn it," Teddy muttered. "If there's drool—or poo— in my car . . ."

"Took her for a walk," the valet said. "Sweet girl."

Ginny slipped him an extra five in addition to Teddy's more grudging tip, and shoved the dog into the backseat, getting a broad swipe of Georgie's tongue across her cheek in return.

"Sit, Georgie. Stay down." She did a quick check for drool or poo, and—relieved but not surprised to find none—sat back in the seat.

They were both sunk in their own thoughts on the way back, the only sound in the car Georgie's breathing. Then Tonica broke the quiet, the words rushing out of him. "Jesus, that was sad. The guy runs—ran—his own company. And he's been sitting there for days, with one change of clothing, waiting for someone else to come in and tell him what he already knows, and handle it for him."

Tonica sounded somewhere between disgusted and surprised, and Ginny felt the weird need to defend the old man.

"It's a family thing. They make you crazy, no matter who you are, or how much money you've got."

That got a snort of agreement. "Amen."

"Most of my clients are like that," Ginny added, thinking about it. "About wanting someone else to do for them, I mean. Sometimes it's time management, about allocating and delegating the things that really aren't worth their time to do, when I could do it cheaper. And sometimes I'm doing things for them they could do themselves just as easily, but they either don't want to, or they think it makes them look more important to have someone else do it—or they know it's going to require telling someone something they don't want to say." She hesitated, then shrugged. "I once had to break an engagement for someone."

She could *feel* Tonica's shock. "What?"

She could remember without cringing, now, but back then it had taken every ounce of professionalism not to tell the client to take a long walk off a short pier. "Yeah, I know. This job is crap sometimes, and people suck. But in the long run, I think I was the gentler option, and she could rail at me and know I was sympathetic, that the guy was scum and she was better off single than married to him." Ginny had taken extreme pleasure in cashing that paycheck.

"Whoops." Belatedly, and a little guiltily, she reached into her bag and pulled out her cell phone, turning the sound back on and checking to see if any messages had come in since they went into the hotel.

"Huh."

"What?" He glanced over at her, and then back at the road. "Wally again? Or another anonymous text?"

"Neither. Someone called, but I don't recognize the number." It was local, but not one of her clients, or her family or friends, or anyone in her extensive address book.

"Still no idea who might have texted you?"

"No. And it's not like it matters now anyway, right? I mean, we found Joe."

"Right." He didn't sound convinced.

"It was probably Zara," Ginny said, holding on to her pet theory. "The woman pulled a gun on us, a little text is totally within the realm of possibility."

He countered with the one flaw in her logic. "How would she have known you were on the case, much less how to reach you?"

"How would anyone have known?" she countered. "You, me, DubJay . . . did you do it?" She stared at him with suspicion.

"No, I did not. Jesus, Mallard."

The irritation and disgust in his voice made her snicker. "It doesn't matter, anyway, like I said. Job's done. This call's probably a new client. Or my mother, trying to reach me in a sneak attack through someone else's phone."

"She does that?"

"If she thought of it, she would." Ginny waved a hand

in dismissal. "My mom. I love her but she's high maintenance."

"So you duck her calls."

"Occasionally, yeah. Guilty as charged. Don't give me
that look, Tonica, you haven't met my mother. And yours,
apparently, is all the way across the country, so shut up."

He shut up.

"If it's a friend, or my mom, they can wait until I'm
home. And if it is a new client, I need to be at my desk,
anyway. There's only so much magic I can work on a tablet."

He glanced at her again, then looked away. "So what are
you going to tell Wally?"

"Nothing. Not yet, anyway." She was, as she'd said,
good at ducking calls when she had to.

"And on Monday?"

"I'll tell him we found Joe and conveyed his message. After that, it's up to Joe himself—and your friend's
friend—what happens. Joe either tattles on his nephew
or keeps his mouth shut, and deals with the fallout either
way."

He started to say something, then shut his mouth with
an audible click.

"Yeah, I know." Ginny knew what he'd been about to
say, and why he didn't say it. "It sucks. My job, sometimes
it's cut and dried, but sometimes you see into the messy
corners of peoples' lives."

"Like the broken engagement?"

"And others, yeah." She had seen and heard things she

would never repeat—it wasn't just the NDA she occasionally signed, but basic decency. You saw too much of peoples' insides, in this job. "The one thing I've learned is that you can only fix the stuff you're hired to fix. Everything else is off-limits. You're not Fixit Advice Bartender Guy, here, Tonica. They don't *want* you poking around there, and they don't welcome advice."

"Yeah, like that ever stops you."

"I don't offer advice," she corrected, a little sharply. She didn't. She commented, and she one-upped, but she never offered advice unless someone asked her directly.

"Okay, yeah. True enough," he said. "That's what keeps you from being insufferable."

"Sweet-talker."

They pulled into Mary's parking lot a few minutes after his shift would have started, but there was another car in the spot Tonica usually took.

A cop car.

"Oh, hell." He pulled into the slot next to it and cut the engine, then stared ahead for a minute before getting out of the car. Ginny understood his reaction: Mary's wasn't exactly a cop hangout, and certainly not while they were still on duty. A cop car probably meant that something was wrong.

Ginny wavered a moment, wondering if she should go in with him, then decided that if anything had happened, it had nothing to do with her, and she'd just be in the way. Besides, Georgie needed her pre-dinner walk, and then dinner. She'd been a very patient puppy, but the trainer they had gone to had been explicit about the importance of a regular feeding schedule for a young dog.

"C'mon, girl," she said, holding the door open and snapping the lead to the shar-pei's collar. "Let's go home."

While Georgie snuffled at the familiar-smelling verge of grass, a tabby-striped gray cat emerged to sniff at Georgie's face in greeting. Although "emerged" would suggest a slow and dignified move, and for the first time since Ginny could remember, Mistress Penny seemed actually agitated. Georgie put her face down within reach, and the two of them seemed to be catching up with each other.

"Nice to know you guys gossip, too," Ginny said, and then curiosity got the better of her, and she took her phone back out and picked up her messages. Five seconds into the first one, her eyes widened and her body language shifted from satisfied exhaustion to worried tension. Ten seconds in, and she was yanking at Georgie's lead, pulling her away from the fascinating smells of the grass and cat, and heading at a fast walk back toward her apartment, the phone—message still playing—shoved back into her pocket.

Behind them, Penny sat in the parking lot, watching them go, her whiskers twitching.

"Ms. Mallard?"

The building manager met her when she reached her floor—had obviously been waiting there for her. Normally Hoyt was a friendly man, his long dark hair pulled into a ponytail, his brown eyes wide and open, but there was a crease through his forehead and a frown on his face that made Ginny stop, even as she held out her cell phone to him, as though to offer evidence of what, clearly, he already knew.

"What happened?" she asked.

"Someone broke into your place."

Ginny knew that already: the message had been from the cops, trying to reach her. She wanted *details*. "I was on a job, I didn't have my phone on, I didn't know until now. What *happened*?"

"I did the best I could: I let them in, told them what I could, but," and he shrugged, clearly helpless in the face of police authority. "You're supposed to call them."

Ginny, realizing she wasn't going to get anything from him, pushed past the man into her apartment. She stopped just inside the door frame, not sure if she could keep moving.

"Oh God."

"Call them," Hoyt said from the doorway. "You want I should make you a cup of coffee?"

"No. Thank you. I . . ." Georgie, aware something was wrong, pushed up against Ginny's leg, the weight almost making her stumble. "Could you take Georgie for me?" And she held out the leash behind her. Taking care of owners' pets was not in his job description, but she'd give him credit for the way he took the leash without hesitation.

Ginny stood where she was, dialing the number the

voice mail gave her, and identified herself, then waited while she was transferred to the correct person. The young man who eventually greeted her sounded too young to be wearing a uniform, as though his voice hadn't even broken yet.

"Don't worry," the boy-cop said, not at all reassuringly. "We've already been through, so you can go in. It seemed as though they were more interested in making a mess than taking anything, since your electronics were still there, but we'd like you to confirm that for us?"

No, she didn't see anything missing, although the state of her once-neat desk made her want to cry. No, she didn't know anyone who would do this as a prank, who would do such a thing? Yes, the filing cabinet that had been broken into held client information, yes, it was confidential, no, nothing was missing and she didn't hold on to anything that could be useful to thieves or—her patience broke at that point, and she asked the boy-cop, flat out, if they—being professionals—had actually gotten anything useful, or if they were going to wait for her to discover a clue?

"Ma'am, I understand that you're upset—"

"Upset?" She wasn't upset. Upset was when she broke a mug in the sink, or missed a bus, or had a run in her stockings. What she was feeling now had nothing to do with upset.

Stepping over the debris of what had been her paper-recycling pile, she braced herself to look into the bedroom.

There was nothing they might have stolen there, unless they wanted her clothing, but . . .

Whoever it was hadn't restricted themselves to her office. Weirdly, that made her feel better. The bedclothes had been pulled off and dumped on the floor, and the pillows were slashed open as though someone had gutted them. The rug had been shoved halfway across the room, and all of her drawers were half open, as though someone had gone through them quickly, riffling dirty fingers through her clothing.

Her privacy had been invaded, in a way she hadn't ever thought of before. Her computer in the office was intact, though—she'd checked to make sure the external hard drive was still attached—but now she wondered if they'd rifled through her files there, too. Her password was strong, but she'd never had any reason to encrypt her digital files. Had they hacked her bank accounts? Her social media? God, had they read her email? Suddenly she wished that she did have scandalous emails. What if they'd read them and been bored?

"Mallard, focus," she told herself, holding the phone away from her ear. "You're getting hysterical."

She backed out of her bedroom, and went into the kitchen. It looked intact, but then she noticed that things were out of order, and there were traces of sugar and flour all over the place, suggesting someone had even searched the Tupperware containers. What the hell? Or had the cops done that?

Her feet dragging, she went into the bathroom, but other than the laundry hamper spilled on the floor, it looked unmolested.

Now the boy-cop was telling her that they'd be in touch if anything came up, but since nothing was taken, she should just change her locks and update her insurance. All the while, a voice that sounded a lot like Tonica's was telling her that now was the time to tell the cops about the text, about the job, about everything. But she couldn't, the memory of Joe's words—his worry about disgracing his family's name—holding her back. She couldn't be the one to bring the cops into this, especially since there was absolutely no evidence any of this was connected. Ginny did believe in coincidences. Sometimes.

So instead, she thanked the too-young cop as politely as her mother had taught her, and put the phone away again.

The thought of staying here, of dealing with the cleanup, faced with the mess, and the fingerprint dust everywhere, was too much for her to deal with just then. She picked up her bag, grabbed a Tupperware container of Georgie's food, and retreated without any shame from the disaster of her apartment, locking the door behind her. The lock hadn't been broken; it was still turning and locking easily. She saw no point, despite the baby-cop's advice, in putting in new locks: if they wanted to come back, it wasn't as if she could stop them, anyway.

Hoyt and Georgie were sitting on the stoop of the building, Hoyt smoking, Georgie sniffing at the grass without much interest. When she came outside, they both lifted their heads and got up.

"You okay?"

"Oh, yeah. Fine. Thanks." She took the dog's lead from his hand, tried not to gag on the cigarette smoke, and warded off any other questions by stepping away and putting a formal distance between them.

She'd thought, at first, randomly, to call a car service and go to her parents, or maybe call one of her friends and ask for crash space. Instead, she turned and headed back to Mary's.

10

The walk to Mary's soothed the worst of her jangled nerves, enough that Ginny could feel her heart rate slow down and, in the process, her common sense return. Living in a city, you expected certain things to happen, eventually. She'd been robbed before—she'd been mugged, too, and had shaken it off after a few hours, since all she'd lost had been her wallet and some jewelry. It wasn't the fact of the break-in itself that so upset her. So what was it?

Part of it was the sheer disruption, the violence that they'd done to her belongings. And then to have nothing gone . . .

They hadn't taken any of the easy-to-haul valuables. Which meant that, contrary to her first instinct, whoever had broken in hadn't been looking for something to pawn or sell, but something else. Something less valuable but—to them—more important. And something that hadn't been in her apartment.

The only things she had with her were her wallet, her tablet, and Georgie, and she didn't think anyone would break in to steal a half-grown dog, no matter how much Ginny loved her.

"Oh. Oh fuck." She stopped dead, and Georgie pulled at the leash, clearly anxious to get to their destination. "Sorry, baby," she said, although not sure if she was apologizing for stopping, for her language, or for thinking there might be something more valuable with her than her dog.

Valuable was how you defined something someone wanted. Badly. And she could only think of one thing that could be of interest to someone, which wasn't in her apartment.

The papers. The papers Joe took, the ones that could prove that Walter Jacobs was up to something not-good.

She didn't have those papers, but someone else might not know that.

DubJay? No. She wasn't going to tell him anything yet, but he didn't know that, and anyway, this had to have happened before they talked to Joe, for the cops to have come and gone already. Even if DubJay was pissed at her for not responding to his email earlier, it made no sense.

Someone else? Someone who wanted to see Jacobs Realty get into trouble? Someone might have figured out what DubJay had hired her for, and thought, like she did at first, that it was to find the papers and bring them back.

No. Crazy conspiracy theory was crazy. Probably the thief was looking for something valuable—a high-end television, maybe, or a huge wodge of cash. That made more sense than thinking someone had broken in to get at her records. The breaking of the file cabinet's lock could just be someone assuming she hid her valuables there—it was the only thing in the apartment that was locked, after all. Never mind that she did it only out of vague paranoia and because the file cabinets came with locks she thought it a shame not to use. But no matter what logical, unrelated explanation she came up with, it all came back to Jacobs Realty, and that text-threat. Did someone else want to get hold of Joe, or at least those papers? Was that quiet, worried old man in real danger?

She needed to talk to Tonica, now.

Ginny checked around the back before going in: the cop car was gone, the parking lot filled up with the usual mix of nice cars and beaters, both the back and front doors open, and the sound of voices falling out into the evening air. Everything looked totally normal.

Georgie, not sure why they were standing in the back lot, pulled her around to the front, heading for the bike rack her leash was usually hitched to. There was another dog there, a large apricot standard poodle that didn't even bother looking up when Georgie came by. Ginny chose another hitch a few steps away, just in case the two decided that they didn't like each other, and tied Georgie's leash to it, then set out the travel bowl, filled it with water from the bottle that came with it, and put down a handful of kibble on the sidewalk. "Stay here, and if someone tries to take you away, you growl at them and bark for me, okay?"

Georgie looked up at her as though to say "of course I will, Mom," and Ginny laughed, gently roughing up the dog's wrinkled head in farewell before going inside.

★ ★ ★

Ginny hadn't even made it to the front door before Penny appeared, picking her way over the sidewalk, past the poodle, to stare up into the shar-pei's face. "You're back. What happened? Were the men still there? What happened?"

"They were gone. It's a mess! She's not happy." When her mistress wasn't happy, Georgie wasn't happy. "Why didn't you scare them off?"

"Me? What did you expect me to do?" Penny's whiskers twitched in disbelief.

"They messed up her desk. I'm not allowed to even touch her desk, or the box she puts things in, and they tore it all up."

That made Penny's whiskers twitch in the other direction. Interesting. She started to groom her left ear, always a sign that she was thinking thinky thoughts.

"What?"

"I don't know yet. But someone tried to tear this place up, too. I wasn't here, but all the humans are angry and worried and excited, fussing about."

Georgie didn't have whiskers that twitched, not the way Penny's did, but if she did, they would have. "I don't like this. I don't like this at all. They talked to people all day, and got more and more worried, and then they went into a place where they didn't bring me, and they came out and Herself was upset. And now this?" A whine escaped her, and she lowered her head to her paws, trying to pretend it wasn't her who'd just made that noise. A sideways look showed that the poodle was ignoring both of them, his head high in the air and focused intently on the door to the busy place. His owner was inside, and the dog wanted to go home.

"Stop whining," Penny said, pulling her attention back to the conversation. "You wanted her to stop being so worried, didn't you? She's up and doing things, on the scent, excited . . ."

Georgie let out one last whine, rested her muzzle on her paw, and stared at Penny accusingly. "Not if it makes her say the bad words! Penny, we have to fix this!"

"We will." The tabby looked unconcerned, but the tip of her tail flicked, giving her away. "We will."

Ginny walked into Mary's and could see nothing different from a usual Saturday night—although she wasn't here often on Saturday. Too noisy, too many people intent on drinking more than talking, or if they were talking it was to stave off the fact that they'd be going home alone.

Ginny was comfortable with the thought of going home alone. In fact, she preferred it. With everything that was going on in her life—and after the way her last relationship had fizzled—she wasn't eager to return to the dating mind-set. Her social life was just fine, thanks, no matter what her parents thought.

As though to prove that, she had no sooner made it through the cluster of people at the door when someone called her name, and a long arm waved her over. "Hey girl, you missed all the excitement!"

"Hi Mac." Ginny accepted the kiss on the cheek from her friend and sat down at his table, squeezing in thankfully on the offered stool before someone could steal it away for another table. "What excitement? Did someone finally break the two-hundred wall?" Mary's had a beer club that kept track of how many different beers you had tried. People had gotten to 130, but never higher. Not that they admitted to, anyway.

Mac was in his element, thinking he finally knew something Ginny didn't. "Someone broke in this morning."

"Broke in?" That explained the cop car outside, when they arrived. She blinked, then said, "Oh shit," under her breath, the possibilities tumbling around in her head. But no, there was no way it could be connected to her break-in. Why would someone look for Joe's papers here? She and Tonica had gone over this in the car, about who knew what. DubJay came here, but he didn't know that Teddy was helping her. Joe didn't come here, and they hadn't mentioned the bar to him at all—no reason to. He'd known Tonica's name but . . . no, the timing was off.

Ian and Zara? They'd sent them off to talk to Joe, while . . .

No, that was insane. She was really starting to lose her mind now.

"Was anything stolen?"

"Hundred or so dollars, and a bottle of Walker Blue. Patrick, for all that he's a shit, isn't such a dummy to leave the Friday-night receipts laying around."

There was history behind Patrick and Mac. Ginny didn't know if it was business, personal, or romantic, and had no intention of asking.

"I bet they were looking to score booze, not cash, but the storeroom was locked tight, and the alarms went off before they could get through that. So they tore things up a little, just to make a point, and ran."

"Huh. And you know all this . . . how?"

"Oh hell," Mac snorted, "Patrick's been telling everyone, all night. He's proud as fuck that the thieves didn't get much. Although, seriously: Who robs a bar on Saturday morning? Friday night when it closes, yeah. Lots of cash on hand then."

"Yeah." She picked up Mac's cocktail napkin and started shredding it into narrow strips, thinking hard. Maybe she was insane, maybe she wasn't. Saturday, some time between when the bar had closed, and before they'd opened. After she had met with Teddy, after they had left. About the same time that someone had broken into her place and not stolen anything.

Two break-ins on the same day? In places connected to her, even remotely? It was probably a coincidence. This area of town was a nice place, but nowhere was safe from break-ins. But Ginny had an orderly, logical mind, and coincidences were messy things.

"Virginia, leave my napkin alone!" Mac took the pieces away from her. "Yo, Teddy! Ginny needs a drink, before she drives me crazy!"

Ginny didn't want a drink. She also didn't want to go home. She'd come here looking for distraction and had gotten it, although not the sort she'd expected. Thankfully, Mac was noisy and exuberant and didn't need Ginny to say anything other than "Uh-huh" or "No!" or "Really?" at the right places, while waiting for Tonica to take a break.

Stacy slid through the crowd, dropping drinks off at tables with an almost-practiced ease. She was getting better—her first Saturday, she'd dropped her tray three times, and almost quit. Ginny's usual landed in front of her, napkin square underneath, without a drop spilling.

"Thanks," Ginny said with a smile, and Stacy was off again.

"So I was telling you about the guy whose dinner we're doing, right? Because he pulled shit again this morning, changed the entire menu. All that, and then the bastard says to me, he says, 'But it's all okay, because Mac, you're our girl, you can do it!' And I'm thinking 'bastard.' He's the client, so I laugh and don't knock him over the head with his own paella. But oh, I was tempted . . ."

Mac's stories were all variations of the same thing: clients who were demanding and insane, and Mac saving the day through sheer talent and the patience of a saint. Ginny would be tempted to chalk them up to dramatic interpretation, except that she'd worked for Mac a time or three when he was overbooked and she'd hit a slow period. She would have brained the guy for being an asshat.

"You're lucky," Mac said, finally slowing down. "You get to keep a screen between you and your people."

"Yeah." She smiled, but couldn't stop thinking about Joe, alone in his hotel suite, while they all waited for Tonica to get in touch with his contact and pull a miracle out of his back pocket.

★ ★ ★

Teddy saw Ginny come in, but he didn't have the time—or inclination, honestly—to say hello. The bar was its usual busy scene, with the added push of having Patrick hanging over his shoulder, muttering about break-ins and the cost of installing new alarm systems. Teddy wanted to tell him to shut up already—losing a couple-three bottles of booze and a hundred dollars in spare change was less than the cost of doing business, and anything short of gunmen busting in and shooting up the place wasn't a disaster. But he kept his mouth shut and poured the drinks, and didn't play favorites or chat anyone up, keeping Stacy moving, delivering drinks, and Seth clearing tables so they could keep the crowd under control. Thankfully, it looked to be a mellow night, for all the morning's excitement—or maybe because of it. People were talking more than they were drinking; not that they were going dry.

"Two slides and a G and T and three Bass," Stacy chanted, sliding under the bar and reaching for three mugs. She pulled the taps; he mixed the drinks. Eventually she'd step up and mix drinks, but for now, the routine was soothing to him, reaching for the bottles in their familiar places, the measurements poured without his having to really think about it, shaking and stirring and garnishing with ease.

It was easy not to think, when you were doing familiar things over and over again. That was half the appeal of bartending for him, the ability to not think.

Except things were poking at his brain, forcing their way in and distracting him from the rhythm of gin and tonic and lime and ice, until he had to stop and think if he'd put the gin in already.

Yes. He had. The wedge of lime went into the glass, to sit with the two slides and the beers, and Stacy whisked it away.

After he'd gotten his briefing on the morning's fun and games—and given the cop his whereabouts during that time, because the bartender, with his access and his knowledge of what was stored where, was always a suspect until he wasn't, and that was just the way the game was played—Teddy had called his friend.

The call hadn't gone too well.

"You want me to do what?"

"Just . . . float the idea past. See if she bites."

Megan had been less than thrilled at the idea. "You want me to call my ex-wife, and ask if her office would have any interest in possible safety violations, without giving her any names or details. And keeping your name out of it. So if she bites, she's gonna bite me?"

"If it's not anything they'd be interested in, nobody gets bitten. If it is . . . then give her my name."

He should have said, "Give her Ginny's name." Ginny was the one who had been hired for this mess. Or better yet, he should just have given Joe Jacobs's name, since he was the idiot who had gotten into this mess in the first place. But the memory of that old man, torn between what he knew was right and what he owed his family, stopped him cold. In the end, it would get ugly. There was probably no way around it, and Jacobs Senior knew that. But for now, at least, they could keep the names secret.

Like Mallard said, family made you crazy. And made you do the crazy, too.

"Just do it, okay?" he'd said. "If it does turn out to be something they can help me with, I'll owe you."

"You still owe me from when we were eleven." But Megan had, reluctantly, agreed.

That had been three hours ago. He couldn't do anything more to help Ginny until Megan called him back. Assuming she even did.

"My place was broken into."

He looked up from the drink he was mixing. "What?"

He hadn't even seen Ginny come up to the bar: he was slipping, and slipping badly.

"My apartment. Broken into. Sometime today. The cops were there, there's fingerprint dust all over the place, it's a disaster."

Her voice was perfectly modulated, the tones as rounded as she could make them, the very model of a debate-club captain. He didn't know if she had been, or if she'd even been on debate club; she probably had. But he knew her, better than he'd thought, and even in the ambient noise of the bar bustling around them, he could hear the edge in her voice. She was holding it together, but maybe too tight, and it was going to crack.

"Where's Georgie?"

The question seemed to throw her for a second. "Outside."

"Go."

She just looked at him, that attractive face utterly clueless, and he sighed in exasperation.

"Go hug your damn dog, Gin, before you lose it."

"I . . ." Her eyes were too wide, her skin too pale, and he realized that she had absolutely no idea how stressed she was. Or, more likely, she knew damn well and would die rather than admit it.

"Go, before I kick you out," he growled.

She slammed her glass down on the counter—it was empty; she'd been using that as a pretext to come talk to him, he guessed, and stormed out. Teddy finished the order he was working on and slid it down the bar, then picked up Ginny's glass and dumped it into the empties cart below the bar.

"Stacy. Take over."

"What?" She looked at him, her eyes wide not with stress, like Ginny's, but with excitement and surprise.

"Ten minutes, starting now. Go."

Too soon, and she would probably screw up, but every bartender had to die on the job at least once, and probably more than that. It would be good for her.

He slid through the crowd, towel still slung over his shoulder, the black apron still wrapped around his waist, and stopped just outside the door, watching Ginny, who was sitting on the city-supplied bench, the damned dog at her feet and Mistress Penny-Drops sitting on her lap, calmly washing one paw.

"My father is always after me to go back to a 'real job.'

He thinks I'll meet someone there, and have a normal life, and work normal hours and . . ."

"And you'd end up taking a hatchet to someone one morning, out of sheer boredom."

That surprised a laugh out of her, and Penny, affronted, leapt off her lap and landed on the ground, staring accusingly at the two of them. Georgie let out a contented sigh, and shifted her head until it rested on Ginny's shoes.

"Did they take anything?" he asked her. "In the break-in?" She hadn't said robbed, he realized now. Ginny was too precise in her words for that not to mean something.

"Tore the place up. But no. I didn't . . . if they took anything, it wasn't obviously valuable. They didn't even open my jewelry box." He'd never seen her wear jewelry, except the simple silver ring she always wore, and sometimes a pearl necklace, when she was dressed up. Her ears—or anything else, far as he could tell—weren't pierced.

"And the change jar was empty," she recounted, "which means they got maybe ten bucks, but mostly they were going through my office, and all the places paper might be kept. Like the recycling bin."

"Shit. The office was tossed here, too."

She didn't seem as surprised as he'd expected. No, of course not. Everyone knew, by now.

"You think the two things are connected," he said.

"You don't?"

He hadn't had enough time to think about it yet. "But, if it's related to Joe, why would someone look here?"

"What about your place?" she interrupted.

"Mine? I . . ." She was right. The only reason they would have come there was if they'd somehow connected Ginny and DubJay with Mary's, and that meant they probably knew about him, too.

"Did the cops call you?"

"No. But my building doesn't have an alarm system—there's no point." He turned his face up to the sky, as though looking for some kind of answer. "If they did, they did. Not much I can do about it now, and not like I had anything they were looking for."

"Do you think they were looking for the papers, the ones Joe took?"

He sat down on the bench next to her, careful not to step on Georgie, and to hell with Stacy, back inside. She'd manage. "Maybe. If Jacobs Junior had that, he'd be home free, right?"

"No. Joe could still go to the authorities, or have copies, which would raise questions, anyway . . . I don't know if copies would count. Would they?"

"I don't know." If Megan's ex came through . . . nobody had called yet, but there was no reason she would call back on a Saturday night. Real-estate fraud wasn't enough to get the wheels of justice churning after hours, he supposed.

"And what if it's someone else, Teddy? What if there's someone we don't even know about yet?"

"Jesus."

Mistress Penny leapt lightly to the back of the bench and walked toward him, reclaiming her usual spot on his shoulder. Her little head rested briefly on top of his own, then she curled across his shoulders like a scarf, her chin next to his.

"You really need to get a collar for her," Ginny said, changing the subject entirely.

"Yeah." He could hear the lack of enthusiasm in his voice.

"You should. I mean, what if she gets hurt? Without a tag, they won't know who to call."

"She's not my cat."

The fact that she was currently draped across him as though all the bones in her body had melted pretty much put the lie to that claim, but Ginny didn't call him on it.

"But wouldn't you worry if she went missing?"

"I didn't say that. I said she wasn't my cat."

"Then have her chipped, at least. It's just twenty dollars to get her registered. Well, thirty dollars if she's not fixed. Is she?"

"I have no idea. It's never been something we talked about."

"Tonica."

"What? I told you, she's not my cat."

She rolled her eyes. "Typical guy—if he doesn't put a ring on it, he won't claim it."

"Hey! That's not it at all. I respect her freedom. Also, do you want to be the one to put her in a cage and take her to the vet?"

There was silence.

"Yeah, I didn't think so. Miss Penny goes uncollared,

219

untagged, unannoyed, and perfectly able to take care of herself. Back to the business at hand, please?"

"What's the point? I don't see what else there is we can do."

"Call him, anyway. Joe. Just to be sure everything's okay." Thinking about the situation, his gut had gone cold, and his skin was prickling. He'd learned to trust those instincts. "I have to go back inside. Bring Georgie around to the back. I'll stash her in the storeroom for the rest of the night. You can call there."

He expected her to argue. The fact that she didn't made the coldness intensify.

As did the fact that Penny, unusually, stayed with him the entire way inside, then leapt to the top of the bar, where she could keep an eye on things.

Cats had instincts, too.

Tonica's tone had made something inside Ginny twist uncomfortably. She didn't believe in premonitions, or omens, or ESP, but human stupidity and greed? That, she believed in, the same way she believed in gravity: inconvenient but inevitable. So once she'd gotten Georgie comfortably secured in the storeroom with an extra pup-tart and an old blanket to sleep on, she called the hotel, giving Joe's room number to be connected directly.

The phone rang once. Twice. A third time, and Ginny was starting to worry, her stomach clenching around the hard knot in her gut, when the receiver on the other end was lifted.

"Hello? Mr. Jacobs?"

"Hello?"

A woman's voice. Ginny's brow creased, and her free hand pressed against her stomach, as though to ease the knot. Had they connected her to the wrong room?

"Who is this?" she asked.

"This . . . who is this?" Utter confusion filled the other woman's voice, and the vocal switch from cautious to defensive triggered recognition in Ginny's brain.

"Ms. Coridan? Zara? Where is Joe? What's going on? Why are you there?" A dozen possibilities flooded Ginny's brain, none of them good, and she could feel her adrenaline ratchet up again.

"Who is this?" the woman demanded.

"Ginny Mallard. The one you threatened, remember?"

"Oh. Right." Zara didn't sound reassured, then she got defensive. "I didn't threaten you, I—"

"Why are you there? What's wrong?"

"What, you mean beyond all the things that are already wrong?" Defensive and bitter. Now she sounded like the woman who had pulled a gun on them.

"Zara, damn it, why are you there? Did Joe call you?" If so, she was going to wash her hands of him, Ginny swore it. Damn the man, anyway . . .

"No. I . . . I needed to talk to him. To try and talk some sense into him."

"Hopefully, not with a shotgun." The words slipped out before Ginny could stop them, but she didn't really regret it.

"Look, everything's fine. Don't worry."

"Uh-huh." No smart-ass comeback to the shotgun crack? Ginny was pretty sure the other woman had been crying, and Zara Coridan didn't seem like the sort of woman, on first encounter, who was likely to cry easily.

Ginny turned, unable to pace in the small room, and tried again. "Let me talk to Joe."

There was a pause. "No. He doesn't want to talk to you. Not to anyone. He's done talking, he says."

Ginny frowned, not sure what that meant, and if it was good, or bad. "Look, someone broke into our offices, we think looking for something that would lead them to him. Do you understand? People—violent people—are looking for him."

"I have my gun," she said.

Oh, great. Ginny closed her eyes, feeling a headache form.

"One person isn't going to do it. Can you . . ." Calling the cops would be out. Joe, with his insistence on keeping everything quiet and not getting the family name smeared, would never go for that, although her instincts were clamoring for uniforms with guns right now. "Can you at least tell hotel security that you saw someone lurking in the hallway?"

A hotel that nice would take unauthorized lurkers seriously. And even though Ginny knew she hadn't left anything lying around that might lead to Joe—how could she, when she hadn't even known where he was until after she left her apartment—it couldn't hurt to take precautions, right? At least until they had someone official working on Joe's situation.

"No. No cops, no security. We're fine. Everything's fine."

Ginny didn't have Tonica's bar-honed instincts, but she knew bullshit when she smelled it. "Zara, nothing about this situation is 'fine.' Please." But she knew it was a lost cause; enough years of talking to her parents had taught her when someone wasn't listening anymore. Zara was scared, which meant that whatever had happened, Joe was scared. And scared men, no matter their age or wealth, did dumb things.

Add a gun to the equation, and dumb could get deadly. No matter how good a shot Zara might be, she wasn't good enough. And she'd probably shoot the wrong person, anyway.

"All right. The door's locked? Stay put, don't go anywhere, don't let him bring anyone else in." They'd told him not to call anyone, not to talk to anyone or let them in, and he clearly hadn't listened . . . maybe Zara would be smarter. Ginny was annoyed: they were busting their asses to get him out of trouble, and he couldn't even follow basic instructions.

The only response she got was a click. She'd been hung up on.

"Damn it," Ginny said, disgust overriding her worry. Georgie, who had curled up on the old blanket and gone to sleep, whuffled as though in response, but that and a twitch of her hind leg were the only reaction.

Pocketing her phone, Ginny stared at the storeroom wall and came to a decision. Now, she just had to convince Tonica that it was the right one.

"Wake up."

"I'm awake." Dogs were sloppier than cats, but Penny had to admit, Georgie went from sleep to alert pretty fast, and without too much useless motion.

"I've been listening. Someone . . ." She thought about what she had heard, and edited it, for Georgie's flopped-over ears. *"The ones who went through your den, they were the same ones who came here."* She wished, for a moment, that Georgie was a scent hound, but there had been too many people here too long to pick up any similarity between here and there. *"They won't come back here, but they might go there, to your den."*

"No they won't!" Georgie got to her feet in an awkward scramble, legs square under her, chest out as though she had bulldog blood in her. Penny had to scramble back in undignified haste to get out of her way, and her tail lashed once in annoyance.

"Don't be an idiot," she snapped. *"What are you going to do against humans? Against more than one human, who probably has a gun?"* She had heard guns mentioned; she knew what they were, that they were bad, and killed people. She had no interest in seeing anyone get killed.

"You have to go somewhere else. Somewhere safe. All of you."

"All of who?"

"You and Ginny. And Theodore."

"Who?" Georgie, taken down from battle readiness, looked at

her with a puzzled expression on her wrinkled face, head cocked at an angle and ears flopping in a way that made Penny want to bat at one, just because it was there.

"Theodore. Teddy."

"Oh. Why didn't you just say so?" Sometimes, Georgie thought maybe Penny wasn't as smart as she thought she was. But the sharpei kept that thought to herself.

"We need to keep them together, and you have to watch their tails."

"How?"

Penny's tail lashed, just once. "I don't know. I'll figure something out."

"What? No."

Tonica wasn't buying it.

Ginny pushed her main point again. "She's there at the hotel, with a gun, and not exactly all that tightly wrapped."

"I am not charging over there like some kind of half-assed knight errant. We did our job. Call the cops, if you're that worried."

"We can't," Ginny said glumly. "Even if that didn't get us fired—and not paid—calling the cops saying there's a crazy woman with a gun could get me sued for defamation of character or something, and then good-bye, business."

"Well then." Like that solved everything. "Gin, we did the job we—you—were hired to do. In fact, we've done *more*. Way more than you're getting paid to do, considering."

"But—"

"Grown man. His own problems. Can only fix the stuff you're hired to fix. Right?"

She swirled what was left of her drink thoughtfully. "Right." She really hated when someone used her own words to prove she was wrong. It wasn't fair.

Tonica turned to serve someone else, and Ginny looked around the bar, not wanting to think about the job anymore, not if she couldn't *do* something about it. Being a workaholic was easier when it was all facts and dates and broken-down details, not people doing dumb things that she might not be able to fix.

After 11:00 p.m., the lights in Mary's were dimmer, the conversation softer, and the drinks were being ordered more slowly, as though people were starting to roll it up for the night. It contrasted oddly with Ginny's memories of last call, but she figured she'd hung out at different kinds of places—and with different kinds of people—when she was in her twenties.

Mac had gone home a while ago, with a wink and a smirk in Tonica's direction. Ginny hadn't even bothered to tell him otherwise: Mac had long been convinced the two of them should hook up, and never mind that they didn't even like each other.

Not that way, anyway. After the past few days, Ginny was willing to admit that, for an opinionated, know-it-all, probable ex-jock, he wasn't too bad.

Something soft brushed her ankle, and she looked down to see Mistress Penny weaving a gentle figure eight around her ankles.

"Hello, you," she said. "Been visiting poor Georgie in purgatory?"

Behind her, she heard Tonica come back, and swung around to face him. He had lifted her glass up off the bar, swishing it as though to determine how much of it was ginger ale and how much was melted ice, and then dumped the mess into the sink, scooping more ice and refilling her glass. She didn't really want more soda, but it gave her a reason to still be there without anyone raising an eyebrow. Although that hadn't stopped Mac.

Not much stopped Mac. Ginny tried to remember that, and take some of that for herself. Nothing stopped her, either. Not even the client—or the client's uncle.

"Seth says the cops are going to send a uniform around at close, to make sure there's no trouble. Not that I expect any, but . . ." He shrugged, and bent down to scoop Penny up, cradling her in his arms. She rested her wedge-shaped head against his chest, and began to purr. One sleepy paw reached out and batted at Ginny's shoulder, trying to tangle in her hair.

"You should come home with me," he said suddenly.

Ginny made an effort to raise her eyebrows the same way Mac had done to her, and failed.

"Stop that."

"You think they're going to come back to my apartment at two in the morning?" She hadn't even thought about the possibility.

"No. But I know you, Ginny Mallard. Now that you're over your shock, you're pissed off, and seeing your apartment, if it's half as bad as you said, you're not going to be able to sleep until you sort it out and clean it up. Which means you're not going to sleep at all. We only have one more day to figure out what to do about all this, and your being sleep deprived and cranky is not going to help."

She wanted to argue—if for no other reason than arguing with him always made her feel better—but he was right, damn it. They both knew it. Finding a way out for Joe—not racing over to tell Zara to put her damn gun away before she shot the wrong person—was the smart move.

Ginny let out a massive, intentionally theatrical sigh. "All right. Anything from your friend's friend?"

"No. Look, you know that's a long shot, right? I'm not even sure exactly what the State Bureau of Investigations does, actually, or if they can be any help at all, coming from another state. And if she doesn't call by tomorrow afternoon, anyway—"

"If she doesn't call, we go back to Plan A, Part Two. Bring in the local cops, no matter if Joe likes it or not, and let the blood splatter. I get that." But she didn't like it. Neither of them did.

It felt like failure.

11

Georgie had been confused when she was coaxed back into the car and driven somewhere else: it was nighttime, and they should be going back to the den. Instead, they had gone to another building, and Herself said they were going to sleep there. Then she'd remembered what Penny had said, and was relieved. Penny had gotten the entire pack together, like she'd promised.

The new den—it smelled like Teddy—wasn't as nice as theirs, but there was a pillow for her, and her bowl and food, and a chunk of rope to chew on. Georgie waited until the humans went to sleep, and then settled herself, determined to stay up all night, watching, in case the slippery man, or the bad men, or anyone else tried to come in, but the whole night is a very long time, and she was very tired.

New place and bad dreams made her sleep restless, though, and well before dawn, a noise woke her.

"Hey."

Georgie got up from under the kitchen table, where Teddy had put down a blanket, and padded over to the window. Penny sat on the fire escape, grooming her paw. She looked up and smoothed her whiskers.

"Hi," Georgie said. "What are you doing here?"

Penny got that offended look on her face. "Why shouldn't I be anywhere I want to be?"

"No, I meant . . ." *Georgie got tangled over what she had meant.* "What's wrong?"

"Nothing. I checked on your place and it's quiet, and the busy place, too. No new smells."

"Quiet here, too. Except the Man snores."

Penny's whiskers twitched. "I don't like it."

"That he snores?"

Penny's whiskers twitched backward this time. "No. That it's quiet. You're sure that she talked about a threat, when she was on the phone?"

"Yes." *Georgie hadn't liked that, but there hadn't been anyone there to growl at. She was no good if the threat wasn't in front of her. That's what Penny was good at.*

"What did they talk about last night, here?"

"They didn't, not really." *Georgie tried to remember. It was hard.* "Not a lot. It was late and I slept most of the way here. About going to the cops, maybe. And the missing-man. And getting some sleep before they made any decisions. But they're waiting for something. When it comes, they'll know what to do."

"Hrm."

"I wish you'd just have come with. I'm not smart enough to know what to listen for. Would it really be so bad, to sleep inside for one night?"

Penny flexed her claws, and her tail lashed once, then stilled.

"You're a dog. You don't understand."

Georgie rested her muzzle against the windowsill. "No, you're right. I don't."

"Hey, Georgie."

Ginny's voice caused Georgie's tail to thump once, instinctively, and she swung her head off the sill to give her owner a lick on the hand that came down to pet her. When she looked back, Penny was gone.

"What were you looking at, girl?" Ginny stretched, looking out the window. The place wasn't a dump—she hadn't expected it to be, really—but it wasn't fancy, either. The view out the window was someone else's window, about ten feet away. The neighborhood was mostly apartments, both multistory brick buildings and repurposed old houses. On a Sunday morning, it was quiet—not even the church bells were ringing yet.

Last night Tonica had tossed a pair of sweatpants at her and pointed toward the bed, and that was about all she remembered before sleep took over. Now, with the faint morning light filling the space, and snores still coming from the lump on the sofa, Ginny explored the studio.

The bathroom was clean and functional, but that was about all she could say for it. The black-and-white tile was chipped, the shower handles were old-fashioned, and the sink had traces of dried shaving cream on the faucet, but the shower curtain was new, and the toilet showed signs of regular scrubbing. The medicine cabinet had shaving cream—he had sensitive skin—and the usual assortment of aspirin, toothpaste, cold medicines, and a pack of condoms.

No prescriptions, nothing incriminating, other than the fact that he used a tooth whitener.

She went back out. Tonica was still snoring, and Georgie had lain down again in front of the window. The main room was pretty barren, too: a kitchen table, and the sofa and a coffee table, plus an old leather armchair that, despite being worn, still looked expensive. A single bookcase was filled with paperbacks and the occasional hardcover. Something caught her eye, and she picked it up, smiling a little.

The only other thing really of interest was a narrow desk against the far wall, less a desk than a narrow table with stacked cubbyholes. Aware in the back of her head that she'd gone beyond investigating and into prying, she walked over, and looked more closely. Based on the style, and the age, Ginny decided that it was a post office cubby, or maybe from a hotel, the cubbyholes where each guest's messages would be placed. It was old, whatever it was, in the way that whispered "antique" rather than shouting it. She hadn't realized Tonica had that much money, to afford something like this, and that leather chair.

No, wait. Hadn't Joe asked about the Tonicas of New Hampshire? Huh.

Ginny touched the desk, running her hands over the satin-smooth finish.

"It was my grandfather's," a voice said. "He had a demolition business, back in the day. Used to pick through the pieces of every building he took down, save what he liked, sell what he could."

Teddy was awake. She turned, torn between brazening it out and apologizing for snooping.

"Find anything interesting?"

"No bodies, no safes, no incriminating letters. You're really incredibly boring."

"Yeah, I know."

Either he didn't mind her poking around in his stuff, or he hadn't expected anything else. Ginny thought it might be a little of both.

"Nice place you've got there. I mean, a little spartan, but nice." She wasn't being sarcastic: in daylight, she could tell that the building itself was in solid shape, and that his limited decor wasn't poverty but aesthetics. Not her taste, no, but it suited him.

"I especially like this." She lifted the book she'd found on the shelf, and tilted it back and forth. The flagged pages fluttered, and it fell open to a page liberally marked with yellow highlights. The same book he'd been reading in the storeroom on Friday. She held it up, marking the page. *"The Moron's Manual for Private Investigation?"*

To her surprise, Tonica blushed.

"You can call it research all you want," he said, running a hand through his hair and making it stand up even worse than previously. "Me, I like having some clue what we're doing, and what we're doing is investigations. Unlicensed and technically without any legal standing, but investigating."

"If it quacks like a duck?" She was trying to make a joke, but he wasn't having any.

"Then it can get cooked like a duck. Ginny, you know we are way the hell over our heads on this one, right?" He waited, staring at her, and for once it wasn't a challenge, no sense of "step into my trap so I can show off and show you up." She couldn't read people the way he did—she was spectacularly bad at it, in fact—but she knew Teddy Tonica well enough, by now.

"Yeah. I know." She'd known since she took the job, deep in her gut, but her pride hadn't let her admit it. "But . . ."

"Yeah." He echoed her, without either of them finishing the sentence. But they weren't going to give up. Somehow, they'd do the job they—she—had been hired to do, and keep Joe out of trouble, too. If they could.

"All right." He practically shook himself down, the way Georgie did sometimes, and started over to the kitchenette, reaching for the coffeemaker as though expecting it to be ready to go.

"Damn, didn't prep it last night. And two, not one. I assume you want coffee?"

"Please. God, yes."

He reached into the cupboard and took out filters and a coffee can. "All I have is dark roast."

"That'll do." She wasn't going to critique the coffee options. Not right now, anyway.

She took a seat at the table, watching him go through the familiar motions of making coffee. Georgie had woken up, and now paced the room, occasionally stopping by the window as though to look for whatever had gotten her attention earlier, although it didn't seem to be the birds calling outside. There was still food in the bowl; she hadn't eaten all the kibble last night, but she didn't seem very hungry, so Ginny didn't bother to refill the dish. There was water left, but not much; she was going to need to walk Georgie soon.

"I'm going to go for a run," Teddy said. "There are extra towels in the closet there, if you want to take a shower. Then we should go back to your place and clean up."

"You're offering to help clean up?"

"Jesus, Mallard. You think I'm just going to leave you to deal with it alone?"

She had, actually. He'd already gone above and beyond; she hadn't expected anything more.

"How long until the coffee's ready? I need to walk Georgie."

"She can come with me, we'll have a nice run." He made the offer, but even with his back to her she could tell that it was a spur-of-the-moment thing.

"Tonica, Georgie's built to walk, not run. And she needs to pee. You really don't know a thing about dogs, do you?"

He shrugged, hitting the BREW button, and turned, looking not at her but her dog, who looked back expectantly, as though she knew what they were talking about.

"Yeah, those legs, not exactly going to keep up," he admitted. "There are spare keys on the hook by the door: the round one's for the apartment, the square head is for the building. Try not to lock yourself out? I'll be back in about half an hour."

★ ★ ★

It felt odd, leaving her there—he wasn't in the habit of letting women—anyone—have the run of his place. But it was *Ginny*. He might not like her much, but he trusted her. So Teddy laced up his running shoes, snapped his iPod to the waist of his jogging shorts, and headed out.

He hated running. He did it, but he hated it. The first ten minutes were torture, the middle section was bearable, and the last five minutes, all he could think was, "Can I stop now?" He had heard of the runner's high, but didn't believe in it. On the other hand, it kept him in shape, and meant he didn't have to deal with a gym, the crush of desk-types working off their pudge, and there was a point in the day where he could simply turn off his brain and think about nothing but the pain.

He turned down the street and headed for the park. There was a series of stairs he used for wind sprints, then he'd turn left and go down Reynold, and—

"Mr. Tonica."

A hundred—or at least three—wisecrack responses flashed through his head, but he repressed the urge, pivoting as his foot came down to face the man who had approached him. A man, the one who had spoken, and a woman to his left. They were a matched set: tall and muscled, and dressed not so much to impress as to repress. He did a quick calculation of his odds, the way bouncers did when they looked at a fight, and held up his hands.

"Ya got me. Did I jaywalk?"

"We're not cops, Mr. Tonica."

No, he hadn't thought they were. Not Feds, either. He would have put his money on the classy end of the crime spectrum, but they didn't have quite the right rough edge to them. More like they were dressed up to play the part, trying to intimidate him into thinking they were tougher than they were. Maybe after they'd broken into a few places, and not found what they were looking for?

All that went through his mind in a split second, along with the knowledge that if anything nasty went down, he was probably screwed. If they weren't armed, he'd eat his iPod.

"But you know my name, and you stop me on the street, in public . . ." He lifted his hands, taking a quick look around while he talked. There was another jogger farther up the road, and someone walking a large black dog down the street, but that was as "public" as this neighborhood got, this hour of the morning. The odds of a cop car cruising down the street were slim to none. "So I'm assuming this is some kind of bizarre Seattle iteration of a planned meeting, where only one of us planned to meet?"

"I'd heard that it was your partner who had the wise mouth."

"Partner?" He was honestly taken aback, then comprehension flashed. "Oh, Mallard. She's not my partner—not in any sense of the word. We're just . . ." Friends? No. But while he was puzzling over the word, the guy spoke again.

"You and Ms. Mallard took a commission from a man by the name of Walter Jacobs."

Teddy waited, sure that the man had more to say than stating the obvious.

"We would like to know the status of that commission."

Guy used a lot of ten-dollar language. "Why don't you ask DubJay?"

"Because we're asking you." Behind him, the woman took a step back, as though she were removing herself from being involved with the conversation. But she didn't step out of range, Teddy noted. In fact, she was just close enough within reach that, if she were to pull a gun from underneath her jacket and fire, he would be hit point-blank.

He didn't think she was going to shoot him. Probably. Not yet, anyway. The fact that his mouth had gone dry and his chest hurt was due to running, that was all. Not fear.

"Look, if you're the guys who tossed Ginny's place, you know we don't have what you're looking for." Whatever that was.

"We think that you do." And the guy stepped forward, until they were nose to nose. "Just tell us, and go back to your run. Nothing to see here, nothing to tell, everyone goes away whole and healthy."

The wiseass comment escaped then. "And if I don't?"

Guy stepped back, his hands spread as though to indicate he was harmless. "Then you don't. And we have to go back to doing things the hard way."

There wasn't any threat in the voice, just resignation, and that made Teddy more worried than if the guy had shown a knife or gun. He either talked now, or he'd talk later, and it didn't matter to them, one way or the other.

"Look, I . . ."

"Is there a problem?"

Another voice, and all three of them turned as though their heads were on pulleys, to see someone approaching. The other jogger, who had minutes ago been at the other end of the street. He was solidly built, wearing a Portland sweatshirt and running pants, and his body looked more thickly muscled than you'd usually get in a dedicated runner.

"No problem," the woman said.

"Huh. Looks to me like there's a problem. You okay, Theo?"

Nobody called him Theo, out here. He'd left that behind, when he came west. Teddy didn't feel reassured. There was way too much going on, and he was in control of none of it.

"These folks stopped to ask me . . . directions."

"Huh." The newcomer came closer and the first man stepped away, not giving ground but reassessing the field. "Not much out here to see. You might want to get back into your car and head for the highway. We're not much for tourists around here."

There was something going on between the three, and Tonica didn't know what it was, but he felt like a T-bone caught between three hungry dogs.

"Thanks for your help," the man said, and just like that, it was over. The two walked back to their car, got in, and drove away.

"Thanks for your help," Tonica said, not sure if he had just gone from bad to worse. "You are . . . ?"

"A friend. One who happened to catch up with you just in time, it looks like."

Yeah, and where were you when a crazy woman actually threatened us with a gun? Teddy thought, but only asked, "Do you make a habit of helping out strangers in the street?"

"We're not quite strangers; we both work for the same person," the guy said. "That person asked me to keep an eye on you, make sure you didn't run into any trouble."

"Or poke into anything we weren't supposed to?" Teddy asked, remembering what Gin had said about her clients not wanting advice or extracurricular poking into their business.

"You seem to be a smart man, Theo. I'm sure you can get the job done without further incident."

"Yeah." So far this morning he'd been threatened by two different groups, and he hadn't even had his coffee yet. "You got a name?"

Caught off guard, the man answered, "Sam."

"All right, Sam, did you have anything to do with the break-in yesterday?"

"The what?"

Sam's surprise and instant attention were telling. He was either a fantastic actor or honestly surprised. Based on how quickly he'd given his name, Teddy was betting on surprise. This guy wasn't a goon. That meant he probably was there to keep an eye on Teddy—and Ginny—rather than cause trouble.

Somehow, that didn't make Teddy feel better.

"You might want to watch those guys, not me," he suggested, jerking his chin to where the dark sedan had been parked. "They might be more of a threat to your boss than we are."

"I'll take that under advisement," Sam said.

By the time Teddy got back to the apartment—his run aborted after that encounter, even if the adrenaline hadn't already started to fade—Ginny had already used the shower, and was dressed in her clothes from the day before and sitting at his table, sipping coffee while the dog slurped up kibble from one of his better dishes.

"When you got that threatening text—y'know, the one that you didn't think it important to mention right away—"

"Yeah?" She looked up at him, and he could practically see the gears shift in her head. Ginny Mallard could single-handedly kill every "dumb blonde" joke on the West Coast. "What happened? You didn't take your phone with you—" Her eyes widened, and she scanned down his form, looking for some sign of injury or scuffle. "Did someone jump you?"

"Jump? No, nobody jumped. I just got approached by two persons who found me a person of particular interest—one they were maybe interested in beating the pulp out of—and then had my bacon possibly saved by a watchdog hired by, I'm assuming, none other than Wally himself."

"What?" Ginny's voice rose high enough to make

Georgie look up, wondering what was going on. "Start at the beginning, Tonica, and leave nothing out."

He told her what happened, ending with the third man jogging away, like they'd just stopped to talk about the weather.

"And then I turned around and came back, like a good little pony." He was still shaking, not from exhaustion or adrenaline, but anger. Anger and, he admitted, a little bit of fear. It might not be macho to admit it, but he'd been scared.

"DubJay hired someone to follow us?" Ginny seemed more outraged by that than anything else he'd said.

"And I, for one, am sorta glad he did, whatever his reasons. Gin, focus. If Sam-I-am was telling the truth, and he—and DubJay—had nothing to do with the break-ins, odds are pretty damn good those two did.

"You were right, yesterday. Someone else wants to put hands on Joe, or the papers he took. Someone *not* DubJay. And someone able to send two not-quite goons out after me. Us."

"The government, maybe? Did your contact—"

"If they were the government, they'd have flashed badges, right?"

"Mafia?" Her voice actually squeaked.

"How the hell should I know? They weren't carrying cannoli." That had been his first guess, too, but . . . "I'm not sure the Mafia would send along a female enforcer."

"A woman? Really?" Ginny perked up a little. "All right, that's horrible, but awesome."

242

"Focus, Mallard," he said. "A guy who did all the talking, and a woman with him. They both looked like bulked-up suits, not straight muscle. Same with Sam-I-am. And all three of them looked like they were carrying."

Ginny was thinking hard; he could practically smell the burning gray cells. "Competition, then. Business, not crime, although I'm not sure where the difference is, some days. Someone looking to get there first and shut down Jacobs . . . is corporate real estate that big a deal? I figured, when he was willing to pay so much for this, that they had a lot of money riding on this particular deal, okay, but overall, are we talking enough money to interest someone enough to use violence? I mean, the company makes a lot of money, yeah, and I could see someone trying to maybe buy them out—or them trying to buy someone else out—but it's not like they're billion-dollar companies . . . although they did have a particularly good year, well, past couple of years, even in this economy . . ."

He didn't want to know how she knew that about a private firm. "Gin, listen to me. This isn't some academic exercise. They were not there to call me names. You ever hear the saying, The smaller the stakes, the fiercer the fight? PTA politics are nastier than the UN."

"You've never been to a PTA meeting in your entire life."

"My mom has," he retorted. "But my point is, if you have half, or maybe only a third of the pie, and you get a sniff of someone maybe doing something that could lose them their third . . ."

"You want to make sure it happens—and that you're the one who benefits." He could practically see the pieces clicking for her. "They don't want Joe, they want the papers he saw. Or whatever information was in them."

"And they think we have them, or know where they are. And they're okay with doing some damage to get that information from us."

"But they don't know where Joe is?"

"If they did, they wouldn't be bothering with us. And it sounds like my shadow just caught up with us, so odds are nobody knows." He hoped. "If we're lucky, they'll believe us, and just keep watching, hoping we're dumb enough to lead them there.

"Last night, you said Zara said everything was fine—do you believe her?"

Ginny leaned back in her chair, thinking. He waited. She had a mind like a filing cabinet, he knew that from the trivia games, and details were her trade, the way drinks were his.

"Yes. She was upset, but not scared. Like they'd been having an argument over him-being-stupid kind of upset." She looked up and scowled. "Oh don't give me that look. I may not be the people-schmoozer you are, but I'm not totally Asperger's, either."

"Nice with the offensive stereotype, there."

"Excuse me, Mr. Mafia with Cannoli?"

"Fine, the PC police can come get us later. She was being straight with you?"

"Yeah. I mean, I have no idea what other crap she's pulling, or why she just had to go see him, but there wasn't anyone else in the room with them, pressuring her, I'm sure of that."

He waited.

"Pretty sure. No, I'm sure. She's a tough cookie. If someone was pressuring her, or threatening him, she'd be mad, not sad."

"Yeah, that matches what I thought, too."

They stared at each other, the weight of everything pressing on them. The break-ins, now this . . .

"I thought Joe was being melodramatic when he asked if we were there to kill him," Teddy admitted.

"He was." But Ginny didn't sound as certain as he would have liked.

Georgie chose that moment to let out an impressive belch.

"Oh, nice dog you have there, Mallard," he said in disgust, grateful for the distraction.

"She didn't pee in your car, Tonica."

"Point." He really wanted to run with the banter, pretend there was nothing else they had to deal with, but they didn't have time.

"I think we need to talk to DubJay and get some answers out of him. About our shadow, and what he's actually trying to hide."

"You mean, without getting fired, or giving him any answers in return?"

"Yeah."

She stared at him, and then nodded. "I'm not going to call him at oh-hell-early on a Sunday morning, though. Let's go get breakfast, because I know you don't have anything other than coffee and stale eggs here."

"Hey," he said, offended, and then paused. "How do you know if eggs are stale?"

"Buy me breakfast, and I'll tell you. Then you can help me clean up my place. And then . . . then we'll deal with DubJay."

12

They'd eaten in a crowded, noisy diner where the food was only okay, but anyone trying to sneak up on them would have to deal with waitresses who looked like they could take on a squad of terrorists without spilling the coffee. Then they'd driven to her neighborhood, both of them self-consciously checking the rearview mirror for any sign that they were being followed.

Which was stupid, because clearly, the bad guys already knew where she lived.

What was in her mind, though, as they got off on her floor, was that it felt odd, bringing Tonica up to her apartment. Never mind that she'd just spent the night at his place, however platonically, this was *her* home. It was filled with . . . *her*.

She unlocked the door, opened it, and winced. "It actually looks worse than I remember."

"You were in shock, the first time around." Tonica looked over her shoulder, the five inches he had on her just enough to see in. "Ow."

Ginny would have sworn that she wasn't the type to go into shock, but she thought about the daze she'd been in, walking down to Mary's, and admitted, if only to herself, that he might have a point.

"It's been a hell of a couple of days," she said.

"Nicely understated, Mallard."

Georgie, let off her leash, immediately pushed past the humans standing just inside the doorway, and went first to investigate her food dish. Finding it empty, she took a few halfhearted laps of water, as though reestablishing ownership of that bowl, and then went over to her bed, where she curled up and, with her wrinkled muzzle resting on her paws, watched the humans as though curious to see what they'd do now.

The apartment was covered with papers. She hadn't thought—doing so much of her work on the computer—that she *had* that much paper. Apparently, she did. The sofa cushions had been sliced open and some of the padding pulled out, then dumped on the floor as well. All the cabinets were open, and there was a layer of gray dust everywhere the cops had dusted for fingerprints.

"All right." She sniffed a little, her nose feeling like it was runny even though her sinuses were clear. "I'm going to work on the papers—I can tell what's what and where they're supposed to go. If you could . . ." she waved a hand sort of vaguely at the rest of the apartment.

"Dust and mop?" He took the direction easily, and she remembered how clean, if spartan, his apartment had been. Whatever else she could say about Tonica, he didn't shirk from work. Which made sense, she supposed: the bar area was always spotless, too.

He was looking around him now with an appraising but nonjudgmental eye. "No problem. You keep your supplies under the sink?"

"No, the closet, over there," and she waved her hand again, this time with more specifics. "I think you might—"

"I got this, Mallard," he said. "Go figure out the paperwork."

If she let herself think, she'd think about crazy women with guns and goons out to break their legs, or whatever goons did to make people talk. So instead, Ginny tightened her focus to "clean up the mess," and got to work. The easiest thing to do seemed to be to gather all the papers together and then sort them out, but she quickly discovered that most of the papers were garbage—they had gone through her recycling bin, too.

"I swear, I'm going to start taking the bin out every couple of days, and not wait for collection," she muttered, adding another handful to the "toss" pile. "What, they thought I was going to toss something that important into the recycling?"

"It's important to them—that doesn't mean it was important to you," Tonica said. He was working on the counters, wiping away the fingerprint dust with careful deliberation. "How many times have you scribbled down something that was vitally important at the time, and then tossed the paper after you didn't need it anymore?"

"I make notes on my phone."

He sighed, almost a laugh. "Of course you do."

"Or on my computer. But it hadn't even been turned on—there was no reason they'd shut down again, not after leaving the place like this, it's not as though they were trying to hide anything, and they didn't take the hard drive, or anything. Why?"

"No time? Easier to toss the place than sit and try to hack through firewalls? Or . . . not everyone's gone digital. Maybe . . ."

"What?"

He left the cleanser and sponge on the counter and walked over to her office door. Curious, she followed him.

"Traditional. Big desk, filing cabinets, that huge bin for recycling . . ." He was ticking off the details of her office as though to himself, turning around in place. Considering her earlier snooping, she really couldn't protest. "I bet they took one look at this office and sussed you out as an old-fashioned girl, one who wrote down everything on paper and then transferred it to your computer after."

"That makes twice the work," she said, instinctively offended.

"Not everyone thinks as efficiently as you, Ginny."

She was pretty sure he was mocking her, but she let it go.

"Are you sure they didn't even turn on the computer?"

"No. I'm not certain . . . I suppose I'd have to check with the cops and see if any fingerprints turned up." It had only been twenty-four hours—impossible to believe, but true. Even if she'd been high priority, there was no way they'd have anything to release, and she was pretty sure that a break-in where nothing was stolen was about as low a priority as things got. She couldn't even blame them for that, as much as it burned. "None of my accounts looked hacked, but I called my banks to let them know, anyway. I should change my passwords now." She hadn't wanted to do that on her phone, on potentially unsecured networks.

"If you touch that keyboard now, your fingers are going to get filthy." It was covered in the same dust as everything else; either they'd been serious about trying to find fingerprints, or they'd been training a rookie on her crime scene.

"It will wash off." Now that she was back in her familiar space, the numbness washed away, the more usual and familiar sense of urgency returning. She had to be *doing* something, something more proactive than sorting papers that were mostly meaningless, anyway, and waiting for someone to jump out of the shadows at them.

He'd been right, she had been in shock. But no more.

She sat down in the chair and touched the ON key, relieved when the display hummed to life. She hadn't even known she was worried—had they done something to her computer?—until it wasn't an issue anymore.

As though drawn by the ON key, Georgie abandoned her bed and padded into the office, taking her usual place under the desk with a contented whuffle. Teddy waited a minute, then, realizing he was now being ignored, went back into the main room, she presumed, to keep working.

There really wasn't anything else to do: they knew where Joe was, so the original part of the job was over. What they were going to say to DubJay, and how she was going to avoid actually telling him anything, or letting him know that they knew—or thought they knew—what was really going on . . . that was another question, and one Ginny was avoiding for now.

She glanced at the time display. Eight thirty. She'd have to deal with DubJay sooner rather than later, but not just yet.

Running through the list of alternate passwords, she chose one and changed the relevant accounts, then stared at the screen, thoughtful. If the twosome who had approached Tonica, and whoever it was who had texted her to lay off, worked for a competitor—

"No, that doesn't make sense. Why would they tell me to stop? They'd *want* me to find the papers. A third player? Oh God, please no. My head hurts enough already."

But if the twosome at least had worked for a competitor, which seemed probable, then narrowing it down should be easy enough. Who had the market share to either threaten, or be threatened? A research problem. Ginny pursed her lips and poised her fingers over her keyboard, caught back up in her own comfort zone.

Corporate real estate? Or someone looking to get into corporate real estate? She entered in the search parameters, and hit ENTER.

"No, wait. Didn't Joe say that Zara worked with a public community group? That had had a run-in with DubJay? What better way to discredit someone than . . . damn. Okay, concrete risks first. Find out what group she worked with, first. Then worry about hypothetical competitors."

Focused on her new search parameters, she picked up without thinking when her cell phone rang, answering automatically. "Mallard Professional Concierge Services. We Do What You Can't. How can we help you today?"

Most people paused before responding to that, as though catching their breath. There was no such hesitation on the other end of the line, however.

"Ms. Mallard."

Her heart stuttered, then started again when the voice enquired as to her rates. Not DubJay. Not some mysterious other figure. Not . . . she didn't know what she'd feared.

Tonica appeared in the doorway, clearly drawn by the sound of the phone. She rattled off her introductory spiel, and asked as to the nature of his problem.

"Oh. Ah . . . no, I'm afraid our service does not cover that." She looked up at Teddy, her eyes round with a combination of horror and amusement. "No. Ah, no, thank you. Yes, good-bye."

She couldn't click the call closed fast enough, but her hands were trembling, and when she put the phone down on her desk her head followed, resting face down on the surface while her shoulders trembled from effort.

"Ginny?"

"He wanted . . ." Her words were muffled by the desk, so she lifted her head enough that the words came out more clearly. "He wanted a surrogate."

"A surrogate?" He didn't get it. She patted her belly, unable to actually say it out loud.

"Surrog— Oh." He got it.

She lifted her head all the way, and they stared at each other with that same mix of horrified amusement, until she couldn't take it any longer and the laughter exploded out of her, a helpless, hiccuping noise.

It wasn't that funny, really. But she couldn't stop.

Finally it ran down, and she leaned back in the chair and looked at Tonica, who was still leaning in the doorway, his arms crossed, a little smirk on his face. "Feel better?"

Yeah. She did.

"I've finished cleaning the main room and the bathroom—I didn't want to go into the bedroom without permission." He blushed a little, just the tips of his ears, like a little kid. "But other than the papers, it's set. You're going to have to upholster the sofa, though. Or just get a new one."

"Yeah. If we actually get paid for this . . . or maybe we should offer to sell the papers to the competition, too, and see how much we can make." She indicated the screen. "I'm looking up potentials."

"Are you seriously suggesting . . . no. You're not."

She sighed. "No, not seriously. Any of these three would benefit from Jacobs going down, but it could just as easily be someone from out of state, or . . . anyone." She hit the PRINT button, and the printer rumbled to life. "We can't do a damn thing about them, anyway, other than finish the case and make them not our problem anymore. I just want to know names, in case they approach us again."

Approach: such a nice word. Much nicer than *threaten* or *assault*.

Tonica seemed to find her logic reasonable. "So. You think DubJay's awake yet?"

"Yeah." She was sure he'd been awake at least as long as they'd been; he had never struck her as being the kind to sleep in.

Tonica clearly sensed her hesitation—well, it wasn't as though she'd been hiding it. "Soonest done . . ."

"Don't patronize me, Tonica, or I'll make you call."

"He didn't hire me."

"Right." Usually she appreciated reasonable people and reasonable arguments. From him, it just irked her.

"He's not going to suddenly read your mind."

"All right, I said." She glared at him, and muttered something Tonica politely pretended not to hear. "Fine. All right." It wasn't like it was her mother. She could manage this.

Ginny picked up the phone and dialed the number on the business card taped to her desk.

A ring. Second ring. A third ring, and then the almost unnoticeable pause-click that meant she was being transferred.

"This is Walter Jacobs. Please leave a message and I will return your call as soon as I am able." Calm, smooth, reassuring. The perfect phone voice. She opened her mouth to leave a message, as requested, and then pressed END instead.

"He's not picking up. And I . . . whatever I say to him, I don't want to give him time to practice his response."

"Ginny."

"It's not avoidance. It's practical. And since, as you so often point out, I'm terrible at reading people, especially someone as smooth as Wally . . . shouldn't I try for every possible advantage?"

He studied her, or the wall behind her, she couldn't tell. But he didn't call her on it. "All right. Point taken. Look, if we can't talk to him, and we're still waiting on my contact's friend, I think we should go back and talk to Joe again."

"Weren't you the one last night saying to leave it alone, not go back there?"

"Yeah. I don't know why, but . . ." He was clearly expecting her to argue with him, to bring up the fact that the original plan had been to not go anywhere near Joe's hotel again, that doing so might lead people directly to him, but it seemed unreal, now, that anyone would attack them in a high-end hotel. And maybe they could convince Joe, after what happened yesterday, that he needed to go to the authorities. If Tonica's contact didn't come through, that was the only way he could be safe.

"Let me get Georgie's supplies."

"We're not bringing the dog again," he started to protest, but Georgie, as though understanding the conversation, had already gotten up to stand by the door. She turned and looked back at the humans, and her body language clearly said, "I'm ready for guard duty. Let's go."

Ginny stood her ground, hands on her hips and a stubborn expression on her face. "You know she's a sweetie, and I know she's a sweetie, but people who don't know the breed look at her and think 'scary.' So far the attempts to back us off have been—mostly—nonviolent. But you got threatened, and my place got tossed, and I don't know about you, but I'm woman enough to admit that I'm scared. Unless you have a concealed carry permit you haven't told me about?"

"I can handle myself in a fight."

"With Georgie, we might be able to *avoid* a fight. Isn't that the point?" She was a little surprised at the sudden streak of macho coming to the fore, but she supposed—she didn't really know him all that well before. She thought she had, but . . .

When she'd thought of Teddy Tonica, she'd seen a bartender who happened to be well-read, with a good eye for people. She wouldn't have expected him to pick up a *Morons* book so he could do things right, or to live in an apartment that was both spartan and tastefully monied, or to have contacts . . . well, no. She had expected him to have contacts who might be able to do things, but she'd thought they'd be more on the seedy side.

"All right," he said, "the dog comes. But I need to stop by Mary's to . . . pick up something."

That something turned out to be a classic sawed-off shotgun, which he took out from under the bar.

"Jesus. You really do have a carry permit? Is that thing legal?"

"I've worked in places a lot rougher than Mary's. Some habits, you learn them hard and never let go."

"Where did you go to college?" She'd never thought to ask, never even assumed he'd gone to college, but she was learning to reconsider a lot of things now.

He laughed, a short bark, as he put the rifle down on the counter, and reached below for the box of ammo. "Yale."

"Yale." Her echo was barely audible.

"Class of ninety-four. Political science. Solid B average, but no real ambition to do anything with it."

The woman's voice reciting his CV was cool, and unexpected. Mary's was still closed—Tonica had made Ginny wait a few steps behind while he disconnected the alarm system and keyed open the door—and they'd closed the door behind them when they came in.

She had come in anyway. Tall—she looked Tonica straight in the eye, so at least five feet eight—with sleek black hair Ginny immediately envied, and skin that looked sallow in the badly lit interior of the bar. She was dressed in dark slacks and a button-down shirt that could have been either business casual or casual dressy; she didn't look like either a would-be thief or anyone's flunky. The badge she offered for inspection with her right hand confirmed that assessment.

"Elizabeth Asuri."

Tonica reached over and turned on another light, so they could see the newcomer better. She blinked, but didn't otherwise react, just stood there with the badge in her outstretched hand, watching them patiently.

Ginny took the offered badge for inspection, but since she'd never actually seen a government ID before, she had no way of telling if it was fake or not. That was something they made look so easy on TV—but really, who saw federal IDs on a regular basis? Was there a class you could take, to identify what all the initials and seals meant? If so, she was definitely taking it.

She handed the badge to Teddy, who only glanced at it before handing it back to Asuri.

"Wasn't expecting the Feds," he said. "To what do we owe this honor?"

"A mutual friend called me last night." Asuri talked directly to Teddy, which pissed Ginny off more than a little, but there was no way in hell she was going to interrupt. The woman, who looked to be in her fifties in better light, unnerved Ginny, although she couldn't have said why.

Tonica didn't seem to have any such hesitation, although he didn't seem too trusting, either. "I thought she was going to call—"

"She did, and was given my name as someone who might find your situation of interest. I did. I would like to speak with Mr. Jacobs, please."

"Junior or Senior?"

Ginny thought Asuri almost but not quite cracked an expression before stuffing it back under federal reserve. "Senior. For now."

Georgie was almost beside herself. She was supposed to go with them. That was her job, Penny had said, to protect the humans, her humans. But they'd gone off in someone else's car, someone whose smell she didn't know, whose voice was unfamiliar, and they'd left her here, locked up! What was she going to do? Where was Penny? Penny always knew what to do.

Awash in misery, Georgie let out a low, pained yowl, packing all of her confusion and unhappiness into the sound. It echoed throughout the bar, and gave no comfort at all, because nobody came to see what the matter was.

How could Ginny do this to her? Didn't she understand Georgie had a job to do?

Settling into an unhappy curl, Georgie let her nose rest on the floor, trying to pick up the faint trace of Penny in the place, and did the only thing she could do. She went to sleep.

13

Asuri had a car that screamed *government issue.* She also had a thing against letting dogs in the car. Ginny had balked at first, but when the agent had indicated an utter willingness to leave her there with Georgie, she relented. This had been her job first; she wasn't just going to turn it over to a stranger because the woman waved a badge around.

Asuri had, at first, simply wanted the address where Joe was staying; either one of them coming hadn't been on the table.

"He knows us, he trusts us. And we told him not to let anyone else in, no matter who they said they were." Ginny had planted her feet and crossed her arms, projecting as much reasonable stubbornness as she could. "Without us to vouch for you, he won't say a word."

"And he trusts you—even though you work for his nephew?" But Asuri had sighed and given in, clearly not wanting to waste the time arguing. "Fine. But the dog stays here."

Now, pulling in to the hotel, Teddy found himself wishing they'd brought the dog and left the agent. She clearly did not think much of having amateurs along, and was rubbing Ginny entirely the wrong way. It wasn't just a female thing. He had no problem with women in positions of power—his mother had been one—but Asuri was . . . irritating.

"So you thought it was just one hop and skip from getting peoples' dry cleaning and setting up kids' parties to investigating a missing person?"

"A personal concierge service is more than party planning." He could practically hear Ginny's teeth grinding from the backseat.

"Look, I'm just saying, you guys managed, but you got lucky. You're good at what you do, but stick to databases and mixing drinks, and let the professionals handle this, okay?"

"Not bad for a bunch of meddling kids and their dog, in other words?" He knew that the tone was going to piss her off, but better she focus on him than patronize Ginny. He could let it slide off—she was about to explode.

Never mind that Asuri was right: he didn't like the woman's attitude.

Asuri handed the keys to the valet, and they walked—or stalked, in Ginny's case—into the hotel, bypassing the front desk and heading straight for the elevator bank.

"I'm not trying to play the role of 'government asshole,'" Asuri said.

"No, it just comes naturally," Ginny muttered.

"Mallard!" Teddy didn't know when he'd turned into the adult in this team, but it wasn't a situation he enjoyed.

"They issue it with the suit and the gun."

The touch of humor seemed to be the right olive branch. "You carry a gun?"

Somehow, he wasn't surprised that information perked Ginny up. Then again, a woman with a gun perked him up, too. He'd take any bet that hers was smaller, sleeker, and more deadly than his, which had gone back under the bar counter, locked up in its case again, before they left.

"What, you thought I did my job by waggling my finger?" Something that might have been a smile touched her face. "Actually, yes, mostly I do. I haven't had to draw my weapon outside of training in quite some time and I plan to keep it that way. What floor?"

"Seven."

The rest of the ride was made in silence. When the doors opened, Asuri took the lead. "Two steps back, and stay quiet," she told them, the hint of humor gone now. Ginny took one look at that expression, and nodded, falling back, Teddy at her side.

Asuri walked up to the suite and knocked on the door. When there was no response, she turned her body slightly, and beckoned for Ginny to step forward, a gesture of her head indicating that the other woman should try knocking. She did so, hitting her knuckles once against the door and calling out, "Mr. Jacobs? Joe? It's Ginny Mallard. Open the door, please?"

There was no answer. No sound came from inside, not even that of someone trying not to be heard. The doors were thick, but not that thick. Teddy had a creeping sensation of something very much not right crawling across the back of his neck.

"Gin . . ." he reached out to touch her shoulder, although he wasn't sure what he would have said or done. She backed up, apparently feeling the same unease.

"Both of you, back away."

Neither of them hesitated; they stepped backward until they were lined up against the far wall, their gaze still on the closed door. Asuri slipped the gun out of her holster, holding it not up and ready, but down, pointed at the ground, and reached for the door handle.

It opened without hesitation, which it should not have done. Teddy took a quick look at the lock mechanism; there was a wad of something stuck there, just enough to disable the automatic lock. Like you would for a party, if you were expecting people to stop by and didn't want to have to keep opening the door. But they had distinctly told him to keep the door locked . . .

Adrenaline spikes were nasty things. Teddy didn't approve of them. He tried to control his breathing, and resisted the urge to back away from the door in a high-speed retreat. Two women were not going to show him up!

The fact that, next to him, Ginny was trembling slightly helped.

Asuri slipped in through the door, the hand with the gun lifting slightly now. The insane impulse to follow her had him taking a step forward, then he stopped. Ginny exhaled, as though she, too, were fighting the impulse to follow.

"Amateurs," he said softly. "Trying not to get shot."

"Yeah."

They waited, ears straining, until Asuri reappeared at the door, her gun now holstered.

"Go get hotel security. Now. And then go home."

"Joe?"

"He's dead."

"He killed himself?" Ginny was in shock. Teddy thought he might be, too. Why else would he feel that numb, as though it didn't matter? Not that he'd known the guy, really . . . but he'd met him. Talked to him. Liked him, even.

"Unless someone else wrote the note, then forced the pills down his throat. It's possible—especially under these circumstances. But I don't think so." Asuri hadn't let them back into the suite, and now the entire place was filled with cops, so they were talking in the hallway, down and away from the action.

"Please." Ginny's voice was thin, soft. "Can you tell us . . . ?"

Asuri frowned, then looked back at the cluster of cops. "There were no signs of any violence, or agitated disturbance. Someone down the hall reported loud noises last night—a man and a woman yelling at each other, about an hour after you say you spoke with the girlfriend. Front desk confirms that she left in a hell of a huff a little while later, all tears and fury. She'll be questioned, but I'm betting he went on his own impulse. From your own testimony, he was on the edge, and pretty much without any good options."

"Were there . . . any papers there?" Ginny asked.

He could *see* Asuri start to say something, and then stop.

"We called you," Teddy reminded her. "We did the good-citizen thing."

"You called someone who called me," she corrected him. "That's not quite the same thing."

They waited, identical expressions of worry and curiosity on their faces.

"There were a number of files, and some media," she said, finally. "They will be given to the right people."

Protecting the Jacobs family name wasn't an issue now, Teddy supposed. The only one left to hurt was DubJay himself. Whatever Asuri had come for, she'd gotten.

"So what now?"

"Now? Now you go home and tell your client the sad news. And you will forget anything you ever knew about this entire incident, or the players involved."

"But—" Ginny started to protest.

"Go home," Asuri repeated. "Cash your paycheck. Be thankful it ended as well as it did."

There really wasn't anything to say to that, except point out that they had no ride home. Which was how they ended up being driven back to Mary's, courtesy of SPD's finest squad car.

"I'm never going to get the smell of vomit and coffee out of my clothes," Ginny muttered as they waved the patrolman good-bye.

"Just be glad you got to sit up front."

They were doing their best to banter like normal, but nothing was normal. Even time seemed askew: it should have been nearly evening, but Ginny's phone told her it was barely 2:00 p.m. Mary's wasn't open for business yet, the after-church drinkers still an hour away.

"Hopefully, Stacy noticed my note before your pooch mugged her," Teddy said, heading for the door. Ginny had never actually been there on a Sunday before; usually she'd be having dinner with her parents—

"Oh, shit." She stopped. "I'll be right in."

She pulled her phone out of the bag, and saw without surprise that there were two missed calls from her mother. Shaking her head, she dialed her stepfather's cell phone, instead.

"Dad, hi, I . . ." She waited. "No, I can't make it, I . . . Dad! Please. My missing dinner every now and again does not mean I'm either stuck in a depressive wallow or out gallivanting. Sometimes it just means . . . I have other plans. Believe me . . . I'd rather be giving Mom grief about her gravy."

She listened to the voice booming through the tiny speaker. Nothing put life back into perspective like disappointing your parents. Joe had been like a father to DubJay, he said.

"Yes, Dad, I'm working on Sunday. We're not going to go into the 'where has your faith gone' thing again, are we?"

She listened again, her lips twitching despite her bleak mood.

"Don't start. I love you both, and I'll see you next week."

When he grumbled a good-bye, she looked at her phone, shook her head, and turned the ringer to OFF before dropping the phone back in her bag. If DubJay—or her mysterious texter—tried to reach her, she was off the clock for the next few hours.

By the time she got inside, Teddy had already settled up with Stacy, and Georgie was comfortably settled on one of the banquettes, a dish of water on the floor next to her. Surprisingly, Georgie's usual companion was nowhere to be seen. Ginny shrugged: the only thing she knew about cats was that they did their own thing.

"You look wrong, on this side of the bar," she said to Tonica.

"It feels wrong. But Stacy won't let me on the other side." He glared at the brunette, like she'd betrayed him somehow.

"Good for you," Ginny said. "Don't let him boss you around when you're the one on duty."

"Your dog was practically pathetic in her gratitude to see someone," Stacy said. "She's a total love."

"Yeah, she is, isn't she?"

"Don't know where she gets it from," Tonica muttered. "Not her mom, that's for sure."

"Leave my dog alone, Tonica. Even your cat won't hang around you for more than a couple of minutes."

"I told you, she's not my cat."

The banter flowed, but it felt wrong. Like there was a

dead body stuck between them, on the floor between their bar stools.

In effect, there was.

Stacy went down to the other side of the bar, unloading glassware, and Ginny drummed her fingers on the countertop, her gaze elsewhere. "We told him we'd help."

"We told him we'd try to help," Tonica corrected her.

"What if he didn't believe us? What if he thought we were going to turn him in? What if—did she know? Why didn't she stop him?"

"Sounds like she tried."

Ginny pursed her cheeks and blew out a long stream of air, making Georgie look up to see what was wrong. "I have to call DubJay. Damn it. If we'd only told him where the old man was . . ."

"Then what? Joe might be alive, yeah. But DubJay would have his evidence back. And I think we both agree that wouldn't be what Joe wanted?"

"Right now, Tonica, I don't know anything. Do you . . . do you think he really killed himself?"

"If someone else had done it, the papers would be gone," he pointed out.

"If the goons who approached you, yeah. But DubJay—nobody would question his right to claim anything on his uncle's person. So he could have left them there, not done anything to make it look suspicious. And . . . this entire thing, hiring us to find him, would be evidence that he was concerned about his uncle, that there was a risk to the old man's life because of depression, or odd behavior . . . we'd be his alibis, almost. God. Is that why he hired us?"

Teddy started to brush off her concerns, or mock her for paranoia worthy of her old movies, but instead stared down into his soda and thought about it for a few minutes. "We can't prove anything, Gin. And if DubJay really did off his own uncle . . . you can't say anything. He can't kill us, not without risking someone putting it all together, but he can make life difficult. Really difficult." The kind of difficult that involved a guy who knew where they lived, as well as the kind that spread business gossip.

"Let him believe that we did just what he asked you to, and nothing more; that we never actually talked to Joe, just scouted him out, and then tried to call . . . he'll have a record that you tried to reach him, but didn't want to discuss sensitive matters on a recording."

Her fingers were back in her hair again, scrunching the curls into a tangled mess. "I feel like we failed."

"We put Asuri on the trail of whatever it was Joe was worried about. She's not going to let that slide. That's got to count for something."

"Yeah. But even if they take DubJay down, it's not going to be for Joe's death."

They looked at each other, a steady, sad look, and Ginny looked away first. "Damn. I'd better put my invoice in fast, before he's under indictment. I'll never get paid, then."

He almost laughed. Almost. "Now that's the Mallard we all know and sorta like."

"Bite me, Tonica." She lifted her glass, and a man's hand

came down gently on her wrist, pushing it back down onto the counter.

Not Tonica's. Not Seth's. A strong hand, with a nice watch, attached to some very strong fingers that were pressing hard enough to turn her skin white under the pressure.

Tonica turned on his stool, even as Ginny twisted enough to see who her assailant was.

"Ms. Mallard. Mr. Tonica." The man stood between the two of them, smiling pleasantly, his female companion a pace behind, covering his back and watching them with careful eyes.

The chair jammed in the door, as usual for the hour before they opened, had given the two access. A quick glance showed that Georgie was sacked out, unnoticed by the newcomers. Ginny wanted to keep it that way.

"Do I know you?" Ginny asked cautiously, not struggling against the pressure.

"Your partner and I have met," the man answered.

"She's not my . . . never mind. What do you want?" Teddy flicked a glance sideways to Ginny, as though trying to warn her of something. She'd already figured out that these were the two who had stopped him that morning. Based on that look, she played against instincts, and kept quiet.

"The same thing as before. Only now we have a little more room to negotiate."

The pressure on her wrist increased, and Ginny bit back a curse, her back and shoulders stiffening with the effort to not react. Already, she didn't like their idea of negotiations. Why couldn't they pick on the big burly guy, instead?

"I told you—" Tonica started to say, and the man interrupted.

"We are aware of recent events. It is a sad thing. However, we also know that you have not had time to report back to your employer. All you need to do is hand over the material now, and tell him that you were unable to locate it. A small, simple lie, and everyone profits."

The guy's voice was so calm and cultured, it made her toes curl, and not in a good way. They thought she and Teddy had been hired to reclaim the papers, not just find Joe. But they didn't have them . . .

"You know the Feds are already on site?" Tonica said.

"We aren't worried about that. Give us the files."

The lock on her wrist tightened and turned, creating an intense, hot friction. Unable to help herself, Ginny yelped in distress, her fingers loosening on the glass and her entire arm spasming, the pain overriding everything else.

The next thing she knew, the pressure on her arm was released as the man fell backward, fifty pounds of irate shar-pei attached to his leg by the teeth. The force of the attack threw him off balance, and he staggered backward even as he bent forward and tried to detach the dog's grip. His action caught his companion off guard, and she turned to him, taking her eye off Tonica for a minute. But when he started to move toward her, she reached under her jacket as though going for a gun.

"Georgie!" Ginny cried out, more worried about the woman shooting the dog, not Tonica, who could take care of himself. Without thinking, Ginny launched herself off the stool, making an ungraceful—but effective—flying tackle, and hitting the woman square in the torso.

The woman went down to her knees, but the impact knocked the breath out of Ginny, adding chest pain to the agony still burning in her wrist, and the woman was able to shake her off, throwing Ginny hard to the ground, her shoulder taking the brunt of the fall.

"Shoot it," the man said, his voice gritty with pain. "Kill it!"

The woman's gun wavered between Tonica and Georgie: she wasn't dumb enough to give Tonica a shot at her. Then suddenly there was a shout—a woman's shout—and Stacy entered the fray, her seemingly slight form revealing some impressive muscles as she grabbed the woman and wrestled her to the ground, holding her there by dint of twisting one arm behind her back in a classic wrestling pose. The gun clattered to the floor.

Ginny rolled to her side, trying to figure out who was where, doing what. Her body hurt, and her eyes were watering, but she saw the man try to stand up, reaching for the abandoned pistol.

"Georgie, hold!"

The three hundred dollars' worth of training sessions they'd never tested were, thank God, still imprinted in the canine's brain. Georgie kept her teeth in the man's leg, not biting down further but not letting go, either, her gaze fastened on his face as though daring him to struggle.

Like any wise rat, he didn't.

"You got the alarm, boss?" Stacy asked.

"They're on their way. And what the hell do you think you were doing? You were behind the bar, you're the one who hits the alarm, not make like some kind of macho vigilante." Tonica sounded pissed.

Ginny shifted onto her side, and winced as the bruises she'd just picked up started to make themselves known. Teddy was on the other side of the bar, rifle in his hand—he must have practically thrown himself over the counter the moment things went to hell, to get to it that fast. He was glaring at Stacy like she was the dumbest thing he'd ever seen.

"I wasn't going to let them rob the place again," she said, equally irate. "And you were just sitting there while Ginny did all the work, so I figured it was girl-power day."

Ginny let out a snort of laughter; it wasn't funny, but it was. Now that they were all safe, anyway. Even better: Stacy's interpretation meant that they didn't have to explain what the two had actually come here for . . . attempted B and E was good enough, especially if they had been the two to break in earlier.

"Now, if you'd get off your male backside and get the cuffs?" Stacy said, still running on bravado.

"You have handcuffs behind the bar, too?" Ginny knew there was a club and a first-aid kit, but like the rifle, handcuffs were new.

"Took 'em off a drunk a few months ago when he tried

to cuff a woman he was interested in to the railing. Funny enough, he never came back for 'em."

Tonica placed the rifle within easy reach on the counter, then ducked under the break and emerged with a pair of metal handcuffs that looked alarmingly official, and a length of narrow plastic. He cuffed the man first, then looked at Ginny.

"Georgie, release," she said.

The shar-pei opened her jaws and let go. Blood seeped through the torn pants leg, but nothing that would indicate he was in any immediate medical need. The man went down to his knees, either in pain or shock.

"Good girl, Georgie. Guard."

The shar-pei squared her legs under her and stood still, watching the bound man as though he were holding an entire bag of pup-tarts.

He glared at the dog, then looked away when she let out a low warning rumble. Ginny had never heard her sweet doofus of a dog ever make that noise before, but she wasn't about to reprimand her for it.

The narrow plastic piece appeared to be another kind of cuffs: Teddy fastened it around the woman's wrists, behind her back, and Stacy removed her knee from the small of her back once she was secured.

"There. All collared and ready for a walkie."

Georgie's ears lifted a little at the word *walkie,* but she held her position.

"My leg," the man whined. "That damn dog bit me! I need to go to a hospital—it probably has rabies."

Ginny glared at him. More likely, he'd given her dog something nasty.

"You might want to shut up until the cops arrive," Tonica said mildly, the tone not hiding the threat. "Anything you say now might just annoy us. Or worse, Georgie."

"You're a hero, Georgie," Ginny said. The dog, her eyes still fastened on the object she was determined to guard, let out a rare *woof,* as though to acknowledge the obvious. With a gentle thump, Penny dropped from the top of the display cabinet down onto the counter, and then down again to the floor, stepping disdainfully past the bound man to sniff at Georgie's ear, then give it a delicate lick, Ginny thought, as though to say "well done."

"Nice of you to join the party, Mistress Penny," Tonica said, even as she heard sirens, and a police car came roaring down the street.

Whatever the cops might have been expecting when they responded, it probably wasn't two figures, bound and face-down on the floor, a delicate gray tabby sitting on the back of one as though she had done all the work herself.

Stacy, still riding on her adrenaline high, was perfectly willing to explain it all to the cops, how the couple came into the bar while they were prepping for the open and threatened Ginny physically—showing her badly bruised and swollen wrist as exhibit A—and how Georgie defended her mistress and gave them time to disarm the gunwoman and call the cops, and wasn't Georgie the hero of it all?

"Yeah, regular superhero," the older cop said. "Just be careful they don't come back and sue you for some crap or another, having a dangerous beast on-premises or something." The dangerous beast, meanwhile, was having her ears pulled affectionately by the younger cop, who had previously pulled a doggie biscuit out of his uniform pocket and fed it to her while his partner was taking down their report.

Ginny, who normally monitored Georgie's diet like a Jenny Craig instructor, decided to let that one go. If nothing else, it would get the taste of jerk out of Georgie's mouth.

"Will we have to testify, or anything?" Stacy seemed almost overeager to be part of the justice process. Ginny, her wrist sunk in the ice sink behind the bar, just wanted them to go away so she could have a well-deserved meltdown. Tonica, sitting on one of the bar stools, had his eyes closed like he had a headache.

It had been a rough couple of days.

"We'll let you know if you're needed," the older cop said, which sounded like "Don't call us and we won't call you."

And like that, the duo was led away, the cop cars pulled out, and Mary's was returned to a peaceful quiet.

For about three minutes.

"Shit, we're supposed to open in ten!" Stacy yelped, and flew into manic activity, intent on getting everything perfect for her first open. Seth, who had been in the parking lot dumping trash when it all went down, and therefore of no interest to the cops, clattered the mop and bucket, and yelled something about trouble always being trouble and hadn't he warned Teddy?

"Let it go, Seth," Tonica muttered, but not loudly enough to be heard in the kitchen.

Ginny, who had been looking out the window after the now-vanished cop cars and the gawkers still hanging around, barely heard him, either.

"What happens now?" she asked, almost wistfully.

"I don't know," he said. "Nothing, probably. Joe's dead. Whoever sicced those two on us wanted whatever we knew before DubJay got it, you heard them. Well, call DubJay, and they won't have any reason to come after us again."

She kept staring out the window, feeling like everything in her body was made of lead—except her wrist, which hurt like only flesh could. He leaned over the bar and put a hand on her shoulder, looking in her face like she had something written on it. "Come on, let it go, Gin. It's over."

"Yeah." She blinked, then winced, looking down at her arm. "Yeah. You think Seth would make me a sandwich? I'm starving."

Seth had been willing to make a platter of sandwiches. And all four of them fell on the food like they hadn't eaten in weeks. Then the doors opened and the first customers wandered in, a couple still in their Sunday best. Teddy set

Ginny up with her usual, Georgie, still the heroine, left unmolested at her feet.

After a few sips of her drink to stiffen her nerve, Ginny pulled out her phone and called DubJay at home. Teddy leaned on the bar and listened as she told their client what had happened—leaving out several details that were both important and no longer mattered. They had tracked Joe to the hotel—only to discover that he had killed himself. The police were called, they were handling things now. She was terribly sorry for his loss, she said, and that she had not been able to help effect a reconciliation between the two men.

Then DubJay spoke, although Teddy couldn't hear what he said, only that Ginny was clearly listening.

"No, I . . . yes. Yes, I understand." The look on Ginny's face wasn't one of understanding, though. It had been, first, annoyance, and then a baffled rage.

"Yes, of course. No, that would be perfectly acceptable, I . . . yes. Good-bye."

The call ended, and she put the phone away. Carefully, as though it were an unexploded grenade or a dubiously poisonous snake.

"So?" She had been worried that he would refuse to pay, or try to harass answers out of her, or blame them, somehow. Clearly, none of that had happened.

"He didn't care. Or he wants to keep things quiet more than he wants real answers. 'The money's already being transferred to my account, thanks for your work, don't let the door hit you on the way out.'"

"Well. That's good, right?" The last thing they needed was DubJay asking questions and raising hell. They'd dodged that with the cops, more or less; he'd be just as happy if nobody ever looked at him twice in relation to any of it, ever again.

"Yeah. Yeah, it's good."

"But?" He knew Ginny, better now than he had three days before. She was too quiet, too thoughtful for a woman who'd just made a large sum of money.

"That was his uncle, Tonica. His *uncle*. And all he could think about . . . all either one of them could think about was their family name. About keeping themselves out of any whisper of scandal, either about the business or . . . because his uncle killed himself. Or got himself killed. Or we got him killed."

"Gin, stop that. You didn't have anything to do with Joe's death. That's all on DubJay—and hell—on Joe, too. They were both grown men, and they made their decisions. Even if the decision was to not deal with shit that needed dealing with." He had been guilty of that, often enough, to accept the bitter truth there.

"I know." She bent down to rub Georgie's ears, then slid off her chair, picking up her pacing. Her drink was still half finished on the counter in front of her. "I'm for home."

"See you Tuesday at trivia?"

There was an awkward pause, when they both remembered that DubJay was on one of the teams, too.

"Yeah. Probably. I'll be there."

14

Teddy opened his eyes on Monday, the sunlight telling him it was mid-morning, and felt a brief moment of unexpected anticipation—until he remembered the events of the day before. The job was done. No mad chasing about today, nobody appearing out of nowhere with threats, or veiled promises. No federal agents, no dogs drooling in his backseat; just a day of calm and order stretching in front of him.

He should be glad about that, right?

He was, he assured himself. Life could get back to normal now. He just wished things had ended . . . better.

Ginny and Georgie had gone home—he hoped to sleep, but knowing Ginny, she'd probably spent the rest of the night straightening the rest of her apartment, down to scrubbing the floors.

He had hung around an hour or so longer, but Stacy had things well in hand and his hovering like a worried daddy wasn't going to let her develop any self-confidence—not that she really needed more, after retelling the story of how she and Georgie caught the robbers to appreciative imbibers.

And now it was Monday. The job was done. The only thing on his agenda was a morning run, some necessary paperwork, hitting the bank, and taking care of the errands he didn't get to over the weekend.

What had once seemed like a pleasant routine felt oddly stale, looking forward. No worrying about who was doing what, no racing around town, no sniping back and forth or trying to solve a mystery—or getting threatened or potentially shot at or arrested, he reminded himself. The past four days had been an interesting change in routine, sure, but that didn't mean the routine wasn't a good one.

He got up and shook it off, sure that by the time he got through his run, life would be back to normal.

"Turn on the news."

"What?" His hair was still wet from his post-run shower, and there was water in his ear, because he was having trouble hearing the voice on the other end.

"Turn on the news."

"I don't have a television, Mallard. What is it?"

"Walter Jacobs. DubJay."

Teddy went on full alert. "What?"

"He's been arrested."

No TV, but his computer was already on. He woke it up, and surfed to the local news station. Breaking local news: prominent businessman doing the walk of shame from cop car to courthouse. And the guys escorting him wore the uniforms of tie-and-jacket that said Serious Feds were Serious.

"Holy shit," he breathed, the phone still to his ear.

"Money laundering." Ginny's voice had calmed down, now that she'd reached him.

"Money . . . is that what the hell this was all about? Not the certificate fraud or whatever Joe was going on about?" Shit, no wonder Asuri had taken them seriously. "How do you launder money in real estate?"

"Shhh, hang on."

He could hear her tapping at the keyboard as she spoke. "No, it makes sense. I mean, once you put everything together, and look at it like . . . well, like someone who looks at things like this. The company was doing a lot of business with buildings that were being transferred from one use to another, which required a lot of renovation work and official sign-offs, and there are so many places where money can get lost, transferred, turned around, and come out without any idea who had originally put it into the system . . ."

Teddy felt his stomach bottom out. "So the guys who hassled us . . . they were really Mafia? Do you think they killed Joe, because DubJay was horning in on their turf?"

Ginny didn't usually let a lot show in her voice, but right then, the uncertainty and upset flowed through the phone line. "God, Tonica, I don't know. But I don't think so. There was another company that was underwriting a lot of these buildings . . ."

She paused, then typed again, then there was the scraping sound of a mouse being moved around. "Speder-Goren Management. Looks like, if Jacobs Realty went down, they'd be in a position to pick up where the company left off, maybe make some serious money. So long as everything was kept clean."

"This wasn't clean."

"No." There was a short pause, and he could hear her breathing. He thought, maybe, that she was crying, but he knew better than to ask.

"No," she repeated, "Joe's killing himself made it all very, very messy. And now the Feds are involved. No wonder those two were pissed."

"Is it definitely a suicide?" He'd assumed it was, like Asuri said, there was no reason to think otherwise, based on the evidence. And Joe had seemed like the kind to go for a dramatic end, rather than just fizzle away.

"They're calling it that."

She was right: the scroll at the bottom of the screen confirmed the death of one Joseph Jacobs, founder of the firm, the night before, by "presumed natural causes."

If despair and pills were natural, anyway.

He didn't want to ask, but he had to. "You believe it? Do you think Joe killed himself?"

He could almost see her, head cocked to the side, her eyes thoughtful.

"No. I don't. If Zara had thought he was suicidal, she wouldn't have left, no matter what he said to her. She was too fierce for that."

He'd hoped that she would say yes. Then, it could all just be a Greek tragedy, and the curtain falls, everyone goes home. But, as usual, Gin's logic was sound.

"Then who?"

"I think your benefactor," she said. "The guy who kept you from being beaten up. He said he worked for Dub-Jay . . ."

"He *implied* that he worked for DubJay."

"Okay, fine. But his whole thing was about making sure that things stayed quiet, right? How much quieter could it get than a dead man?"

"No fuss. That's what DubJay wanted, all the time. Quiet, quiet. Everyone so concerned with reputation. But, to the point of murder?

"Joe kills himself, DubJay could throw the blame for anything that was discovered on Joe, say the suicide was guilt. And Joe . . ." She went silent. "I don't think Joe would have killed himself. But he wouldn't have stopped someone else from killing him. You know?"

He did. And he wanted to take that sick, sad note out of Ginny's voice. "It's a good theory. Just a theory, though. No way to prove anything."

"No." Her voice was still sad. "Not a shred of proof. I think the spin is going to be that Joe offed himself out of a sense of shame, as his nephew was being arrested. And nobody's ever going to look further."

There was a long silence from both of them, and then she said, "I need a drink."

He wasn't working today. He almost suggested meeting somewhere else, but the thought was oddly disloyal, as though the bar would know, and be insulted.

"Yeah. Okay. I'll be there in an hour."

* * *

By the time he arrived, the late-afternoon crowd had already assembled. If anyone was surprised to see him there on his off day, nobody said anything.

Then again, the gossip already had a focus.

"Did you hear?" he heard, the moment he walked in the door. Not to him: someone talking to another person at the bar, and not quietly, either.

"Yeah, I heard. Hell of a thing, huh?"

Snippet from another conversation: "Never trust anyone who wins that often at trivia. Arrogant know-it-all."

"Ah, you're just pissed your team's always last."

Teddy moved through the crowd, his ears as sharp as ever for what the crowd was doing, but his eyes were on the figure at the far corner of the bar, in her usual spot by the window.

She was nursing a martini, playing with the olive, which the bartender had—despite Teddy's frequent reminders that that wasn't how they did it at Mary's—speared on the end of a toothpick.

"I don't think they're going to skate," she said, not looking up at him.

He slid onto the seat next to her and easily into the conversation, despite the time that had passed since. "What, then?"

"I've been thinking about it."

Of course she had. "And?"

"I think they're going to be baited. I think there's going to be an entire sting going on, and DubJay's arrest—it's just the surface, the chum in the water to attract bigger sharks."

He thought about it while Stacy brought over a nicely poured beer for him, serving it without a flourish, but also without dislodging a drop of the head. He nodded at her approvingly and took a sip, then said, "I think we should stay out of the water for a while, then."

"Yeah." There were layers in that one word, making him look sideways at her.

"You're thinking something, Gin. That always worries me."

"Hah." But she didn't deny it.

He was having an odd cognitive-dissonance flare at being on the wrong side of the bar again, but shook it off, and asked, "What?"

"I'm bored."

"What?" Whatever he'd been expecting, it wasn't that.

"I'm bored. Last night I went home and took a long, hot shower, and submitted my invoice, and had a new client waiting in the queue—the same bastard who I was waiting on last Thursday, in point of fact. And I thought hey, great. Back to normal. A nice, basic job, no crime or violence or trickery . . . twenty-four hours of looking up this and checking on that, and I'm *bored*."

He would have laughed at her, or made a comment, but the truth was, so was he. The stale taste of that morning hadn't gone away. Even the dark, bitter stout tasted stale, and he knew damn well it wasn't.

"It will go away," he said, talking to himself as much as her. "You love your job."

"I'm good at my job. That's a different thing entirely."

"You don't love your job?" That surprised him.

"Oh hell, I don't know. I just . . . I woke up this morning and it was all . . . flat, stale, and unprofitable."

That sounded like a quote, but he couldn't place it. Probably Shakespeare. If it sounded familiar but off, it was usually Shakespeare. Stale. That word again. Flat and stale, like all the fizz was gone.

Her face lit up, like she'd just thought of something wonderful. "We should do it again."

"What?" He shook his head, not sure he'd heard her right.

"Investigate. Research other peoples' problems and solve them."

"Um." He backpedaled furiously. "No. Did you not hear what I just said? The Feds got involved in this case! Helping you out one time, okay, we did our good deed, even if it didn't end well. But I like my job. I don't like getting broken into, or threatened, or shot at, or having the cops giving me the fish-eye."

She ate the olive with a clean, careful bite, and put the toothpick down on the counter. "Afraid of a little trouble? And you're a bartender?"

"I'm a bartender at Mary's," he said, like that settled the argument.

"All right. Point to you." She sat for a minute, her pointed chin sunk in her hands. He looked away, watched Stacy working with Bill, the afternoon guy, restocking the speed rail, while he waited for whatever came out of Ginny's mouth next. She had that Look again. The Thinking Look.

"We were good at this. Together, I mean. Really good."

He shook his head again. "No."

"And don't even try to tell me you couldn't use the money."

"I'm set."

"Uh-huh. I've seen your place."

"You never think I might like a pared-down lifestyle?"

The look she gave him was brilliantly scathing. No, she didn't think that. The sad thing was, it was the truth.

"You live in a monk's cell, you spend all your time keeping this place running . . . and you have not just a degree from Yale in poli-sci, but honors—and a government career waiting for you, if you'd wanted it."

The scathing look turned into satisfaction at his obvious astonishment. "I'm a researcher, Mr. Tonica, and you're just another topic. No matter how well you thought you covered your tracks. And I know for a fact that that brain"—and she leaned over to tap him smartly on the forehead—"is dying in there. Even with the reading and the bartending, and the trivia games . . . dying."

"I don't have any interest in being a private investigator."

"And we're not! You got a license? I don't have a license. We're . . . problem solvers."

"Problem solvers. What kinds of problems are we solving?"

Ginny played with her toothpick, now denuded of olives, looking up at him with a coy look that—if he didn't know better—might have been innocence.

"I have no idea. That's half the fun."

He shook his head, and sipped at his stout. He wasn't considering her proposal. He wasn't thinking about it. He was content.

"No," he said again, finally.

Ginny just smiled.

Georgie had been dreaming of chasing the biggest, fattest squirrel— wearing wool dress slacks—when something tapped her on the nose. She batted at it, and it tapped her again, this time with claws.

She wasn't surprised to see Penny sitting there; Herself had left the door to the balcony open, so Georgie could go out and relieve herself there, instead of on papers in the kitchen like when she was a puppy.

"Hi," Georgie said sleepily, rolling over on her side and looking up at the cat. "What's up?"

"She's at the busy place."

"I know that." It was rare she knew something when Penny told her, so Georgie said it again. "I knew that."

"They're talking about doing it again."

"Doing what? Oh, no." Georgie got up, as though she could do something about it, then and there. "No." She shook her head, her left ear flopping over. "No."

"What? It's a good thing. Humans are like dogs, they're happier when they have something to chase after."

"*The den got broken into! They almost got killed! I had to bite someone!*"

Penny sat on her haunches and licked one paw delicately, paying particular attention to the area around her claws. "*Almost doesn't count.*"

"*What do you mean it doesn't count?*"

"*You almost got killed, too, when that woman pulled the gun, but you didn't. Does that count?*"

"*Yes!*"

Penny sighed dramatically. "*Dogs.*"

"*You . . . you're doing this for your own entertainment, aren't you? You don't care about any of us.*" Georgie whined a little, and both of her ears flopped.

Penny looked insulted at that, her tail lashing in irritation. "*Of course I care about you. You're my friend. They're our humans. We have a responsibility to them. But that doesn't mean it shouldn't be fun, too!*"

"*You call this fun?*"

"*Yes.*" Penny looked at her, wide-eyed and innocent. "*Don't you?*"

Georgie just sighed, and put her head back down on her paws.